THE DAY AFT

Whitley Strieber

THE DAY AFTER TOMORROW

The right of Whitley Strieber to be identified as the author
of this work has been asserted by him in accordance with
the Copyright, Designs and Patents Act 1988.

First published in Great Britain in 2004 by
Gollancz
An imprint of the Orion Publishing Group
Orion House, 5 Upper St Martin's Lane,
London WC2H 9EA

Second impression 2004

A CIP catalogue record for this book
is available from the British Library

ISBN 0 575 07603 8

Printed in Great Britain by Clays Ltd, St Ives plc

CHAPTER 1

Jack Hall stared into his microscope, trying not to let his freezing cold hands shake the equipment. Outside, the Antarctic wind shook the tiny mobile lab. He'd come far for these precious ice cores. The story they had to tell was urgent, maybe very urgent. And now at last he was looking back along the years, back past season after season, layer after layer of ice.

Back his eyes swept through time, past the middle ages and the Roman Empire, to the time before Egypt, when the ice got clean and pure and then – not.

There it was, the layer he was looking for, the year hell had ridden the winds of the world. The ice was thick, the layer was complex, full of particles, irregular. To his expert eye, it told the story of a monster that had marched through planet Earth back then, a storm beyond the wildest limit of the imagination.

He'd read the fossil record, of course. He even knew the time of year the storm had taken place. It had happened in June. North polar temperatures were spiking to eighty degrees Fahrenheit. The fossil record revealed that a herd of mammoths had been feeding placidly on daisies not far from a blooming apple tree when, literally as they chewed their food, they had been frozen solid and the world around them transformed into a roaring arctic hell.

There was no ice in the Arctic deep enough or pure enough to confirm the fossil record. But this – this was

1

the gold he needed. He looked up from his work and gazed out the frosted window of the lab. As far as he could see, the amazing, twisted, sweeping ice of the Antarctic shelf stretched, ice that had been attached to the continent for thousands of years. Overhead, the deep blue Antarctic sky spoke eloquently of profound, absolute cold. He laughed a little to himself. The truth was that it wasn't as cold as it should be. Not nearly.

He saw his assistant Frank Wilson come down off the drill rig carrying an aluminium case he knew contained more ice cores. That was good. They needed those critical cores from the same depth, because Jack's case had to be airtight. Everybody from the White House on down was going to try to demolish it. They didn't want to hear what he had to say, he knew that. He was not a politician. His job was to reveal what had happened in the past. It was up to them to act.

He stood up, watching the rig more closely. The drill was still running. But Frank—

'Hey, Frank, what's going on?'

Frank began opening the cores, preparing them for a clean transfer to the Cat's storage locker. 'Jason's running it.'

Jason was a good kid, but he was also a grad student with next to no field experience. 'Is that—'

At that moment, there was a sort of shudder. It wasn't much, but it shouldn't have been there at all. What the hell was happening?

Then there came a screaming sound from the drill. Jack could see that it was turning free. A distant shout echoed. 'Oh, shit,' Frank said as he burst out of the Cat, down the ladder and began to sprint across the ice.

What sounded like a ragged, endless volley of rifle shots

shattered the profound Antarctic silence. Jack leaped up onto the drill rig.

'I didn't do anything,' Jason screamed above the screeching of the drill and the explosive cracking sounds.

Behind them, Frank shut the drill down. As the bit whirred to silence, there was a crash just below the rig and what felt like an earthquake. Jack forced himself not to shout the furious curse that came to his lips. The damn *ice* had given way. This supposedly solid chunk of ice shelf had just – there was a damn hole under the rig the size of a car. He peered down into the blue ice.

Again the drill shifted, and Jason, in his terror, grabbed it. It swung towards the hole, grad student attached.

'Let go of the drill!'

The kid's face peered back, eyes huge, skin as pale as the death that was clawing at him.

Jack leaped forward, balancing on the edge of the rig itself, and gripped the kid's parka. As the drill fell away, he manhandled the scrabbling, terrified student up onto the stable part of the rig. But it didn't stay stable for long. An instant later, the three of them had to jump a four-foot gap just to get off the rig. It yawned below them, easily a couple of hundred feet deep, sudden death waiting inches from the least slip.

Now the rifle shots changed to deeper roars, crunching, and echoing booms. The whole damn shelf was disintegrating right under their feet. Jack watched as the rig started moving away from them, carrying Jack's ice cores with it. He lunged towards the edge.

Frank grabbed his shoulder. 'Forget 'em, Jack. It's too late.'

What was happening right here and now – a whole ice shelf unexpectedly disintegrating around a group of skilled scientists – told him that they were essential. He did what he had to do. He leaped across the widening crevasse to reach them.

'Jack, don't!'

Jack landed on the far side of the crevasse, stumbled, slipped, then regained his footing. He gathered cores as best he could. Some of them crumbled, but there was nothing he could do about that, not without proper carriers.

When he turned to jump back, he was shocked to see that the gap was widening fast. It was at least ten feet. And then he saw it, hundreds of feet below – the dark, shadowy presence of the sea. He stared, almost hypnotised by the impossible, unbelievable sight. Nobody had tested the temperature of that water, but it must have been high, way too high, for years.

The ocean currents were already going haywire. What he was trying to warn the world about must already be well under way. He flung his cores to Frank. Even if it meant his life, those cores had to get back to the lab. If he couldn't publish the crucial paper, Frank could and would.

Jack saw that he had exactly one chance to escape. He unsheathed his narrow, sharply pointed ice axe. He was a powerful man, he made damned sure of that, living and working as he did in some of the world's most dangerous places. He leaped, reaching with all his might, and felt the axe drive into the face of the cliff at Frank and Jason's feet. He dangled there, feeling the axe begin to slip.

Then Frank had him, and he was coming up over the edge.

'You're out of your mind.'

'I knew you'd catch me.'

Frank shook his head, then both men smiled.

'What the hell is happening?' Jason was not amused.

Frank dropped a fatherly hand down on his shoulder. 'The whole goddamn shelf is breaking off, that's what's happening.'

'We've got to get out of here!'

'That would be true.'

The International Space Station smells like a whole lot of things, but not roses or clean sheets or new mown grass. You get used to it, though. Slowly. Yuri Andropov would remind himself, when the toilet overheated or the air cleaner went down, that *Mir* was a whole lot worse. But he wasn't thinking about creature comforts now. He was a professional observer, and he was observing something that was quite interesting. Looking down at the gigantic storm below, he worked the station's cameras.

'You want to see storm,' he said into his mike, 'this is storm.'

From the nearby space shuttle, which had just completed a docking manoeuvre with the space station, Commander Robert Parker said, 'Most incredible sight, Yuri.'

Far below them, a WP-3D Hurricane Hunter from NOAA's Pacific Squadron moved towards the storm, looking no bigger than a gnat against its towering clouds. Superficially, the plane looked like a C-130 cargo craft, but the fat instrument cowling on its belly and its huge, churning props told a different story. Those instruments fed no fewer than 250 separate weather readings a second to the plane's array of onboard computers, and what they were saying right now was getting some extremely serious attention from the meteorologists hunched over their stations inside the plane.

'Is this normal?' a nervous rookie scientist asked as the plane seemed to leap and flounder across the sky.

'Once we dive in there's less bounce, more shake. Don't have any loose fillings, do you?'

Up front, Commander Michael Daniels stared steadily ahead. He was recording some very powerful gusts across the plane's wings, and he was thirty miles from the storm's perimeter. He'd been doing this for fifteen years, and this was not a usual pattern, not at all.

'Get Goddard on the horn,' he said to his first officer, his voice maintaining a calm he did not feel.

At NASA's Satellite Command Centre at the Goddard Space Centre, Janet Tokada was also reading data output from the plane. But she had even more information. Thanks to NASA's ultra high-tech scatterometer instrument aboard Japan's Advanced Earth Observing satellite, she could measure wind speeds inside the storm, in areas the plane had not yet reached.

Commander Daniels' voice crackled in her ears. 'Control, this is Recon One, do you read me?'

'This is NASA Goddard, go ahead.'

'We may lose you in a few moments. Do you have updated stats for us?'

Janet glanced at her Science Officer. 'Here's the TRMM data,' he said, holding out a sheet. The estimated internal wind speeds leaped off the page at her.

'Recon One,' she said quickly, 'we advise that you turn around immediately.'

She listened . . . to static.

'Recon One, do you read me?'

'What's the matter, Janet?' her Science Officer asked.

6

'This thing is off the charts. It could rip the wings right off that plane.'

Daniels continued to fly into the storm, and to listen to the static. The radio automatically searched frequencies, but they were over a thousand miles out in the south central Pacific, over one of the most isolated areas on the planet, the vast stretch of empty water that spreads south of the Hawaiian islands. 'We've lost them,' he said. 'Tell the guys to release the dropsondes.'

Measuring instruments dropped out of their containers as the plane entered the storm. This was the rookie's moment. It was his job to read and record their transmissions. He sat rigidly at his station, fighting the wild gyrations of the aircraft as he tried to call out his readings.

'Transmission is up and good. I am seeing wind speed at – at – one ninety. That is one ninety! Hold on. That is one ninety-five.'

Up front, Commander Daniels heard the unbelievable, fantastic numbers but could not react, he was too busy keeping the airplane running. He gripped his controls, struggled to read his vibrating instruments. Beside him, his skilled co-pilot adjusted the bite of the props. They reduced airspeed, increasing the shake, rattle and roll but diminishing the threat to the airframe.

'Two hundred,' came the young voice from behind, 'two ten, two twenty, *two thirty*!'

This was a typhoon with wind speeds equivalent to that of a tornado. It was fantastic, unbelievable. But it was also no place to turn an airplane, not one that was so close to its design limits, and probably past them when it came to crucial areas like wing roots. Commander Daniels flew on, largely because there was nothing else he dared to do.

The wings fluttered so wildly that the sound of creaking metal rose over the surging roar of the props. Commander Daniels thought helplessly of his people. If the aircraft disintegrated, they were all dead. Chutes would be useless in this maelstrom.

'How far to the eyewall?' he asked his co-pilot, his calm, decisive voice betraying nothing of his inner feelings.

'Eight niner clicks.'

Less than a minute. That would be a maybe.

In back, they burst through the wall of the eye into a silence so deep that the rookie laughed with relief. 'Wow, that was some ride!'

The others were silent. They all knew the same thing: this airplane had to make it out the other side or they were going to have a real bad day. 'Let's hope this monster never makes land,' one of them said quietly.

It was pitch dark at noon on the Big Island, and Aaron was damned concerned. No, he was scared. Shitless. And he was doing something he normally would have considered a total waste of time. He was watching the news. This typhoon was, like, some kind of a sea monster. Hundred and ninety mile-an-hour winds? What was that about?

He could hardly hear what the weather maven was saying, though, because ole Zack had surf-punk music blasting out of his monster Jensens loud enough to actually drown out the damn storm.

'It's gettin' gnarly out there, Zack. Maybe we oughta split.'

Zack belched. They had done about umpteen quarts of beer last night.

'I'm serious, man. Everybody else is gone already.'

Zack looked over at him. Zack's eyes were red. 'Don't be such a wuss. How bad can it be if the damn TV still works?'

Bang. Then darkness. Silence. Then, as Aaron's ears adjusted to the absence of the Dirt Surfers, he heard the roar of the wind, and Oh My *God*.

And then something else, which was – damn *ripping*? Plus, crashing noises, glass breaking.

'What the hell *is* that?' Zack said.

'It's the house getting torn apart, man.'

This whole part of the island had been evacuated yesterday. But Zack had not believed, not in anything except what promised to be the most humongous surf in the whole history of the world. And Aaron had stayed with him, because he was that kind of guy, and plus Zack had said, 'do you *believe*' and that had always done it for this surfer. Now he was feeling damn sick about it, oh, yes.

He peered out into the darkness and flying rain. No way was he going anywhere near the beach in this. Yeah, there would be surf all right, surf enough to grind you to pulp. Then he saw a door tumbling through the air like some giant had tossed it. The next house over was right up at the end of the road. It would be taking the storm head-on. Then he saw a piece of a window, then a whole damn *couch*.

'Jesus Christ, Zack, that's our neighbour's house going past, is what that is!' They had to get the hell out of here, and right now. He went to the door, threw it open – and had it just grabbed right out of his hands by a wind that was like a living thing . . . that knew they were there.

'Come on, man!'

This time Zack did not argue. Not even he was that insane.

They struggled down the stairs, heading for the carport. As they reached the ground, Aaron felt water come up into his shoes, then up to his calves. The whole place was flooded. He jumped into his ancient jeep and dragged the key out of his pocket. So scared he could barely function, he jammed it into the ignition.

Click.

Okay, do not piss in your pants, that would not be good, boy-o. Zack would not forget that, nossir! He turned the key again. But then he realised that Zack wasn't in the car. There was a noise, he turned around, and saw that Zack was tying his damn board to the roof-rack.

'What the hell are you doing? Forget the board, Zack!'

At that moment, there was a series of noises like fire-crackers going off – big firecrackers. The slats that closed the side of the carport tore away in rapid succession. Now the storm came roaring in, a creature with an evil voice, and it was calling their names.

As Zack jumped into the car, the house above them groaned and actually damn well lifted, and blew right off into the darkness and the spray. Frantically, Aaron turned the key, and the starter ground and ground, and finally – *finally* – the engine fired. He pulled out into where the road used to be and started out towards the highway. Something black came bounding towards them, looking like a cardboard box being blown by the wind, except that it was no box, it was a huge steel dumpster coming down on them like death itself. It hit fifty feet in front of them, then rose up into the air, its lid clanging open and closed, open and closed. All they could do was watch as it came closer and closer. They heard it smash into the surfboard and rip it away.

Aaron hit the gas, the tyres spun, screamed, then caught, and they shot off up a road that had become a wind-whipped river, praying to God that they'd reach the highway before the ocean did.

It was a sunny day in Arlington, sunny and kind of hot, actually, as Sam Hall went up in the elevator to his dad's apartment. He had Laura and Brian with him because it was pretty cool to basically have this, like, entire apartment to yourself, which he did.

'Where's your dad?'

'Who knows? Halfway around the world somewhere, as usual. Last email I got was from McMurdo Sound.'

'Does he know you come here when he's out of town?'

They thought he was completely uncool. He knew that. Like, a professional wuss like him would never be allowed to come into his own dad's apartment unless he was under total supervision. Okay.

'Actually, yeah. I'm taking care of his plants for him.'

And also actually, the African Violets were not doing so hot.

'I see,' Laura said touching one of them, 'you've got quite the green thumb.'

Uncool again, totally uncool. Sam got a damn glass of water from the kitchen and soaked them. Their dead bodies, that is.

'Uh, I think you're overwatering them,' Brian said.

'You think?'

They were floating, actually, dead sticks in muddy goop. It was not pretty. 'Uh, Sam, my boy, where are we supposed to sit?'

The living room was a trifle messy. Sam swept a pile of *National Geographic*s off the sofa and cleared some space.

If you wanted *National Geographic*, this was the place to come. His dad had every *National Geographic* that had ever been printed, and possibly a few more. They were interesting, though. Sam had been looking for pictures of the Antarctic. He wanted to see where his dad was. Truth be told, his dad was incredibly cool. Not many fathers, like, dared the edge. Brian's dad worked somewhere deep in the Agriculture Department. He looked like a big fat loaf of bread in a suit. And the only time Laura's old man sobered up was to go to the liquor store.

'I think we should start with English Lit,' Laura said, 'and then tackle art. We need to – Sam?'

Sam had turned on The Simpsons, in part to actually watch the show, in part to display the incredibly cool gas-plasma TV that was hanging on the wall like some painting or something. It was like Dad to sort of automatically buy the coolest thing in the world and then forget he even had it. Dad was very neat that way. There was something about knowing what the best stuff was and having it and also being very uncaring about it that just made him – well, fact was, Sam was a teenager who really liked his father. So call him crazy.

'Sam, you can't study and watch TV at the same time!'

'I'm multitasking, Laura, my dear. It's great mental exercise.'

Brian muttered, 'My dear . . .'

Laura said, 'New York is in four days!'

'You make it sound like the real, actual Olympics. It's the Scholastic Decathlon.'

'Decathlon sounds like the Olympics.'

'It's a ridiculous name, Brian.'

'My mom always calls it the Quiz Bowl,' Brian said. 'I hate that.'

'What they ought to call it is glorified Trivial Pursuit,' Sam muttered. It was a good episode. He wanted to watch this. Homer was going to save Marge from a destruction derby by drinking beer. Sort of.

'If it's so meaningless, why'd you join the team, Sam?'

'What can I say? Because it was there. Life is essentially meaningless.'

'Existential philosophers for five hundred,' Brian yelled. 'Who is Jean-Paul Sartre?'

'Don't encourage him.' Laura picked up the remote and muted the TV.

'Stop that.'

'No. You want to watch TV or you want to get ready?'

He snatched the remote back and she fought him for it, which was kind of nice while it lasted. But it didn't last long.

'Do not turn on that sound.'

Instead, he turned off the TV entirely. 'It's off. See?'

'Okay.'

Now she would find out the grim truth. 'So quiz me.'

He'd almost said 'kiss.' What would that have done? Nothing good, probably.

CHAPTER 2

It was a strange day in New Delhi, even a bizarre one, and it worried Jack Hall, who had begun, as he raced around the world from conference to colloquium to conference, to make note of weather anomalies that he was finding on his stops. What he was finding was worrying him. It was worrying him a lot. And this snow – sure, it was November, but this was New Delhi, for God's sake.

The fact that there were snow flurries in a city that averaged 77 degrees Fahrenheit in November wasn't going to show up on Fox or CNN – unless it was to laugh a little at the irony of anti-US protesters at the UN Conference on Global Warming freezing in a subtropical climate. In a city where January brought the occasional day in the fifties, the irony of snow flurries during a global warming conference probably wouldn't be lost on the media.

As Jack sipped a Royal Challenge Lager, a very smooth Indian beer, in the lobby bar of the hotel where he was shortly going to get himself into some serious political hot water, he watched the protesters on the other side of the large plate glass windows and wondered if, in this wild city, somebody might decide to make their point by, say, driving a truck through. Hopefully not loaded with *plastique*. In the background, a CNN International reporter droned on about how global warming was largely caused by human generated emissions, and the US was the biggest offender.

A glance at his watch told him to put down the rest of the beer, which he did. He walked to the back of the lobby and strolled into a room full of conferees who, quite frankly, looked scared. He tried to decide if it was the violence of the protest or the strangeness of the weather. Probably both. He took his seat. There were greetings, muttered, no introductions. The meeting had been going on all day. Jack had taken a break, extended it a bit in hopes of getting rid of his usual conference headache, or at least tamping it down.

He had not. The Saudi delegate looked balefully at him. Probably jealous about the beer. Not to be blamed. Now there was a stir. A real stir. The reporter who had been visible on the bar TV was in the balcony overlooking this conference area. He said, 'Delegates from all around the world have gathered to hear evidence from leading experts in climate research . . .' And then huge TV lights transformed the conference room into a stage and the Vice-President of the United States took his place behind the placard marked United States of America.

Jack took the reporter's introduction as a cue. Why not? It was as good as any. 'What we've found locked in these ice cores is evidence of a cataclysmic climate shift that occurred ten thousand years ago.'

He got up as he talked, and walked towards the formal dais. This needed to be a soundbite. He tried not to think that half a billion people might see him in their evening or morning or noon news, from Sydney to London to Washington by way of Singapore and Rio.

He looked out over the assembly. 'The concentration of natural greenhouse gases in the ice cores indicates that runaway warming pushed the planet into an ice age for two centuries.'

Now the Saudi delegate leaned into his microphone. Jack put on his earphones for the translation. 'I am confused. I thought you were talking about global warming, not an ice age.'

'It's a paradox, but global warming could trigger a cooling trend.' Jack then explained what had become his pet theory and the main advocacy of his scientific career – that global warming could flood the northern oceans with fresh water, which would disrupt ocean currents and cause the parts of the planet nearest the poles to become very suddenly much colder, which included places like Australia, Canada, Europe and the northern half of the US. In other words, all the richest, most developed countries in the world.

He thought again of those mammoths, dying of the cold so fast that the food they were eating had remained frozen in their mouths ever since. He looked out across the room. None of these people could imagine the violence of such a calamity. None of them.

The Brazilian delegate asked the ace question: when might this happen?

'Maybe in a hundred years, maybe in a thousand. Maybe next week, for all we know.'

All of a sudden, Raymond Becker's throat worked. Jack sensed the old political water starting to boil. 'Who's going to pay the price of the Kyoto Agreement?' he said in his choked, nervous voice. 'It'd cost the world's biggest economies hundreds of billions of dollars.'

'With all due respect, Mr Vice-President,' Jack said. He paused, waiting for the cameras to complete their sweeps back to the podium. He thought: every time you start out with that 'due respect' stuff, fella, you get your ass in a sling. 'With all due respect, sir, the cost of doing nothing could be even higher. Our climate is fragile.' He thought of that collapsing ice shelf, remembered his leap out of the cold arms of death. 'The ice caps are disappearing at a dangerous rate.'

Becker had finally realised that he was in a debate, and with a member of his own delegation. He was frantically shuffling papers, obviously trying to find a name. An aide whispered to him.

'Doctor Hall,' he said, 'our economy is every bit as fragile as the environment. Perhaps you should keep that in mind before making sensationalistic claims.'

How dare he. What a grandstanding jerk. Sensationalistic, indeed. 'Well,' Jack said, outwardly as calm as a tropical lagoon, 'the last chunk of ice that broke off was about the size of Rhode Island. Some folks'd say that was pretty sensational.'

A ripple of applause, some appreciative laughter, but not from the Vice-President of the United States. No, indeed, not from him.

Being a stockbroker was not like being a mugger, not to Gary Turner. He didn't put the squeeze on his clients, browbeat them, grab their orders then churn their accounts dry. No, he took their money another way, by getting them to buy what a friend of his in distant Tokyo was selling, or sell what he was buying. And then when the unexpectedly bad (oh, my!) or unexpectedly good (oh, my again) news came in, he and good old Taka split the profits in their separate Cook Islands accounts.

Beauty of the Cook Islands account: it's illegal, in the good ole Cooks, even to *ask* who owns one, let alone find out what's in it. Money that moved from Tokyo to Rarotonga did not become visible to the IRS, the SEC or anybody. It was just so damn pretty, was his and Taka's little system.

Too bad it was in the process of blowing up in their faces. Gary said into his headset, 'Those shares are gonna triple. Three months, max. Six. Hold on a sec.' He yelled out into the bullpen, 'Does anybody here know why the goddamn AC isn't on? I'm sweating like a pig.'

A moron called Tony, with enough meat on his forehead to feed a football team, said, 'It's November, they shut it off.'

Gary's other line rang. He knew who it was, wished he didn't. He pulled off the headset, killed it, grabbed the phone. 'Hello?'

'We've got a problem, Gary.'

Go ahead, play your part, buddy. 'What kind of a problem?'

'Call me back on your cell . . .'

Uh-oh. The worst had happened. He held up the headset. 'I got Partridge holding, Paulie. Cover me?'

The other broker took his client. Gary got the hell out of the office, went out into the sweltering Manhattan street. What was this, some kind of heatwave? Was the sun broken or what? A panhandler with a dog that looked like a scruffy old lion tried to get something. 'Die,' Gary muttered as he dialled.

He knew Taka was jammed into a crowded noodle shop a block or so from his own office building. He didn't want anybody to hear this, not any of it. He had a horror of small enclosed spaces, and prison cells in Japan were exactly that. Steel doors. Little peepholes. Six feet by four. God help you if you were taller than average, which he was.

Gary listened as Taka's phone rang. He only hoped that

the myth that digital cellular was secure from being tapped was not a myth.

Then the damn panhandler jostled him from behind. 'Fifty's my opening position. I'm willing to entertain a counter-offer.'

Could this be real? A panhandler with a damn sense of humour? 'Buddha, work,' the panhandler said to his mutt. The dog did a begging routine. So cute.

The phone started yammering in Jap. The call hadn't gone through. 'Why don't you try a job,' Gary snapped at the panhandler as he redialled.

'I had a job. Just like you, shiny shoes, big office, secretaries, all that shit. I'll tell you, it's the secretaries did me in . . . and the elevators . . .'

Gary hurried away. The guy had a horrible scent of the future about him – his own future as a broke broker, his licence to steal a memory in the SEC's ever-vigilant computer banks.

Finally, Taka heard his phone ring. He grabbed it out of his pocket, flipped it open. 'I think they know what we're up to.'

'Oh, God.'

In Japan, Taka noticed – barely – that the street had suddenly gone into shadow. He also noticed – even less – the fact that a gust of wind suddenly came out of nowhere, bringing with it dust and street dirt, gum wrappers and crushed cigarette packs. 'The SEC called me—'

'Called *you*? The American SEC?'

'They want to know about Voridium. The options.'

'I knew it. I've sensed this damn thing coming. I swear, I knew this one was gonna go south on us.'

A police car stopped beside a small truck which a family of shop owners were frantically loading with their precious fruits and vegetables. Unlike Americans, Japanese took their produce very, very seriously. The least good of those melons would sell for fifteen American dollars and be worth every penny. But why were they loading up like that, in the middle of the day? The cop sure as hell wanted them to get that truck out of there.

'Sell them. Sell them now,' Gary yelled.

'It'll be a red flag.'

'They can't nail us if we don't make any money. Sell it all now!'

Taka heard a loud sound behind him, a thud. The cop and the shop owner both looked. So did Taka. There was a dent, a huge one, in the hood of the police car.

What the hell?

Gary's tiny voice shouted, 'Taka, did you hear me?' Taka was looking at the impossibly huge hailstone that was rolling at the feet of the shop family. It was bigger than one of their damn melons – a *good* melon. 'Taka!'

A horn blared, a woman screamed, Taka heard glass shatter, realised that it was the windshield of the shop owner's truck. He couldn't believe what he was seeing. He just stared, frozen.

A drum roll came thundering down out of the sky, and with it a bombardment of huge hailstones. They slammed into cars, blasted against walls, shattered windows. The street became a maelstrom of falling glass and hail. A sign shattered, spraying Taka with bits of neon dragon.

Then the cop got hit. He dropped like a bag of rice and lay there with blood pumping out of his head. Taka leaped towards the truck, hoping to shelter under it with the shop family.

Gary held his phone away from his ear. 'What the hell's going on? Taka?'

But Taka did not answer. He lay in the street, dimly aware that the blood flowing away and down the drain was not only the cop's, it was also his. Then another huge hailstone exploded in his face, and he thought, 'This is a wonder of nature.' Then a third hit him, and darkness came. The next one took his life, and then more came, and more, and like so many others in the streets of this stricken city, he ceased even to be recognisable.

Nature's wonders can be very, very hard.

The Hedland Climate Research Centre overlooked a broad expanse of the Scottish Highlands, and, on this day, speeding black clouds, low and mean. Only two cars were present in the car park, and inside, the years of budget cuts and official inattention had taken their toll. Exactly two technicians were on duty, one watching Arsenal defeat Tottenham and the other dead asleep with an old Derek Robinson novel open in his lap.

Far to the north, in the angry waters above Scotland, waters that once killed the Spanish Armada, and that claimed many a U-boat in their cold grey jaws, a buoy sounded, its whistle joining the screams of gulls, its rusty chain clanking as it was swept by wave after wave. Lightning flashes revealed its rust, its age . . . but not the dire message that it was sending to Hedland, to the two terminally bored guardians of mankind.

'Simon,' Dennis said, 'you're snoring.' He wondered just how deeply Simon was asleep, and the statement was a test of that. What he really wanted to do was to take out his flask of Bushmills and consume about half of it in three delicious swallows. But not if Simon was conscious enough to know. Simon would like to get his pal George Holloman up here. Simon would like to see

Dennis transferred, and being damned good and drunk on the job might be enough to do it. Assuming that the inspector was not himself drunk while taking the report.

Dennis watched the bastard. *Was* he asleep? Maybe he was the one needed a bloody transfer. He reached over and picked up the book, held it between his two hands for a moment, then slapped it shut in Simon's fat-filled face.

Simon jerked awake, shook his head. 'I just closed my eyes for a moment.' He smiled. 'The baby kept us up all night.'

Dennis said nothing. What was there to say? He went back to his game. Neither man saw the yellow warning signal on their control panel, which linked to radio telemetry from the 'study buoys', which had been deployed by the British Meteorological Office five years ago to record water temperatures, as a way of determining what no satellite could really see, not on a moment-to-moment basis, which was how the Gulf Stream was actually functioning at its crucial northernmost extent.

If it failed, and oceanographers and meteorologists were afraid that it might, a maelstrom would descend on England as cold air normally held back by warm air rising off the current came gushing down from the Arctic. Already, starting in 1999, the British Isles had experienced some truly terrible precursor storms. All of Europe had. But they would be nothing compared to the big one.

Professor Gerald Rapson knew all of this. He knew it and he lived with it every day of his life. He was a friend of Jack Hall and had supported him at Delhi. Now, as he drove along the twisty road to Hedland, as always enjoying the magnificent views of sea and sky and sweeping highland that disclosed themselves around every bend, he worried about Jack and he worried about the bizarre weather.

A super-typhoon had just smashed across the Hawaiian Islands, leaving death and fantastic destruction behind it, reducing a legendary island paradise to a twisted mass of wreckage. Bizarre storms had erupted in Japan when a moisture laden Siberian cold front had smashed into the hottest November Tokyo had ever known. Huge hailstones had killed people all over the country, even in downtown Tokyo. So far, the Japanese government hadn't released a death toll, but back-channel sources were saying that it was going to be in the neighbourhood of two thousand.

As Rapson pulled into the car park, he confirmed another odd phenomenon. Sea birds were migrating southward, creatures that normally did not move at all. He listened to their haunting cries, and wondered what they knew. Out there beneath the dark mutinous waters, what was happening? What secret was nature about to reveal?

Shuddering, he hurried towards the red-brick facility with its roof covered with antennae and satellite dishes. Maybe Hedland would have some secrets to reveal.

Inside, Simon was thinking about brewing a new pot of coffee. This was always an issue. His coffee was no good, Dennis said. But Dennis didn't even drink coffee. He preferred his Brodie's bloody Scottish Teatime Tea, even though the Manchester laddie was no more Scots than the Queen. Preferred fancy tea, and preferred to criticise simple old coffee as provided by the Met.

Simon had just dumped the coffee into the Kona when he noticed that amber light on the console. He walked over to the monitor station and read the flashing line of text.

'Nomad buoy forty-three-eleven is showing a temperature drop of thirteen degrees.'

Dennis asked around the game, 'Where's forty-three-eleven?'

'Looks like . . . George's Bank. Over towards Canada.'

'That's rough seas out there. They've had a nor'easter brewing up for about a week. Must have knocked it out.'

'We'll have to file a request to get it fixed.'

Professor Rapson had entered too quietly to get any notice from the techs. He was a little embarrassed. They wouldn't care to have a superior sneaking up on them. 'Are our boys winning?' he asked, by way of announcing himself.

Dennis almost fell to the floor. He turned off the game immediately. Laughing, Simon said, 'Hello, Professor, how was India?'

'You know scientific conferences. The dancing girls, the wine, the parties . . .' He shook his head, pretending a bit of a hangover. Then he, also, saw the amber alarm light, quietly flashing.

CHAPTER 3

Jack Hall was now living through at least the sixth weather anomaly he had personally experienced in the past three weeks. It was hot as hell right here at home in Alexandria. Thanksgiving was just weeks away, and it felt like August. What few people strolling the streets in their shirtsleeves knew was that if they'd decided to go to the beach, they would have found the ocean so cold that they couldn't stay in for more than a couple of minutes.

That worried Jack Hall.

He tossed his bags on the floor and picked up his mail as he entered the apartment. And look at it. The place was a damn wreck. His *National Geographic*s were scattered all over the living room, his African Violets looked like they'd been both drowned and parched, and there were crumbs and other evidence of heavy-duty teenage eating everywhere.

Sam was going to have a little explaining to do, he thought as he flipped through his mail. He stopped at an envelope from the Arlington County School District. Sam's grades. As he opened it, he felt more cheerful. Sam was a really good student. Where it counted, in the grades department, Sam Hall delivered. He scanned the list. A, A, A+, A+, very nice. Then he saw something that he could not believe. A misprint? He picked up the telephone and dialled his ex-wife's house.

Sam was gobbling cereal. He was late, he knew that,

but also hungry. He was always hungry, but maths, lit, and Am. History would prevent him from eating even a Snickers bar until noon.

'Will you get that?' his mom called.

'Gotta eat,' he hollered around a mouthful of corn-flakes.

Lucy was in a hurry, too. This family was not fabulous at getting rolling in the morning. ''Lo,' she said into the cordless phone as she walked back and forth loading on her white doctor's coat, her stethoscope, car keys, purse and all the other little things she could remember.

'It's me.'

'Hi, Jack, when did you get back?'

In the kitchen, Sam practically choked on his cereal. Milk and bits sprayed across the table.

'You didn't tell me Sam got an F in calculus!'

Sam was making frantic gestures at her. She shook her head. His efforts to keep her from giving his dad the grim news were for naught. 'All right,' Lucy said, 'calm down now.'

'Sam is a straight A student,' Jack barked. 'Since when does he fail?'

That was not a question she cared to deal with at the moment. 'I can't talk about that right now,' she said, hoping he'd understand. But Jack was probably in another time zone altogether. India, Antarctica, Siberia, who knew?

'Maybe you should make the time.' His voice was soft, even gentle. That was a warning sign, big time. Soft words meant only one thing in the world of Jack Hall: a major earthquake was on the way. Well, let it come. She'd divorced Jack for a reason. A lot of reasons. And this kind of implication that she was somehow a lousy, second-rate

26

parent was for sure one of them.

She let him have it, a small dose of what he needed to hear. 'Excuse me, but I'm not the one who's always gone for months and months!'

There was a silence on the other end. Then something happened that she thought was quite surprising. Very damn out of his box. 'You're right,' he said. 'I'm sorry. I just don't understand how Sam could get an F.'

Neither did she, but she didn't care to tell Jack any such thing. 'I'll let him explain it to you. Can you take him to the airport tomorrow?'

'Sam's getting on a plane?'

He who hated to fly was indeed getting on a plane. She spoke in an undertone, glancing at Sam, who was sitting on a barstool across the kitchen pass through, straining to hear every word. 'He joined this Scholastic Decathlon Team.'

'Sam joined a team?'

'I think there's a girl involved. Listen, I'm gonna be on call all night. Pick him up at seven thirty tomorrow morning, will you? And don't be late. I don't want him to have to take a taxi to the plane again.'

Now it was time for big ears to do his darndest to de-infuriate his father. 'Have you packed yet?' she asked him.

'I have all night.' He grabbed for the phone.

She held it away. 'Pack.'

He got it, took it to his ear. She kissed him on the fore-head. 'I'm gonna miss you.'

'It's only a week, Mom.'

She couldn't delay any longer. She had many hours ahead of her at the hospital, doing one of the notorious twenty-four-hour shifts that were the lot of residents in these days of budget cuts. Sammy was still her little boy, though, and a week was a long, long time for ole Mom. She did not let him see the moisture in her eyes. No way was she going to be one of those clingy mothers. As far as she knew, he'd inherited his father's travel gene and this would be one of a lifetime of trips.

It was so damn good for Jack to hear Sam's voice. The hope of youth was in his tone, the energy and fun of being a teenager. Too bad his grades had tanked and he'd left this place a sty.

'Hey, Dad,' Sam said, 'so you just got in and I'm taking off?'

At least Jack would see him on the way to the airport. He wanted that ride to be all fun and no fights, so he decided to get the rough stuff out of the way right now. 'Thanks for taking care of my place, Sam.'

'No problem.'

'It's a disaster zone!'

'I was gonna clean it up. I forgot when you were getting back.'

Now came the biggie. 'And what about your report card?' This one grade could keep him out of MIT or Caltech. He didn't realise it, but his whole future as a scientist was at stake here. Sam was brilliant, and he had an extraordinary career ahead of him in whatever discipline he chose. But not if he didn't get a top, top school. That was essential. 'So, buddy, what about—'

'Hold on, there's another call.'

There was a click. 'Sam?'

'Dad, it's Laura! Gotta go. See you in the morning.'

'Sam!'

But he was gone, which was the damnedest thing. Sam hero-worshipped his dad, hung on his every word.

Something had sure as hell changed, and Jack had a feeling it had a name, and that name was Laura. He laughed a little to himself. What the hell, his little Sammy had a girl. That was very damn cool. Probably a real looker, too.

Jack wanted to clean this place up, but there was no time for that now. He had to get to the 'office', which was a space tucked away in the basement at the National Oceanic and Atmospheric Administration. It was where they buried the resident paleoclimatologist. Out of sight, out of mind. Just as well. His entire budget was no bigger than a computer glitch. NOAA could go out of the paleoclimate business without so much as a peep of protest from anybody of any importance at all.

Thing was, paleoclimate was the whole story. You figure out what happened in the past, you are going to find out what NOAA *really* wanted to know, what it lived to know, which was what in holy hell was going to happen in the future.

He passed through security and parked, then went down to his digs. The joke was that he was so far underground that you had to go down from the basement parking lot to find him.

True enough, but at least he was here. He existed. He went through building security, then down the long, neon-lit hallway to the door with the slightly crooked 'Paleoclimate Laboratory' sign in the sliding holder. What they did not know was that Jack's people had glued it in with crazy glue. If Gomez ever ditched paleoclimate, he was going to have to replace this door.

Jack punched in his code and went in. He was greeted by the usual neon and silence. He went down the hall, turned to the room where his ice cores were being unloaded. He was nervous about this operation. After the catastrophe on the ice shelf, a lost Snocat and all that blather, he was not going to be doing any more of this shallow coring anytime soon. The sexy science was being done by the deep-core teams located deep in the Antarctic fastness, drilling down to half a million years ago and more. Those were the boys who got the dollars and the news stories. Some jerk with a cracked theory about something that had happened ten thousand years ago was no fun. What about the air *Tyrannosaurus rex* breathed? That was what CNN wanted to know.

The he heard Frank's tired voice say, 'You should be cataloguing those samples. The boss said he wanted them done by the time he gets back.' He was in the massive freezer that would house the cores they had managed to save from the Antarctic debacle. Good, that meant that the cores had got here on time and in good shape.

As Jack started into the freezer, he heard Jason reply, 'He won't come in before tomorrow. Even Taskmaster Hall has to sleep.'

'Taskmaster Hall?' What the hell was that supposed to mean? Jack didn't want to eavesdrop, so he stepped into view, and into the ice-cold air of the freezer. 'I slept on the plane,' he said.

He surveyed the boxes. And that was it for Jack Hall. All time, all space, all commitments, all needs disappeared in an instant. It became him and his ice, beginning and end of the world. He measured, he prepared, he moved, he tagged.

At some indeterminate time, Frank and Jason went to lunch. Later, somebody held a turkey club under his nose until he yelled at them for getting contaminants near his ice. Later, he heard whispers concerning pizza. All he knew was that this project could not be completed until this ice was in order and secure, and that was going to happen as fast as possible, because Jack Hall had a point to prove, and he was damn well going to prove it.

As far as Jack was concerned, he'd been working for about half an hour when Tom Gomez, the director of NOAA, came striding into the freezer.

'I know you have an innate talent for rubbing people the wrong way, Jack, but why, for the love of God did you have to aggravate the Vice-President of the United States!'

'Because my seventeen-year-old kid knows more science than he does.' Way more, as a matter of fact.

'Perhaps, but your seventeen-year-old kid doesn't control our budget. It doesn't matter if he hates you.'

Wheels clicked in Jack's head. He realised that the six-forty on the clock was not evening but morning, which explained why he'd got all the samples processed, and also why his staff had disappeared on him, which he had been going to raise hell about.

Sam. Oh, God, no.

Jack went for the door, brushing past Gomez. He had to reach Sam in time. He needed that half hour alone together in the car with his kid, needed it bad. He drove like a bat out of hell – which, unfortunately, meant very slowly anyway in DC's morning rush. There was no such thing as an easy reverse commute in Washington. With government offices spread halfway from Wilmington to Richmond and up to Baltimore, every road in every direction was jammed from six to nine every damn morning, and this one was no exception.

As he turned the corner onto Lucy's street, he saw the cab already there and Sam giving his suitcase to the driver.

He leaped out of his car and took the suitcase. 'Sorry I'm late, Sam, I—'

'Dad, the cab's already here.'

No, that would not do. He had to have this time. 'I'll take care of the cab.' He gave the driver twenty. 'Will that cover it?' Another ten and the driver pulled out. Actually looked kind of happy. Happy-ish.

Jack looked at his boy. He'd grown so damn much, it almost broke his heart. He wanted to be with Sam, to spend every waking moment, in fact, with Sam, but that was not the way Jack Hall's world worked. He was racing time to convince the powers-that-be to begin a massive planning effort to prepare for sudden climate change, maybe even to stop it, at least for a while. But nobody believed him and nobody cared, and boy, this was one paleoclimatologist with the world on his shoulders.

Where Sam had ridden when he was five and they'd gone to the Virginia State Fair and ridden the tilt-a-whirl and eaten cotton candy, and whacked the Whack-A-Mole with the best whackers at the fair.

Times, oh, good, good times.

Now Sam sat quietly beside him, his teenage secrets hidden behind his careful eyes, hidden in his silence. Jack would love to have met Laura. He dared not even ask.

'So, is being late your way of getting back at me for failing calculus?'

Oh, my love, how far that is from the truth. 'Of course not.'

'It sounded like you were pretty angry yesterday.'

That wasn't true, either. He couldn't be angry at Sam, not for more than a few seconds. 'Not angry, just disappointed.'

'You want to hear my side of it?'

'There are sides?'

'I got every question right on the final. The only reason Mr Spengler failed me was because I didn't write out the solutions.'

'Why not?'

'I do them in my head.'

Pure Sam. His mind was breathtaking. 'Did you tell him that?'

'He didn't believe me. He says he can't do 'em in his head, so I must be cheating.'

Now Jack did get angry. He got very, very angry. *Very* angry. All of Sam's life, they'd come up against teachers who resented his brilliance or feared his brilliance or just plain thought bright kids got in the way. Spengler was obviously another one of these pinheaded pricks. 'That's ridiculous,' Jack said, trying to keep his rage inside. 'He can't fail you for being smarter than he is.'

'That's exactly what I said.'

Which must have gone down just wonderfully. 'You said that? How'd he take it?'

'I think the answer to that question is an F.'

Boy, had he ever misread this boy of his. He'd thought that Laura had gone to his head. 'I'm sorry I jumped to conclusions, Sam.'

Sam's expression did not change. He wasn't ready to say it was okay because it obviously wasn't okay. He knew the stakes, and he knew that, unless his dad could work a miracle, that F might really get in his way. Unspoken between them was what they both knew: if Jack had been there to reason with Spengler, maybe things would have been different. But Jack had not been there.

'You have to go to the right!'

'What?'

'Dad, to the right! Departures!'

Jack had almost driven through the airport, his mind had been so far from the reality of the world around him. He had to swerve across lane after outraged, honking lane to reach the departure area. He saw security people watching him very carefully and thought, I don't have a carload of dynamite, fellas, not exactly.

'I'm gonna call this teacher and have a word with him. We'll straighten this out.'

'Forget it, Dad, I'll handle it myself.'

Sam got out, heaved his bag out of the back seat, and headed for the terminal. Not even a goodbye, not even that. Jack's heart just about broke. 'Sam . . .'

Sam disappeared into the terminal.

CHAPTER 4

Captain Parker was riding an exercise bike in the International Space Station. The fact that he was upside down not only didn't bother him, he kind of liked it that way. He was going home in a few days, and he didn't want to come out flopping around like a deboned carp, which is what happened to astronauts who didn't follow a strict physical routine up here. As he rode, he listened to the Flight Director, who was no doubt uplinking to tell him about the incoming shuttle mission.

Then he heard that it had been scrubbed, weather.

What the hell? Surely it was only a delay. A scrub meant a lot more than that.

Nope, the orbiter had sustained a lightning strike and the safety committee had called for a complete inspection. Every tile, every rivet, every wire. So this was going to be a no-go mission. A whole new mission was going to be declared.

'How long until they reset the launch, then?'

'Doesn't look like you'll be coming home this week, Parker. Your wife's going to be giving me an earful.'

He'd like to have done the same thing. Couldn't NASA handle a lightning strike, even yet? All he said, though, was, 'Roger that.' Discipline was tight aboard the station. It had to be. You were living in zero gravity with zero space and zero privacy. The best emotions up here were no emotions.

Hideki, the Japanese astronaut who'd been on station for three weeks, was looking out a window while shaving. He was still enjoying things like letting his razor float beside his head while he checked his beard. Wait until he got a little of that thick lather involved with his sinuses. He'd be shaving with skin oil like everybody else did, once he'd discovered just what sneezing did to a weightless body. Hideki a go-go. It was gonna be fun.

Then Hideki turned around. Lather or no lather, there was concern on his face. 'Come take a look at this cloud pattern.'

Concern over a cloud pattern? This was going to be interesting. At first, as he peered down towards the earth, Parker did not understand what he was seeing. When he realised that it was a thunderstorm, an actual shiver of fear went through him. The damn thing must be thirty miles high. The top twenty miles of it were – were they made of ice? What the hell was going on down there? What must it be like under that thing?

Then he saw another one farther north, over the Yukon of all places. What hath God wrought?

Sam ate peanuts because they'd been in the ground and he liked the ground, he liked it so much. No matter what it felt like, the floor of an airplane was not the ground, and he could sense the vast, empty air a few feet from his shoes. He'd made a morbid study of air crashes, and now his complex mind was going through the catalogue of engine failures, fires, and disintegrating airframes that filled one particularly dark little corner.

There was a bump, just like hitting a pothole in a very good car. But this was not a very good car, it was an air-plane, no doubt a very bad one, maintained by people who knew all kinds of amazing things you could do with duct tape, and that bump was not a pothole, it was a hole in the air and it basically had no bottom.

'Are you all right?'

'He's afraid of flying,' Brian said, casually staring at his laptop.

That was the last thing Laura needed to hear 'I'm fine!'

Wham!

That was a big one, that was serious. God, had the tail fallen off? Sam waited. No, the plane was still under control. Of course, it took a lot more than a few bumps to make these babies turn to confetti in the sky, so—

Wham!

Dear God, we're dying. We're dying, it's over. A bell rang. The 'Fasten Seat Belts' sign glowed in his face like a branding iron being held by a sadistic maniac. His hands went down, grabbed the belt, ripped at it. Fastened. But did it matter?

As discreetly as he could, Sam checked the airsickness bag in the seat pocket in front of him. That was there, thank God. If he had to use it, he'd be very quick, very efficient, they would not be offended.

They would be offended and they would laugh and it would become a Story. Laura, it was nice knowing you. Laura, I thought – never mind what I thought.

'If you're going to be sick, turn the other way,' Brian said.

He couldn't turn the other way! The other way was Laura! And he felt green, definitely. Damned peanuts, damned Coke.

'Shut up,' he muttered. Definitely green. Oh, God.

The plane was now dropping and rising, dropping and rising. A stewardess wobbled past. 'Peanuts?'

Oh, please, no. Not even the smell of peanuts.

'Statistically, the chance of a plane going down because of turbulence is less than one in a billion . . . or was it a million. I can't remember . . .'

Laura leaned across Sam. He inhaled essence of some kind of wonderful perfume. How did they manage to smell so good, women?

'Shut up, Brian,' she said. Then she touched Sam on the shoulder. 'Don't pay any attention to him. Everything is fine. Look, they're still serving.'

EEEEeeee, slammm! Plastic cups spilled, ice cubes bounced along the floor like a panicked crowd that couldn't escape, and there were screams. Yes, actual screams. And this was the shuttle. These people flew all the time.

It was bad. It was the end. The stewardesses hurried aft behind their carts. So much for all right. And look at them, they were pale, they were just about ready to run.

The intercom hissed for a moment. Then the pilot spoke. 'Folks, we seem to be passing through a bit of turbulence. Please remain in your seats with your seat belts fastened. Put your seats and tray tables in the upright—'

The whole plane shuddered, then it slid to the right, then Sam's stomach arrived in his mouth. He watched an ice cube, an olive and *Time* magazine float gracefully up past the seat back in front of him. He heard voices, a chorus. It was a chorus of screams.

Then, *thuddd*! Stomach to feet, here I come! Clatter, snap, and oxygen masks were coming down. Laura's came down. She sat staring at it, her eyes practically popping out of her head. Brian had shut that damn laptop of his at last. He looked over at the oxygen mask, his jaw in his lap.

Finally, the plane levelled off. Finally, the flight became smooth again. Stewardesses appeared, telling everybody not to touch the oxygen masks, helping the folks who'd put them on remove them.

Laura turned to Sam. He turned to Laura. 'Sam,' she said.

'Yes?' Was this the moment, so close to death, that she confessed that they shared the same secret, that she declared the love he dreamed of getting.

'Sam, you're hurting my hand.'

He looked down. Her fingers looked like trapped, red worms. He snatched his hand away. There were white marks in her skin, he had been gripping her so hard.

'Sorry!'

Brian opened his laptop again. At least one thing could not be disputed, Sam thought, the guy had guts.

At Hedland, the weather was finally becoming normal for the time of year. It was no longer bizarrely hot. On the contrary, a light snow was falling. Simon had seen Rapson's car in the car park, so he decided to say goodbye to his wife here instead of prolonging matters by going inside. They were almost always together, and as far as he was concerned, he was not looking forward to two weeks without her. Jeanette was the luckiest thing that had ever happened to him, the treasure of his life.

'I can't believe I'm spending two weeks alone with my mum,' she said, gazing up at him from her car.

He couldn't either, but he also knew that her mother was incredibly excited about their trip. 'Be patient with her,' he said, 'she's been looking forward to this holiday for months.'

Jeanette smiled, more than a little ruefully. Her mother

could be a trial at times, especially for the daughter she always found a little wanting. 'I know,' she said softly.

Simon leaned into the old Vauxhall and kissed her. 'I love you,' he said. He really wanted to kiss her again – many agains – but she pulled away.

Laughing a little, she said, 'I love you, too.' Then she reached out and touched his cheek. 'Promise not to call every ten minutes, though. All right?'

She knew her husband. He was already thinking about that first call to her cellphone, to make sure she was okay on the snowy roads. 'I'll try not to,' he said.

He watched her drive off, then headed into the Centre. The control room, as always, was dim and quiet. But Rapson was standing up, staring at the bank of data monitors.

'It's very odd,' he said as he heard Simon approach, 'but this buoy is registering a thirteen-degree drop in ocean temperature.'

Simon thought he'd told Rapson that. He was sure he had. Maybe the old man had forgotten. He covered. 'I forgot to tell you. That buoy malfunctioned the other day. I'll put in a call to see if there are any ships near George's Bank to get it.'

'This buoy isn't in George's Bank,' Rapson snapped. 'It's just off Greenland.'

That was very odd. Simon went closer to the monitoring station. A dot was flashing near the Greenland coast. He zoomed the view out to see just where the buoy was – and picked up another one flashing a steep temperature drop. 'What are the odds of two buoys failing?' he said, thinking aloud.

There was a low beeping sound from another monitor, the one that covered buoys in critical navigation waters, that would require immediate attention if damage or failure occurred.

'Make that three,' Rapson said.

What were they seeing here? Simon looked over at his boss. Rapson was staring at the monitors, deep in silent thought.

As Sam, Laura and Brian sat in a cab stuck in a traffic jam, Luther threaded his debris-heaped shopping cart among the cars. Or rather, Buddha led the way. Luther was pretty miserable, what with the sudden end of the bum weather that New York had been enjoying since last March.

Hearing a weather report coming out of a radio, he drew near a yellowback. The driver had the window partly open, and it was possible for Luther to listen. 'The temperature at La Guardia is a chilly thirty-eight degrees right now,' the announcer said. 'That's a record breaking fifty-four degree fall from yesterday's high of ninety-two.'

The driver rolled up the window and the traffic started moving at the same time. Luther and Buddha had to get out of there fast. He wondered if he had an overcoat somewhere down among his treasures. And what about Buddha? He hated cold weather. He began searching for a grate. He needed a grate.

Sam was enjoying sitting hip to hip with Laura so much that he was unaware of the time, certainly unaware of Luther and Buddha.

Laura leaned forward. 'Excuse me,' she said in her most polite voice, 'but we're really late.'

'We're almost there,' the cabbie snapped.

Brian opened his Manhattan flashmap. 'We're only two blocks away.'

Laura grabbed it from him. 'Lemme see. Okay, guys, let's walk.'

They got out of the cab into freezing cold wind. No wonder the flight had been so horrible, with all these wild weather changes. Secretly, Sam thought they were lucky not to have become a statistic. As he paid the driver, he heard a strange sound overhead. Everybody around him was looking up, so he did the same, despite being told by his dad never to do that in New York. 'Looking up in Manhattan marks you as a tourist. Don't do it unless you're willing for your wallet to go bye-bye.'

Yeah, Dad, but this is *weird*. There were millions of birds overhead. *Millions* of them. He made out the dots of little birds like sparrows, the quick soaring shapes of swallows and larks, the ominous forms of hawks. Their voices echoed among the skyscrapers, raising a strange, screeching din that was unlike anything Sam had ever heard before.

Above the birds, the long ribbon of sky between the buildings looked real dark. Sam could see the clouds actually rolling. They looked like black, fast-moving smoke. And yet here on the ground the air was still and cold.

What Sam did not know – what nobody knew – was that the intensity of the changes were so great that they were triggering latent instincts in animals of all kinds. Normally docile dogs paced and growled if their owners came near, cats hid and hissed, and slapped and bit anybody who tried to pull them from behind the sofas and the closets where they had gone. At the Central Park Zoo and the Bronx Zoo and all the zoos, in fact, from Toronto to Richmond, animals strode their cages, apes beating their chests, lions roaring, captive eagles flapping their hobbled wings.

Visitors at the Central Park Zoo were thrilled when the wolves began to howl. The keepers were mystified. They'd rarely heard it before, even at night. During the day, never. But what a day it was, dark, lowering, with even the park's pigeons agitated, flocking in endless, twisting loops that moved slowly south across the park. Pigeons are not migratory birds – at least, not normally.

In Gary Turner's office on Wall Street, the brooding, uneasy weather might as well have been happening in Samarkand, not right outside his window. He sat hunched over his cellphone, his free hand hiding his mouth.

'I know this must be a difficult time for you, Mr Masako, but this is really important. Your son would have wanted you to help me on this—'

The line went dead. Gary gasped with surprise, then almost doubled over, fighting to keep his guts from turning inside out. Had Masako hung up on him, or what had happened here? Oh, dear God, he was one inch – one damn *inch* from jail, here. And all he had was this damn Jap who only understood every tenth word and probably hated him anyway.

'Hey, Gary, bogey incoming three o'clock.' From his adjoining cubicle, Paul spoke in a quick whisper. And then Mr Foster appeared. He didn't look too concerned. But then again, he never did.

'Gary, Gary, Gary. You're a clever boy, Gary, but not as clever as you think.'

Gary sat, frozen. Mr Foster leaned down, his knuckles on his desk. Gary could count the pores on his nose. They were pits. Canyons. He smelled faintly of some kind of horrible hair cream. 'I just got a call from the SEC, Gary me boy.'

Gary controlled his throat, trying desperately to work

up enough spit to talk. 'Really,' a high little boy's voice chirped, 'the Securities and Exchange Commission?'

Foster was sweating now. His eyes looked like they'd been borrowed from an angry rat. 'They know all about the Voridium options you've been buying offshore.'

Gary wanted to ask, 'What Voridium options?' but that, he feared, would not be the right thing to do.

Mr Foster turned as red as he would have if Gary had asked it. 'You know the ones,' he snarled. 'They'll be worth a fortune after the merger.'

He was caught. Dead to rights. They had him at the end of a rope. Stonewall. Only choice. 'I didn't buy any—'

'Don't be stupid, Gary. Tell your friends in Japan to dump them before the merger goes through and the SEC will have nothing on you. Otherwise, get yourself a good lawyer, 'cause they will throw your ass in jail for this.'

He stood up, ran thick fingers through that bizarre hair of his. What was in it, Brylcreem? Clubman Hair Oil? 'Personally,' he said, 'I don't give a rat's ass what happens to you – but if you go down, it puts a stink on all of us. So do the right thing, Gary.'

He turned and strolled away, just as calm and cool as he could be. Paul, who had been filing every word in those deep memory banks of his, asked what the hell was going on.

Gary didn't dare say anything. He shot back a 'don't ask' look and hoped the moron understood.

What was jail actually like? Either he got through to Mr Masako or he was going to need to find that out. Ironic, he was going to get rich even though he desperately did not want to, because a guy had been killed by a damn *hailstone*. He would have laughed. Not today.

*

Pinehurst Academy had stood on bluffs overlooking the Hudson River for a hundred years. In contrast to the wild and crazy city on the other side of its high brick walls, red and aged, but topped by masses of cut glass embedded in concrete, the broad campus lawns were normally an oasis. But not today. As the storms rolled, one piling on another, crashing southward like an avalanche from the sky, the tossing trees and rainswept lawns, the sidewalks awash in runoff, were far from peaceful.

In the gym, a lovely old structure with a barn roof held up by huge, dark beams, the rain roared so loudly that the nervous teams of academic competitors had trouble hearing their own answers, let alone the questions being asked. Behind the 'Woodmont High School' sign, Sam, Brian and Laura sat with the others at the long competitors' table.

It faced a single podium, on which a referee neatly dressed in a dark suit with a maroon tie read a question. 'In 1532, Spanish conquistador Francisco Pizarro defeated this Inca Emperor at the Peruvian highland town of Cajamarca. What was his name?'

Sam thought disdainfully to himself that it *was* just glorified Trivial Pursuit. If it wasn't for the lovely Laura, he would never in a million years be involved in this stupid kiddie contest.

'Montezuma,' Brian whispered.

'Montezuma was in Mexico, not Peru,' Laura shot back. 'No, it's Ana something. Ata?'

Sam watched them struggle. He watched the other teams conferring, saw the looks of fear up and down the table. Actually, he was doodling. He was drawing a galleon sailing across the Spanish Main. Maybe it was Pizarro's ship, on its way to Peru to exterminate one of the world's great civilisations for what turned out to be about sixty thousand pounds of gold, all of which the Spanish kings spent within a single generation. By the time another five years had passed, half the Inca population would be dead, the other half enslaved. In ten years, Peru would be a ghost nation.

Laura poked him in the ribs to stop the doodling.

'Atahualpa,' he said absently, returning immediately to his bowlines. Accurate or not, for a 1532 galleon? He wasn't entirely sure. Laura scribbled on one of the Official Answer Sheets.

'Time,' the referee said.

She thrust their answer into the hands of the judge who stepped from behind the table. The referee asked, 'Correct answers?'

There were only two: Woodmont and the Pinehurst Academy itself. But of course, Pinehurst was the host and founding school. In fact Pinehurst Academy was the New York Yankees of the Academic Decathlon. Their trophies lined the entrance hall. Then Sam noticed something he didn't like too much. J.D. White, the captain of the Pinehurst team, made eye contact with Laura and gave her a little salute.

He'd better start keeping those eyes of his to himself. He'd been devouring Laura with them ever since she walked into the damn room.

CHAPTER 5

As Dr Lucy Hall hurried into the Paediatric Intensive Care Ward, she thought for a fleeting moment about Sam. How was he doing up there? Were they ahead? She hoped so. Her son was a fierce competitor. He would not like to lose. He was also an almost infinite source of knowledge. It was not possible to play Trivial Pursuit with him. She'd wished that they would allow kids on some of those high-dollar quiz shows. Sam would start his adult life rich, if they did.

Her son left her mind as she approached the bed of one of her young patients. Silently, as she always did, she thanked God and her lucky stars that her own precious child was so healthy and so strong. People did not realise how hard things could get.

She looked down at Peter. Brain tumour affecting his optic nerve. No surgery possible, chemotherapy ineffective. The weapon of choice was thus radiation. Peter looked real tired.

'The treatments have shrunk the tumour twenty per cent,' Maria said as she handed Lucy the clipboard. 'How's his eyesight today?' Lucy asked softly.

'No change,' Maria said quickly.

That was not good. Not good at all. She moved closer to his bedside. 'Hello, Peter. How's it going?'

'A little better, I guess.'

Coming from a young patient, that meant its opposite. Peter felt a little worse. She wanted to just reach into his head and drag that dark offending mass out of there with her bare hands. How had it come to this beautiful little boy? Why? Was God asleep at the wheel, or what?

When she saw he had a well-worn copy of *Peter Pan* opened, a wild sort of a hope leaped up in her heart. Maybe, just maybe, the professional assessment of his vision was wrong. 'Can you read that?'

'Nah. But I know the story from the pictures. My mom used to read it to me.'

Like most of the kids on this ward, Peter had a large support team of parents, brothers and sisters, aunts, uncles and cousins who were there for him and for each other. Friendships blossomed in the family waiting room outside, hopes rose and fell, laughter broke out like sunshine and tears flowed like a waterfall. As the storms of disease passed, Lucy thought of it as a sort of lifeboat. Strangers wept on each other's shoulders and everybody bailed for everybody else.

If you wanted to know something about the nobility of the human species – if you believed for a second that the greed and the cruelty and the violence were all she wrote, then you needed to spend a shift here where children lay dying and getting well, and you would find out two things: saints are a lot more common in this old world than sinners, and the eyes of a sick child shine with higher love. Few people could leave a place like this still believing that the universe was void of spirit, and when you died, that was that.

'I know your mom's been very proud of you,' she told Peter. 'You've been very brave.'

As if reacting to her words in some obscure way of its

own, the building shook. Then came a sound she'd never heard at the hospital before, a long wail of wind speeding, perhaps, around a corner or whipping through the eaves, a banshee wail on a stormy, unsettled day.

Los Angeles in the evening was bizarrely silent. It was quiet in the way that London used to be quiet, when all sound was absorbed by fog. It was beautiful, though, the fog rolling in from the Pacific, blanketing the Santa Monica beaches, turning Venice into a ghost city, sweeping then up Sunset and Wilshire and across the Ten, slowing traffic on the 405 from the usual evening crawl to a creep.

It came like a living creature made of damp and shadow, slipping and sliding along, bringing with it magic and danger in a place where the traffic boomed and rush hour was all hours.

Inside the Fox news chopper, Bart Tonnies worried that LA was about to get a dose of weird weather like New York and Tokyo were seeing. He thought maybe this had something to do with Typhoon Noelani, which had dissipated north of Hawaii a few days ago. He began to make his report.

In the studio, Tommy Levinson stood in front of his blue screen, listening as Bart reported. He was damn glad he wasn't up there in that chopper. A helicopter was not a nice place to be in fog, for sure.

'This layer of fog is very unusual for Los Angeles,' Bart said. 'It occurs when warm, moist air collides with cold ocean water. Surface temperatures in the Pacific must be abnormally low right now to create these conditions.'

Tommy's camera came on and he said, 'Thanks Bart, that's really something.' But it wasn't the number one story. No, the story of the day was connected to Noelani.

49

They had got a heavy surf warning from NOAA a couple of hours ago. Even the email was strange. You didn't get emails from NOAA marked 'EMERGENCY' too damned often. He continued smoothly on. 'And later today, the experts are telling us that we're going to be seeing some record breaking surf along the southland's beaches, from Santa Barbara all the way down to San Diego.'

His pause cued the co-anchor, Lisa Richards. As always, Lisa was ready. 'Just how big is this surf going to be, Tommy?'

'Lisa, we don't know for sure, but it's coming off Hurricane Noelani which hit Hawaii last week. My guess is that it should be massive.'

'Thanks, Tommy. I hope nobody gets hurt.' She turned to Kevin Garner, her co-anchor.

'That's it from us,' he said. 'On behalf of all of us here at Fox Eleven news, good night and we'll see you tomorrow.'

Fat chance nobody was going to get hurt, Tommy thought. There'd be half a dozen surfers swept away, was his guess. His camera went off. He was done. He hurried out of the set. He had a mission to accomplish, and there was no time to lose.

Bernie's office was empty. Tommy moved fast, and caught up with him in the parking lot. 'Hey, Bern, you said you'd wait.' He needed something from this man, something it looked like Bernie was not ready to give him.

'You're a weatherman, Tommy,' he said.

Was he ever sick of those words. A producer says 'weather,' he means 'trap'. It was a job with no steps – except down. If his ratings should ever slip, a thousand smaller markets beckoned. He'd clawed his way this far up the greasy pole of television. He needed just this one little push.

He forced himself to smile at Bernie, made himself radiate the cheerful good humour that kept his audience coming back. 'It's a weather story,' he said. 'My guy in the forecasting centre tells me this is gonna be the biggest surf ever.'

'Surfing is not a weather story.'

Tommy kept smiling. Inside, he thought 'moron', he thought 'jerk'. 'I can do more than weather, Bernie. Just give me a chance. You know I want to get on the network some day.'

'Sorry, I already promised it to Jaeger.' He started to get in his car.

Jaeger? What was wrong with this picture? Jaeger got funerals and cats in trees, for Chrissakes. Then he knew. Oh, Bernie, you are bad. You are so bad. 'All right,' he said, 'I'll give you my Lakers tickets.'

Bernie stopped getting in his car.

'Courtside, two rows back. You take a shower.'

Bernie frowned.

'From the sweat, Bernie. The players are that close.'

Bernie smiled.

The Pinehurst Jazz Quartet played what Sam thought was probably supposed to be music as waiters in white jackets moved around the room with trays of canapés. Outside, the rain rained, as it had, it seemed, for at least forty days. Sam was feeling highly vulnerable, to say the least. How were you supposed to act at an adult party for kids? Pretend to be an adult? He couldn't even button his ancient sports jacket. He saw Brian and sidled up. Please, engage me in conversation. Save me from this rabble. 'This is so retro,' he said into Brian's ear, 'it might actually be cool if it was on purpose.'

51

Brian's top shirt button was so tight his neck was folded. His face was red. At least there was one person in the room who looked stupider than Sam Hall. 'Yeah,' Brian said, his voice a nasal whine, 'look at all these nerds.'

Then something so fantastic happened that Sam could not believe it. Brian actually started bobbing his head to the music.

No, it was impossible. Nobody could flame out this badly. Dorktown. Unbelievable. He looked like a drunk turkey. Sam slid off, wishing that some god of teenage embarrassment would have mercy on him and drag him right up through the ceiling and the rainstorm and the stratosphere into space. Very far into space.

And then a vision appeared. Its name, officially, was Laura Bowden, but it was not an ordinary, earthbound girl. In that amazing antique dress, she looked like she'd just been painted by Renoir or somebody. He knew that his jaw had dropped, because he had to snap his mouth closed. How could anybody look that hip and that just achingly beautiful both at the same time? 'This place is incredible,' she gushed. 'Can you believe this is their *cafeteria*?'

Oh, my beloved, please don't be impressed with this incredibly impressive place and these incredibly cool kids, not when I can't even button my jacket! He said, 'I suppose it's all right for nineteenth-century robber baron décor.'

Her eyes flashed. 'Don't be so caustic.'

He had to be. It was his only defence. 'What's that supposed to mean?' he asked, trying desperately to maintain a cool he did not feel at all.

Brian, sensing his weakness, stopped doing the Turkey Trot and chimed in. 'Caustic. It means capable of destroying or eating away by chemical action. Corrosive. Marked by sarcasm.'

'I know what caustic is,' Sam snapped. He turned to Laura. 'You think I'm all those things?'

She stared to answer, would have answered, but now the unthinkably awful happened. J.D., resplendent in his perfectly tailored school blazer, moved on her. 'You played a great first round,' he said. To her. Not to the team. Absolutely not. He offered Laura his hand. Sam could smell the manicure from here.

'Thanks,' Laura said from behind the stars that were suddenly swarming in her eyes, 'so did you.' Then she said, to Sam's total amazement, 'These are my teammates, Sam and Brian.'

Class. She also had class. Sam decided that he was enough in love to actually go crazy.

'Welcome to New York, boys,' J.D. said. 'I'm J.D.,' he added pointlessly. Who did they think he was? Sir Paul McCartney? The Pope?

Sam found himself examining J.D.'s nametag. He sensed that this was not going anywhere good, but his fingers were already on the thing. 'That's it,' he heard himself say . . . caustically. His brain screamed SHUT UP, but out of his mouth came 'No name, just *initials*?'

It was so not funny, so utterly lame. And it made him realise that his own amazing, childish stupidity in filling in his own tag as 'Yoda' was going to haunt him for the rest of his life. 'Sam,' his brain screamed at him, 'the name is Sam!'

'Nice name tag,' J.D. deadpanned. 'You should meet my little brother.' He smiled so smoothly that it might have been done by a movie actor. 'You guys could swap booger jokes.'

She laughed. Brian laughed, too, but who cared? *She* laughed. Then Sam was looking at her back – and at J.D. on the far side of it. J.D. gave him the slightest of winks.

'Your school is amazing,' Laura said with a little tremble in her voice. He was so super cool, so far up there, that she was nervous.

J.D. was as smooth as a destroyer on a glassy, moonlit sea . . . and as lethal. 'You should see the library,' he crooned. 'Would you like me to give you a tour?'

'That would be great!'

Great. We'll all go. Then she'd shoved her punch into Sam's hand and sailed away on the arm of Apollo the Sun God . . . in the damn rain.

'Man,' Brian said, 'you've got some serious competition.'

Oh, yes he did. Yes he surely and disastrously and miserably did. 'Please,' he said.

Brian knew when to lay on the coal. 'Bet he's rich, too.'

That was enough. 'Shut up,' Sam said.

Brian started to ignore him. Then he saw Sam's face. He shut up.

Thunder boomed and lightning stalked Washington's monuments, striking the Capitol, the Washington Monument, the Lincoln Memorial. It didn't matter. A little lightning wasn't even enough to make these stout buildings vibrate. But the wind that swept through the streets and shook Jack Hall's townhouse windows gave more than a few people pause. At Reagan, the National Weather Service was recording eighty-mile-an-hour gusts. The Cherry Trees around the Jefferson Memorial were taking a beating, and some of the old oaks in Rock Creek Park were shaking like saplings.

Jack was asleep, something he'd been wanting to be

for about forty-eight hours. So, when the phone started ringing, he started by integrating it into the sound of the thunderstorm he was dreaming about.

The thunderstorm was on an island somewhere just this side of heaven. There were big tropical flowers, the rain was warm, the wind was sighing gently through the coconut trees.

And the phone was ringing. In the coconut trees? No, in the bar. Yes – but that was another dream. No bar here.

Then his hand was moving, grasping something, bringing it to his ear.

The multicoloured tropical flower became a very black telephone receiver. He started his throat, tried to make it work. Nope. He started it again. Careful, though. Mustn't flood the engine. 'Who is this?' he heard some kind of very hoarse old gorilla rumble.

The phone said, 'It's Gerald here. Rapson.'

'Whoson?'

'Gerald Rapson. I'm sorry to call so early.'

Calling from England. Jack's eyes opened. All traces of sleep evaporated. He sat up. 'No problem, Doctor, it's all right.'

'I really hate to bother you, but I'm afraid – well, we've found something extraordinary. Extraordinary and disturbing. You recall what you said in New Delhi about how polar melting might disrupt the North Atlantic Current?'

What in the world? Why did this rate a five a.m. phone call? Jack wasn't sure he wanted to know. 'Yes,' he said guardedly.

'I don't know quite how to say this, but I think it's happening.'

The room swayed. 'What do you mean?' Lightning

flickered against the drawn drapes. Jack quelled an urge to rush to the window.

'One of our Nomad buoys registered a thirteen-degree drop in temperature the other day.'

That was no big deal. What the hell was this about?

Rapson continued. 'At first we thought it was a malfunction. But four more across the North Atlantic are showing the same thing. I've sent you an email.'

The Nomad buoys were part of a complex system that the Brits were deploying. Unlike the current bonehead US administration, they took the North Atlantic Current damned seriously. It was the lifeblood of their country. Kill it, you killed the UK.

Jack called up the email. 'Jesus. I can't believe this.'

'You predicted it would happen.'

'Yes, but not in our lifetime! This is so fast.' But he'd feared it, he had. It had been worrying him for months. It was why he'd started collecting weather anomalies. He needed a drink. No, he didn't. He needed coffee. Quad expresso, very damn hot. Now.

'There are no forecast models remotely capable of plotting this scenario,' Rapson said. 'Except yours.'

His? His was nothing but a rough model of climate as it might have been ten thousand years ago. 'My model constructs a prehistoric climate shift. It's not a forecast model.' A forecast model would have millions of data points and run on a super-computer. His had a couple of hundred thousand and ran on a damn laptop. This laptop.

'It's the closest thing we have. Nothing like this has ever happened before.'

Jack pulled up his model, began keying in water temperatures as they must be at present across the North Atlantic. 'Or at least not for ten thousand years,' he said slowly. He did not like the way this looked. No, he surely did not, not one little bit.

LA had recorded over six hundred accidents in the fog-bound madhouse of the past twenty-four hours. Eleven fools had been pounded to bits by their own surfboards, and the cliffs in front of Santa Monica were being eaten by surf that wasn't even starting to get tired when it slammed into them.

Tommy was on the story, clutching his mike in the wind, staring into the minicam. This was what it was all about, a story like this. Behind him, he knew, surfers were still working the waves, madmen all.

'These waves are even bigger than I imagined them,' he gushed. 'Just take a look. Wow, look at that wipeout.' He kept hoping that the guy would reappear. He did not. 'That's gotta hurt.'

Were these people out of their minds? Yes, damn right. That guy had probably just drowned, for the love of Mike, and there were *still* guys floating boards. It made him kind of sick to think that his story might be drawing more of them down here to this deathtrap.

'I spoke with several people earlier who say this is the best surfing they've ever seen in Southern California.'

'We're not on,' his cameraman said.

'We're not on?' Not even Bernie would pull this. Nobody would pull this. But they had damn well pulled it.

The National Weather Service's Los Angeles Weather Centre was a comfortable station for a meteorologist, but not one that was going to get you real far. Weather was not an issue, here. Smog was an issue. But the weather was cookie cutter perfect except when an *El Niño* sent some storms up this way. Then there could be landslide dangers, for sure. But weather, as in, 'seek shelter immediately' – no.

Which was why Bob Waters was making out on the couch with Tina the administrator from Ojai. They were down to their underwear, too. Bob was very pleased. Things were moving right along.

Then Tina broke away. 'I don't know about this,' she said around her fantastically smeared lipstick, 'aren't you supposed to be monitoring something?'

Oh, dear. Dear, good girl. 'This is Los Angeles, California. It has no weather.'

He got back down to business. She needed to have her temperature increase, pronto. He slipped her bra off and re-ignited her lips with the best kiss he knew how to administer, slow and full of eager, persistent tongue.

She talked around the kiss like she would have around a cigarette. 'What's that noise?'

He pulled back. 'What noise?'

But he heard it, too. What was that? He got up from the couch, tucked in his shirt and zipped his pants as best he could, then stuck his head out into the hallway. They really didn't belong in the supervisor's office, but it had by far the best couch. Still, he didn't want the janitor who was waxing the hall floor to see him.

What *was* that? Not the floor waxer. He stepped out into the hall. 'Excuse me,' he yelled. 'Could you—'

The janitor turned off the machine. 'Yeah?'

At first, Bob couldn't believe it. Then he had to. Every phone in the building was ringing.

He ran into the Command Centre, such as it was. The public was going crazy. He snatched up the first phone he reached. A voice started screaming. The guy was yelling something – 'tornado.' It was the word, 'tornado.'

Oh, Christ. 'Sir, you're seeing a dust devil. No, sir – okay, look, just stay calm.' He hung up and went quickly to the next phone. 'We don't get tornadoes in Los Angeles. But thank you for calling. Really.'

Now the red phone rang. Okay, great. He picked it up. 'It's Tommy,' the voice said. 'I'm at the beach.'

'Look, Tommy, I'm kind of in the middle of something. What do you need?'

Tommy was huddled under a lifeguard stand, frantically using his cellphone. 'There's hail the size of golfballs coming down here!' As he spoke, Manny Wolff handed him a bigger one, then another that was bigger yet. 'Make that tennis balls and oranges. What's going on, Bob?'

Bob was staring at the Doppler radar, staring in disbelief. He was looking at a monster of a kind he had only learned about in college, and it was right over the Los Angeles Basin. As he watched, a red area appeared, shaped like a long hook. 'Oh, my God,' he said vaguely as he hung up the phone, 'I've gotta go.'

His next step was to call his supervisor, Jeff Baffin, at his house in the Hollywood Hills.

Jeff responded immediately to the ringing phone. He hadn't really been asleep, not with all this thunder. He was a meteorologist for a reason: weather fascinated him. It was the world's last out-of-control wild thing, proof that nature was bigger than man. He'd been hearing thunder before the phone rang, and telling himself that he ought to get up and open the curtains and take a look at what sounded like a really neat storm.

'It's Bob. Turn on the Weather Channel. Right away.'

The Weather Channel? Bob had access to far more

information than the Weather Channel. But Jeff found his remote and did as he was asked.

'I think we've got to issue a tornado warning.'

What the hell? This was Southern California. 'What are you talking about?'

Then he saw, on the TV, the same Doppler that Bob was probably looking at. He had done a stint at the National Severe Storms Lab in Oklahoma, and he knew instantly what he was seeing. Instinct caused him to jump to his feet. 'Why didn't you call me sooner?'

'I didn't realise—'

Thunder bellowed. Jeff went to his French doors, pulled the drapes aside, and opened them onto his deck. Wind poured in, wet and dank, the kind of wind that flails and leaps around at the base of a big storm, the wind that worries between the gusts that crush.

Before him there unfolded the most magnificent and terrible thing he had ever seen in his life. The monster was sliding across the Hollywood Hills, its cloud bottoms bulging down at him like the teats of some sort of demoness of the sky. As he watched, circulation formed in one of them, then probed downward towards Hollywood Boulevard. It snaked left and right—then swept his way, moving across a couple of miles of air in seconds.

Instinct made Jeff crouch. The scared animal that lives in the back of every human mind cried, 'Hide, don't let it see you!'

He heard it hissing, a steady sound that rose to a kind of thunder.

Then he came to his senses. He took his cordless phone to his ear. 'Bob,' he cried, 'issue the goddamn warning!'

And then he got the hell out of there.

CHAPTER 6

President Richard Blake said, 'You're sure a five iron will get me there? I was thinking maybe a four.'

'Five's your club,' Tim Cooper said. The President took the club, addressed the ball, and knew that the swing was exceptional as soon as he felt contact. He watched the ball sail perfectly down the centre of the fairway. When it bounced on the green, his Secret Service guys applauded. 'I should never question you, Cooper,' the President said.

He thought to himself, 'I can get in another nine if I'm fast.' Orders were strict: the President took his golf seriously. He was not to be disturbed on the course. The truth was that he used the time to think. Since he'd taken on this killer of a job, he had lost all privacy, all personal space, and it wore on him.

Of course, there were three helicopters overhead and probably fifty minders of various kinds making themselves invisible all around him, but that was okay, that was tolerable. As long as all he saw was Cooper and his following guards, the game was doing its job.

Then he heard a loud humming. He looked around, and realised that golf was done. 'Maybe we can finish the back nine later,' he muttered miserably to Cooper as six carts loaded down with everybody from Secretary of State Angela Linn to the – was that guy the head of NOAA? – anyway, loaded with major players, came bearing down on him.

'Yes, Mr President,' Cooper said.

What in God's name had happened this time?

Tommy was reporting and driving the news van. 'I'm currently moving east on the Ten,' he yelled over the thunder, the horns and the roar of the storm. 'What you are seeing behind me are two actual tornadoes striking Los Angeles International airport – no, wait, they joined and formed one large tornado.'

It seemed to stand dead centre of the runways, like a gigantic black column stretched between earth and sky. Tommy wondered if the debris he could see in the air around it consisted of pieces of airplanes . . . or maybe of people.

Then he saw, not half a mile ahead, another tornado, this one blowing across the freeway. His chest fluttered, he felt air being sucked out of his nose, and the distant noise of the LAX twister was replaced by a cataract of sound so loud it was like a living thing.

A Ford Focus appeared in midair, the driver clutching the wheel. Tommy could see his teeth, his twisted-shut eyes. He swerved, causing cries of terror from the equipment bay in the back, and the Focus hit beside him, and went skidding away on its roof. 'I just saw a guy die,' Tommy thought. And then the tornado was off the road, and thank God.

An aged Honda started honking behind him, its panicked driver trying to literally crawl up the van's tailpipe.

Then the tornado seemed to stop. He looked at the wall of black wind, at the shadow of an eighteen wheeler flashing past inside. Or was that a mobile home?

With sick terror, he realised that it could be coming back.

*

Jack Hall caught up with Dr Gomez and Janet Tokada in a corridor. Excellent manoeuvre as far as Jack was concerned, much more efficient than doing the old interoffice two-step. His conferences with Gomez tended never to actually happen, and this had to happen – now.

'I need to talk to you,' Jack said, standing in Gomez's path.

'Not now, Jack, I'm busy.'

At least he didn't pull his punches. In fact, he actually turned aside and attempted to bypass. Jack was having none of it. 'Gotta be now, Tom.'

Gomez sighed, but he stopped trying to get away.

'We're building a forecast model and we're going to need—' He turned to Jason, who knew all the technical details. It was Jack who knew what the end product meant, kids like Jason who understood what kind of digital massage the data would need before that end product could be created.

'We'll need priority access to the super-computer for two days, maybe three.'

Jack swallowed his own shock. That was a taller order than he'd expected.

Gomez's eyes widened. 'Oh, is that all? Anything else?'

'Yes. We need to start immediately.'

Tom looked up at him. 'I'd say you'd lost your mind. But you've been this way for the past twenty years.'

That made Jack mad. He didn't like being thought of as an overbearing eccentric, not one bit. He was trying hard to conceal it, but the truth was that he was frantic. 'Tom, this is important,' he said smoothly.

Tom looked at him, and Jack looked right back. He did not smile, he did not banter. He wanted to communicate everything he could about the urgency of this project without appearing to browbeat his own boss.

The woman with Tom asked, 'What is this model you're building?'

Who in hell was she? Some congressperson over here to find a budget to slash, a few more scientists to send off to teach high school instead of doing the research for which they'd been trained?

'Janet Tokada,' Tom said, 'Jack Hall. Janet is a hurricane specialist with NASA. Jack's a paleoclimatologist and I have absolutely no idea what he's up to.' He turned towards the double doors that led to the tracking lab. 'Janet, let me show you—'

He opened the doors into total pandemonium, with technicians yelling at each other, people frantically keying information into computer stations, and knots of scientists clustered around monitors.

'What's going on in here?' Gomez asked, amazed. Normally, this was a very quiet sort of a place, an electronic laboratory, really.

Atmospheric specialist Glen Voorsteen yelled, 'They've just issued a tornado warning in Los Angeles!'

Jack thought, 'Oh, God, I don't even need a model. This is my model.'

Jason stared with his mouth open, his face as pale as death, towards a news monitor. Jack followed his eyes to the words at the bottom of the screen, words in bright blood-red: BREAKING NEWS BULLETIN. A young woman was saying, 'The first tornado was spotted twenty minutes ago. We have live coverage from our Fox Eleven chopper. Are you there, Bart?'

'Oh, Jesus, they have a chopper up,' somebody yelled.

*

Bart was so excited that the fact that the chopper was all but doing somersaults in the sky meant nothing to him. He stared out at the massive beast. What was this called, anyway, Category 4, Category 5? It just plain towered into the sky. 'Lisa,' he said, struggling to keep his voice even as the helicopter took another leaping slide closer to the wall of the funnel. 'Lisa, I've never seen anything like this.' These tornadoes are forming so fast—' The pilot grabbed his arm, pointed. 'What?' Bart snapped. They were on live television, here.

A tornado swept along the ridge of the Hollywood Hills. It had a strange, gliding motion, like it was a leaf being blown along. They all moved like that, almost like a snake moves, that same sort of sinister, questing motion.

This one quested right into a very famous sign, and they got it, they got it all right out over the live feed, as the churning funnel ripped the Hollywood sign to pieces, sucking its letters up thousands of feet, then dropping the remains like confetti that blew away in the angry, random gusts of wind that surrounded the central funnel.

The engine of Jeff Baffin's classic Porsche whined as he raced down towards Sunset. Ahead, he could see the single most amazing thing he had ever witnessed. Spread out before his eyes was a vast storm, its blackness spreading from horizon to horizon. All over Los Angeles, lights were gleaming as if it was midnight, but the sun should be up, the streets flooded with morning light.

In the far distance, he saw the pale, iridescent streaks of a hailstorm. But closer – that was the incredible sight, the unbelievable, terrible and awesome sight.

The funnel was not a funnel, but a thick black piston of a thing that towered easily a thousand feet into the sky. It was surrounded by so much dust that the actual structure of the tornado was invisible. Surrounding like satellites were tiny objects, twisting and whirling, bright against the darkness. Jeff saw a pick-up truck, roofs, a police car with its light bar still flashing, and bodies, easily recognisable because of the flailing legs and arms, all sailing upward with majestic grace, then plummeting hundreds of feet down into the streets of the stricken city.

Over the screaming of his engine, he thought he could hear the screaming of people. He tore out on to Sunset and he heard screaming all right.

It was excitement, delight even. A couple of kids, the youngest probably not yet twelve, were standing there laughing wildly and videotaping the storm, which was now so close the ground was shaking. He screamed at the innocent, crazy kids, 'You can't stay here! Run for cover! Go! Go!'

They looked at him like he was insane, then went right on taping. There was a tremendous crash and a small explosion as a motorcycle hit the middle of the street. An office door followed, then a Coke machine, which exploded into a fizzing mess.

They looked at each other. They ran.

Jeff watched the funnel move towards the Capitol Records Building, famous for being round, shaped like a stack of records. He didn't have all that good a view, so he raced the car a couple of blocks. He wanted to keep the monster in sight.

His cellphone rang. 'Yeah?'

It was Bob, wanting to know where he was.

The storm started ripping panels off the building. Jeff could see offices being exposed to the outside, papers flying off desks, chairs and equipment not far behind.

The funnel seemed to be slowed by the building, like a lawnmower hitting high grass.

As it chewed the building to pieces, it made a continuous series of dull thuds, like some kind of automatic artillery piece pounding away in the distance. Then the building completely disappeared in a black mass punctuated by millions of white sheets of paper. The tornado briefly looked like a ticker-tape parade arranged by Satan himself. Then it passed, and the building reappeared. It was a skeleton, clean iron with a ragged bit of something dangling here and there. He could see *through* it, as if it was just a frame, waiting for its walls, its windows, all the signs of life.

'Jeff, where are you?'

'Yucca and Vine. I'm on my way—'

Ahead of him, a taxi lifted off. It looked like a car from Back to the Future. It went up in the air, its brake lights flashing, its front tyres whipping from side to side as the driver instinctively struggled for control he would never get.

Then it fell. Jeff saw it coming. He thought, 'Oh.'

The cab smashed into the Porsche, which was also yellow. But not just yellow, not anymore. Both cars were also stained by red, running blood.

For Tommy Levinson, the catastrophe was also a dream come true. It was a TV reporter's opportunity of a lifetime, and he knew it. He was off the 10 and speeding down a residential street near downtown. He wanted to get in front of the oncoming tornado, dangerous as this might be, to capture the human drama of people fleeing as the deadly storm rampaged towards their homes.

As he leaped out of the cab, he practically knocked

down an old lady hobbling along carrying an equally old cat. The cat was vomiting.

'Hey,' his cameraman yelled, 'the network's gonna take your feed live!'

Wunderbar! Perfect news. Tommy Levinson was going national. 'Are you serious?' he asked, trying to keep his voice from squeaking with excitement.

'You're on in five!'

People were pouring out of houses now. Immediately north and west, the sky was a black wall raining roofs, bicycles, cars, and everything else from Chinese food to a damn horse, which was sailing slowly downward, its tail streaming.

'Do a three-sixty around me and get them all in one shot!'

The wind was kicking up, it felt like some kind of a muscle guy shoving at him, slamming into his back and shoulder. But who cared, this was *national*!

'Three . . . two . . . one!'

'This is Tommy Levinson reporting live from downtown Los Angeles. The devastation and destruction around me are incredible.'

A billboard ripped to pieces and came flying at him. A new movie, he couldn't see which one. Around him, panicked residents ran frantically. The storm would be here in a matter of minutes.

'It looks like some sort of huge Hollywood special effects movie here, only this is the real thing!'

Plywood from the billboard came angling in like a runaway wing. Tommy never felt it slice into him. But the camera caught the action as Tommy and the plywood went skittering off down the street, the blank wood square and the limp, lifeless body.

Inside the Fox News set, Lisa talked into her microphone. 'Tommy? Tommy? Are you all right?'

From off camera, Kevin shot her a look that said, 'Drop it right now.' She shut up. Their director saw he was ready to cue in, and turned his camera on.

'I think we've lost that connection, Lisa. Let's go to Bart.'

The chopper was standing off about two miles south of downtown. The air here was slightly less turbulent, so at least Bart wasn't going to experience the embarrassment of spreading his breakfast all over the instrument panel. From his vantage point, he could see a number of tornadoes, most of them churning right towards downtown.

'I've heard of F-fours and F-fives. I have no idea how big this one is, Kevin. Is there such a thing as an F-ten?'

Kevin's reply from the safety – maybe – of the studio crackled in his ears. 'I don't know, Bart, but I'd keep your distance.'

For sure. The damn tornado chewed into a skyscraper, scraping off its glass wall like a kid tearing the icing off a cake. People came pouring out of this one, no doubt torn from their desks by the suction. Bart felt queasy, but not from turbulence. He hadn't seen much death, and certainly not wholesale death like this, never.

'I'd advise anybody on the ground to stay as far from this area as possible,' he shouted into his mike, hoping that he was still on the feed.

In the LA Weather Centre, Bob was wishing to God his boss would hurry up and get here. Jeff was never late, but he hadn't answered his cell for a long time. Could he not get through because of traffic? Surely he would call in, given the emergency situation. Of course, there was another possibility, but Bob did not want to think about that one.

He listened to the whine of the floor waxer outside. What, exactly, was he supposed to be doing here? He'd sent the warning. All that involved was activating the emergency warning system with a key. Piece of cake. But now what? The storm was bizarre. It was killing lots and lots of people, for sure. So what did he *do*?

Jeff, get your ass in here! He called the cellphone again, listened until the message came up – and then listened more as the line went dead.

He looked down at his feet. The building was vibrating. And now there was a new sound, a big mother of a sound, like some hell-demon pounding on an organ the size of Mount Rushmore, drowning out the floor waxer and everything else in the world.

Tina crouched behind a chair. Bob ran to the conference room window and threw open the curtains. Before his eyes was a black wall. Nothing else. Just pure black. Then something came out of it, tumbling end over end. It was yellow. It was somehow . . . familiar. Dimly, he was aware that Tina was beside him, that she was clutching his shoulder.

A yellow traffic light weighs over a hundred pounds, so when it came crashing through the plate glass window, it did so with the force of about four sticks of dynamite, given the fact that it was moving at over a hundred miles an hour.

The janitor turned off his floor waxer. He looked along the hallway to the closed doors that led into the conference room and control centre. Things had been really noisy a moment ago, but now they'd gone quiet. Awful damn quiet, as a matter of fact.

He headed quickly towards the doors. He had to get in there, anyway. There was cleaning up needed before the day crew came on duty. These night folks took a fair amount of looking after, the way they spread the pizza boxes around, and never mind what those two kids tended to do to the couch in the conference room.

He opened the door and almost fell out of the building. He stood there, his mouth wide, his eyes almost pleading that this not be true. Where the rest of the building had been, he was seeing outside. He was looking at buildings, not a room. He realised that he was looking at downtown, but it didn't make sense because – oh, Jeez, where were those two kids?

On the east coast it was already ten in the morning, but the Olympic Decathlon at the Pinehurst School was not in session, not right now. Sam was, frankly, scared. Something was very wrong here. Laura knew it, too. She sat close to him, close to her friend. J.D., not so conscious of the strangeness of what they were watching on TV, hovered nearby, looking for an opening.

The TV showed a helicopter image of the most terrible thing that Sam had ever witnessed, the destruction of Los Angeles by some kind of weird tornado swarm. They kept just materialising out of the sky and swooping down, sending the black clouds and glittering debris that meant more death and destruction.

Brian came in. 'I was just on the phone with my mom,' he announced. He grabbed the remote and changed the channel.

'—a second aircraft has apparently crashed, also as a result of extreme turbulence . . .'

The image cut to a long shot of the LA airport. Smoke

was rising from many fires, most particularly on the runways. When Sam thought of the turbulence they'd gone through, he almost threw up. Laura squeezed his hand. He leaned over and kissed her cheek. She squeezed harder.

CHAPTER 7

Camp David was founded by Franklin Delano Roosevelt in the Catoctin Mountains near the District of Columbia. It was re-created by Dwight Eisenhower as a much needed place to escape to from the rigours of Washington DC. It was a quick trip by Marine helicopter, and there was not a President since who hadn't been grateful to FDR for his foresight and to Ike for his old-fashioned good sense.

Over the years, though, one president and then another had taken his work with him to Camp David. Some, like Johnson, Reagan and Clinton, had used it more as a conference centre than a retreat. Richard Blake had tried to emphasise its retreat aspects, but not very successfully. The presidency tended to follow you like the most loyal pooch you could possibly imagine. Sometimes. Other times, it was more of a tiger hunting you down – like now.

He was still dressed for golf as he entered the conference room with its pine panelling and its bank of TVs. It looked a little bit like a rustic living room on steroids, but make no mistake, it was all steroids. The Camp David communications system duplicated that of the White House.

Vice-President Becker hung up a phone. 'The FAA wants your approval to suspend all air traffic.'

Becker was the authority on things like the weather

and the environment, things that should not be of any concern to a President, and had been too much of concern to too many of them for too long. Becker's brief was to assist in whatever way he could to disentangle industry from the morass of environmental regulations that were socking too many of Blake's supporters in the pocketbook.

And do the country a favour in the process. This was a damned economy, this United States, not a nature preserve. He sought eye contact with his Veep, but said only, 'What do you think we should do, Raymond?' There were a lot of things he didn't care to say aloud, not even among trusted aides. Another thing about presidencies – they leaked. If the two of them had been alone, he might have added, 'about an asshole demand like that?'

Becker got the meaning of that look. He shook his head tightly and said, 'Until we can figure out what's going on, I don't think we have a choice, sir.'

Well, hell. There *were* some big momma storms brewing this morning, to be sure. And there had been crashes, maybe because of the weather. *Maybe*.

He sighed. If Raymond thought they should go for it, they should go for it. 'All right. What's the National Weather Service say?' He could predict that: 'Maybe hot, maybe cold, could rain, maybe not. Global warming, natural causes. Or not.'

The Vice-President looked grim. Real grim. The President knew, then, that he didn't yet have the whole story, and it was not going to be a good story. Becker was about to 'suggest' a briefing.

'I've already asked Tom Gomez to meet us at the White House. He'll give us a full briefing when we get there.'

Tom Gomez, the head of NOAA, was a professional

scientist, not an administration appointee. He would normally brief his bosses at Interior, not the President. 'What about the Secretary of the Interior?'

'He'll be there, too, sir.'

Something was up. Sure as hell. And bad. That, too, for sure. The President understood that there would be no back nine, not on this day.

Jack Hall was thinking about an apple tree. It had stood in what was now tundra in northern Alaska around ten thousand years ago. On the fine June day that world had ended, it had been in bloom. It had died in bloom, quick frozen by a storm so intense that it had pulled supercold air from fifty thousand feet to the ground in a matter of minutes. Temperatures had probably dropped from around seventy-five above to a hundred and fifty below in seconds. Thus, mammoths frozen solid with delicate plants in their mouths and stomachs, and the apple tree.

His mind snapped back to the present moment, the conference that was going to be about not quite what was happening, and was going to drive him nuts.

Tom Gomez got up on the podium. 'Listen up everybody. We don't have much time, so let's get started. Dr Vorsteen?'

The director of the Hydrometeorological Prediction Centre jumped to his feet like a soldier coming to attention. 'All our grid models are worthless,' he all but screamed. 'We're baffled.'

Okay, that was a step in the right direction.

Now Walter Booker with his wild hair and his Einstein glasses popped to his feet. 'I don't think grid models are going to be a lot of help here. We've got serious circulation moving down from the Arctic, two storm cells in the

Pacific, and one developing in the Caribbean.'

Tim Lanson, the sharp young hotshot from the Severe Storms Lab, interrupted. 'Are you suggesting that the Arctic events are somehow connected to what we're seeing on the West Coast?'

It was an excellent question that Jack knew that nobody in the room could answer, except him. And he didn't have his data yet.

Booker said bravely, 'We have to consider the possibility.'

Now Vorsteen chimed in with some gimcrackery. 'The only force strong enough to affect global weather is the sun,' he announced. Oh, yeah, buddy, that and your big beautiful Lexus and a few billion other smoking machines . . .

'What's NASA say?' Gomez asked.

The ridiculously beautiful Janet Tokada said, 'We've already checked. Solar output is normal.'

Jack tried one. Not that it would help. 'What about the North Atlantic Current?'

Eyes turned his way. He leaned up against the back wall, arms folded. He wished that he had his Indiana Jones fedora. Too bad.

'What about it?' Vorsteen asked.

'Well, I got a call from Professor Rapson at the Hedland Centre at about five this morning. He believes that the current's chasing south like a scared puppy.'

Booker shook his head. 'Come on Jack, how could that be?'

Might as well float a little idea. 'Well, the current depends on a delicate balance of salt and fresh water.'

'Okay,' Vorsteen said. He was on the record that the current wasn't anywhere near doing anything unusual.

Jack continued on. 'Nobody's taken into account how much fresh water has been dumped into the ocean by melting polar ice. I think we've hit a critical desalinisation point.'

He could taste the scepticism. His theory, unfortunately, had captured the imagination of popular authors and filmmakers. Right or wrong, that was a major strike against it in the scientific community.

'I don't buy it,' Vorsteen snapped, correctly reading the silence as doubt.

A surprising ally appeared. Janet Tokada said, 'It would explain what's driving this extreme weather.'

He heard Lanson warn Booker. 'If he's right, all our forecasting models are useless.'

Jack decided to try a frontal assault. Old debate technique, not a good one. But what the hell, the weather he'd been predicting was sure as hell out there. 'Hedland has some pretty convincing data. They've asked me to feed it into my paleoclimate model to track upcoming events.'

That got Gomez rolling. 'Hold on, Jack, are you suggesting that these weather anomalies will continue?'

Time for a little reality check, folks. 'Not just continue, get worse.'

'Worse?'

'I think we're undergoing a major climate shift.'

There was a moment of total silence. He watched various pairs of eyes widen. He saw a smile cross Vorsteen's thick face. Then the place erupted into debate. Gomez saw that it was over, and left the podium.

Jack made his move, the one he'd been planning since he planted himself near the door. He followed his quarry into the hallway. 'Tom! Hi. What are you going to tell the White House?'

Gomez was not a happy camper. But he stopped. Barely. 'What do you think I should tell them?'

Passion welled up in Jack, an emotional fire burning so hot that he almost shouted out his words. 'They have to start making long-term preparations *now*.'

'Jack, all you've got is a theory.'

'Give me that super-computer time, Tom, and the theory will become fact.'

Gomez thought about it. Vorsteen had the ear of the administration, he knew that. He also knew that something was damn well wrong, big time. 'All right. You can have it for forty-eight hours.'

A generous gift, worth about sixty grand in budgetary terms. Jason and Frank had come running up to support their boss. 'That's not much time,' Jason warned.

Gomez raised his eyebrows. 'I can't—'

'It'll do,' Frank assured him.

Janet Tokada had been standing close by, obviously listening. 'Does your model factor in storm scenarios like what we're seeing?'

Actually, they were worse. A lot worse. But there was still so much he didn't know. 'We haven't had time—'

'Maybe I can help.'

He thought about that. She sure as hell could. On a number of levels, he suspected. No, hoped. Go slow, fella, you're too much of a bull, you scare 'em off. He gave her his best smile, extended his hand. 'Welcome aboard.'

Jason hurried along beside Janet as they headed for the lab. 'Hi, I'm Jason,' he babbled.

Okay, son, Jack thought, do your worst. Or best. It isn't going to matter.

*

At Hedland, the weather had been deteriorating for hours and was now in a most unusual state. This part of the world was born and raised on ferocious winter storms, so the locals weren't too concerned. They didn't know the stats, though. They didn't know that this station had never before recorded this much snowfall at this time of year. Never.

As Dennis worked to clear the satellite dishes, he listened to the Beeb on his earphones. 'It has been twenty-four hours now since snow began falling across the British Isles,' he said, 'and it shows no sign of letting up.'

Inside the control centre, Doctor Rapson also watched the news. One of his assistants had a taste for good tea, and he was happily making a brew up that smelled quite promising. His genes were too English for coffee. When the going got rough, what he thought about was a nice cuppa, like right now.

On the telly that was built into the control console, a reporter was reading some quite disturbing news. 'An elite RAF search and rescue team has been deployed by helicopter to airlift the Royal Family to safety . . .'

Dennis came in, banging his boots on the floor, then rolling them off. 'You think they'll come and get us if we get snowed in?'

'Not likely,' Rapson responded. 'Luckily we have our own generator and enough tea and biscuits to sink a ship. We'll be fine as long as the loo doesn't back up again.'

A BBC reporter speaking from Paris said that the temperature there had fallen well below freezing overnight. This was without question the most radical weather change that Rapson had ever experienced. He did not say it to his assistants but he thought that they were trapped here, and that they would not survive.

At NOAA also, they were watching the report from Paris. 'Coming in on the heels of the recent floods,' the reporter continued, 'the sudden drop left roads literally covered in ice. The weather is equally severe in the rest of Europe.'

Jack was glad to see the coffee that Jason was bringing in. They'd been tweaking the model round the clock and even he had to admit that he was more than a little tired. Just how tired became clear when he fumbled and dropped his cup as he tried to drink his damn coffee. He didn't like his body to fight him like this. Work was always more important than physical welfare, and at the moment that was more true than it had ever been.

They had to get this thing finished, and they had to do it yesterday.

'Jack,' Frank said as he helped him with the mess, 'you've been working for twenty-four hours. You're the only one who hasn't taken a break.'

That was true, and Jack had to admit that he was losing effectiveness. A man who couldn't successfully pick up a cup of coffee could not be expected to be all that accurate entering thousands of data points off paper readouts and identifying their positions and relationships in the model, which was what he had been doing all night. And all yesterday.

'Maybe I'll close my eyes for a few minutes. Wake me as soon as we get the first results.' There was a sofa in his office that worked pretty well as a substitute bed. Jack headed for it.

Janet watched him go. For such a big man, Jack Hall was really wound up tight. 'Is he always so obsessive?'

The young assistant, Jason, answered almost as fast as his partner Frank, and they both said 'yes'. She was fascinated with Jack. He was brilliantly skilled at modelling, and also had a vivid way of describing paleoclimate that was very unlike the way most of his colleagues in his dry profession talked about their work. As he'd told her stories of mammoths grazing by a lakeside as supercold gusts from hyper-cells froze them solid, her mind had vividly pictured the scene.

It was not a scene that she wanted to see repeated, say, in the middle of New York City, and she was tremendously worried.

Jason said, 'Frank's been with Jack since the stone age. I've only endured five years of servitude.'

Was he chatting her up? The kid in the group? How fun.

'If he's such a tough boss, why do you stay?'

'Because he's the best scientist I've ever met.'

Then Frank said, 'We're done.'

Janet looked at him. She did not like the expression on his face. Somewhere deep inside herself, perhaps she felt that their finishing the model would somehow unleash the disaster it implied on the world. Or maybe she was just damn tired, too, not to mention damned scared. Without another word, Frank rose from his chair. The three of them headed for Jack's office.

Rain was literally gushing down the windows at Pinehurst. The lovely grounds had become a sheet of grey water punctuated by trees and, here and there, the upper part of a car. The road out was still clear, though, as most of the flooding was confined to the athletic fields.

The corridors were crowded with students carrying

suitcases, and Sam was totally revolted by the stench that permeated the building. Old was not entirely beautiful, it seemed. The reek of sewage did not go very well with beautifully tailored school blazers and all the rest of the ritz, and that made Sam feel a little better.

'I guess the school's plumbing is really old or something,' Sam said into his cellphone. 'Anyway, all this rain's backed up the sewage system.'

Jack wanted Sam home. He wanted him home right now. He did not think that he should tell him why, though, because he also did *not* want Sam to attempt any journeys that were going to be too dangerous. Jack had been concerned about all this for some time. But now he was more than concerned, he was scared. No, terrified.

In the background, visible on a TV in the super-computer room, the President was addressing the nation.

'Where are you going to stay tonight, Sam?'

'They're going to find places for us with the kids who live here.'

It was as he'd feared. 'Are you sure you can't get any tickets for today? Why does it have to be tomorrow?'

If he was right, this thing was about to turn real, real mean. Tomorrow could well be too late. 'Believe me, if I could, I would. This stink is, like, unbelievable.'

'This is serious, Sam.'

'So's the smell!'

He didn't get it, not at all. Jack wanted to blurt it out, but then he would have to add the truth, that he thought that there was a good possibility that the world as they had known it was ending; indeed, that they might never see one another again. 'Sam, I want you home.'

'I stood in line for two hours to get these tickets, Dad.'

Jack's heart was breaking. He glanced over at the

82

President on the TV screen, then started to tell Sam the truth.

Sam said, 'Don't worry, I'm not gonna miss the train.'

Maybe the lines would still be open tomorrow. Maybe it would even be safe. 'Okay.'

'Gotta go, Dad!'

'Okay. I love you.'

Sam closed his cellphone. Laura was saying, 'Guess what, we've got a place to stay.'

There was J.D., grinning away. So they would be going to his place. At least the invitation wasn't just for Laura. 'Great,' Sam said. He raised the edges of his mouth in what he hoped was a believable approximation of a smile.

CHAPTER 8

The lowest temperature ever experienced in the United Kingdom was recorded at Braemar, not far from Balmoral Castle in Royal Deeside. On January 10, 1982, it reached −17 Fahrenheit, but a glance at the external temperature monitor told RAF Flight Lieutenant Scott Harrow that it must be far below that on the ground right now.

Minus 44 at eighteen hundred feet meant that it was probably around minus 35 on the ground. It must be ungodly cold in Balmoral Castle, where they were headed. The Royals had got snowed in and the heating system had failed. This, extraordinarily enough, was a rescue mission to pull the Queen and her spectacularly grumpy husband, Prince Philip, out of a very dangerous situation.

One did not think of them as really old until you saw them up close. Scott, as a member of the Queen's Flight, had been close to them many times, and they were frail old people in very nice clothes, basically.

'Look at those cars, they're not moving,' his co-pilot said.

The chopper was passing over the A93, the Old Military Road, that connected through Royal Deeside. Scott gazed down at the long line of vehicles. It looked as if the entire town of Braemar was trying to convoy out. And it looked as if they were snowbound. That was death down there, probably a lot of it.

'Radio HQ, tell them to send somebody out to check on it.'

It was getting damned cold in the helicopter, despite its heating system, and Scott could see why. They were at minus 52. Flight Officer Williams said, 'This can't be right.' But his gauge and Scott's agreed.

Minus 58.

Now the stick became sluggish. 'What the hell's going on?'

A spiderweb of cracks appeared on Scott's external temperature gauge. It was connected to an external pitot tube, which would be directing a thin stream of outside air onto its measuring filament. Obviously, the temperature inside the instrument was dropping below its tolerance minimums.

The stick was not properly responsive. Scott was a little afraid, frankly. It was not a good sign, this sort of control issue. Instinct made him glance again out the window. This was no place to attempt a counter-rotation landing.

Williams yelled, 'The bloody hydraulic fluid is starting to freeze!'

A moment later, a Christmas tree of warning lights began flashing. Everything that required hydraulic pressure was beginning to malfunction.

Hydraulic fluid freezes at minus one hundred and fifty degrees Fahrenheit. Scott tried to reduce altitude, on the theory that he might get a slightly higher temperature closer to the ground.

'Pan! Pan! Pan! Royal two-zero flight controls are not responsive,' he said into his microphone. 'Attempting autorotation. We're going in. Repeat, this is Royal two-zero—'

He heard the Voice of Safety start, 'Your fuel pressure

has dropped below the required safety limit. Please correct this condition. Your fuel pressure—'

He hauled the stick back with every ounce of strength in his body.

Nothing whatsoever happened.

He heard the beginning of the crash, a long, sighing crackle as the fuselage went sliding along the steel-hard surface of the snow.

That was the last thing he heard.

The other two choppers in the flight closed position. Squadron Leader Wilfred Tyne was appalled at what he had just seen. Scott and Willie had plunged out of the air like a bloody stone. They had not lived, he knew that. He'd seen the aircraft break up on impact. There was no smoke back there, though, meaning that it hadn't exploded. Which was odd, considering that all three helicopters were fully fuelled for the trip out here and back, given that Balmoral's fuel depot might not be operating if their power generators had all failed.

Suddenly he heard chopper three sing out, 'Port engine pressure dropping.'

The pilot shouted, 'Attempt relight on one.'

They'd damn well lost an engine, and Wilfred knew why: these helicopters were below their operational minimums on temperature. They were freezing to death.

He saw chopper three fall back, wobbling in the sky. Then he heard, 'Flameout on starboard engine as well.'

He began circling. His third chopper dropped, then a fairly good counter-rotation started. They got it back under a semblance of control. Excellent, they were going to at least be able to make a crash landing.

Then he saw the rotor slowly just stop moving. No

rotation, no counter-rotation, nothing. For a long second, the helicopter hung motionless, as if it was taking a moment for it to realise that it had to drop.

It fell away gracefully, drifting lazily to one side, and then plummeted towards the ground. It disappeared in a spray of snow. He'd just lost his flight. He was too stunned to grasp it. Six men were dead and the rescue mission was in a shambles.

Then his own instrument panel began flashing emergencies.

'Entering autorotation,' he said, 'select emergency fuel.'

'Emergency fuel selected on both.'

Wilfred pressed the collective lever. He might as well have been pressing on a brick in a wall, for all the movement he got.

'Come on, you bastard!'

He could not lose his whole flight. Then what the bloody hell would happen to the Queen?

'Come on!'

'Selecting manual pilot override.'

Using all his strength, he managed to keep the chopper under a sort of control as it descended. A quick glance told him the altimeter was unwinding in a blur. He fought the wing, seeking to get some kind of dihedral going, feeling just the slightest response as air pressure over the twisting rotor blades increased.

Then there was a sharp *bang*, followed at once by a terrific jolt to the left, then a ferocious tumbling that never seemed to end.

When it was over, though, there was movement inside the twisted airframe. A moment later, a broken door fell off into the snow with a dull thud, and Wilfred climbed out. He stood in his shredded flight suit staring off down a long, snow-choked vale.

Was that smoke down there? Perhaps a wisp of it was coming from a house otherwise buried in the drifts. He started down. As the shock of the crash wore off, though, he realised that his thigh was burning. It felt like coals were being pressed against him. Instinctively, he clutched at the rip in his flight suit that was letting in the super-cold air.

But it was too late, far too late. He kept plodding, but his movements slowed. He was so cold that his sensations failed him. It didn't feel as if he was freezing, but as if he was burning.

He came to a stop. He knew that this had happened, but distantly, the way a man knows a thing in a dream. Then he knew no more.

He'd frozen solid, a stick of gum still in his mouth. Like the mammoths of Alaska so long ago. But they'd been chewing daisies. Wilfred favoured Doublemint.

The wind came across the vale, howling down out of the north, drawing graceful snow ghosts with it across the ridges and the rounded hilltops. It hit Wilfred in the face, causing his helmet's plastic visor to shatter.

Wilfred swayed with the wind, then toppled back. When his body hit the chopper's exposed left landing gear, it shattered like glass, falling to the ground in pieces. In time, they would be reduced to bones, this strange scattering of limbs, head and torso. But first there would be snow, racing, tumbling out of the sky, smothering the crash site beneath a blanket of white and silence.

Jack and Tom Gomez hurried through the metal detector into the Old Executive Office Building. The security guards hardly looked up from their TV. A reporter was telling about how people were buying up provisions all over Washington. People were not stupid. They didn't need to be told that something was terribly, terribly wrong.

'You better be sure about this, Jack. My ass is on the line, here.'

'You saw the model.'

'Yeah, and I hope to God it's wrong.'

Jack wouldn't have minded a disguise right now, because Becker was coming this way. Tom plastered a huge shit-eater across his face and said, 'Mr Vice-President—'

Becker didn't even slow down. 'Hey, Tom.'

Tom dragged Jack along, keeping up with the striding Becker. 'You know Dr Hall?'

What a moronic question. Had Tom forgotten what had happened just a week ago? Or had New Delhi been before that? It seemed like the conference had happened in another lifetime, on another planet. Hopefully, also, to Becker.

Becker glared at him. Jack gave a little smile. 'We've met,' the Vice-President snapped.

'Doctor Hall has some new information I think you should look at.'

Jack held the folder in front of Becker as the three of them shot down the long corridor. 'We just got these results from our simulation. They explain what's causing this severe weather.'

'I'll have to look at them later. The director of FEMA is waiting.'

'This is urgent, sir,' Jack said, 'our climate is changing violently and it's going to happen over the next six to eight weeks.'

Becker gave him a look out of the side of his eye. Jack realised that the Vice-President wasn't just vaguely aware of him. He was acutely aware. 'I thought you said it would take hundreds of years.'

'I was wrong.'

Becker smiled slightly. 'Maybe you still are.'

'Look what's happening around the world. Europe is already in serious trouble.'

'We're making all the necessary preparations. What more do you expect?'

Jack actually entertained the idea of slapping some sense into this mutton-head. There were probably twenty million lives at stake in the United States alone, and half again as many in Canada. 'You have to start thinking about large-scale evacuations.'

That stopped Becker's forward motion, at least. He turned on Jack. '*Evacuations*? You're out of your mind, Hall.'

Aides, who had been waiting for Becker at the end of the hall, began marching forward.

'Excuse me, I have to go, ' Becker said.

Jack had to keep trying. He could not give up on those lives on a point of politeness or whatever it was. 'Mr Vice-President, if we don't act soon, it's going to be too late.'

Becker did not turn around. Jack and Tom found themselves staring at a closed office door.

'Thing I like the most about you,' Tom said, 'I think it's your people-handling skills.'

'Hey, I tried.'

Gomez shook his head.

'He's an idiot, Tom.'

'Rule number one: the boss is a genius.'

'Oh, come on, Tom!'

'The boss is a genius!'

Yeah, okay, he could see that. He got it. 'Brilliant,' he said, 'just awesome.'

How long does it take twenty million Americans to freeze to death?

J.D.'s apartment made his school look like a real dump. Never mind what it did for Sam's digs in Arlington. Even the halls had half-panelled walls. And was that actual silk on the walls or just wallpaper that looked like tan silk?

He decided that the wallpaper in the foyer probably cost more than every stick of furniture in his mom's house put together. Dad's didn't count. Neatness was his obsession, not decoration. His couch looked like it had been won in a third-rate raffle circa 1990 or so, sometime back in prehistory.

Laura just gushed. Oh, she simply *loved* it. 'You live here?' she asked breathlessly.

'Only on the weekends. It's my father's place but he's hardly ever around.'

Laura shot Sam a look that almost melted his heart, it was so wanted and so very, very welcome. She had remembered one of their conversations, when he'd confided to her how much he missed his dad.

'Is your dad here now?' Brian asked.

'Skiing in Europe with Cindy.' He gestured towards a picture on the hall table, of a distinguished looking older man and a girl of maybe twenty-eight. At most. 'My step-mom,' J.D. said tonelessly.

'Plenty of snow in Europe right now,' Sam said. They went into a sort of solarium that was full of plants, orchids and bromeliads in full bloom, and something that reminded him of what tropic nights ought to smell like. Frangipani?

'Somebody knows how to take care of his plants,' Brian commented.

'There's a housekeeper,' J.D. said. 'These things are my dad's hobby.'

'Where do we sleep?' Sam asked.

'There are six bedrooms. Take your pick.'

Six bedrooms overlooking Park Avenue and Sixty-Eighth Street. What, Sam wondered, would be the tab on that? Ten mil, would be his rough guess. Could a nice smile and a lot of love compete with ten million dollars?

J.D. smiled – very nicely. He had noticed Laura pick up another of the photos.

'That's my little brother. I was teaching him to ride his bike.'

Okay, so he was a nice guy, too. This was so not good.

Brian had walked to the large window. The rain was so intense that you couldn't see more than half a block. In fact, you could hardly see across Park. It had been raining like this now for twenty-four hours.

'How long can this keep up?' Brian asked.

Sam had been wondering that. His dad had wanted him home, and his dad knew an awful lot about weather. He sure wanted to be home right now, with his mom and his dad. He stood beside Brian staring out at the pounding, cold rain, and wondering.

Jack was standing around a speakerphone with his team. Dr Rapson's voice crackled from the far north of Scotland. 'About two hours ago, three helicopters went down on their way to relieve Balmoral. They crashed because the fuel in their lines froze.'

Jack felt sick. Was he talking about the kind of temperature that might be recorded during a supercold downburst? 'At what temperature does—'

'Negative one hundred and fifty degrees Fahrenheit,' Rapson said. 'We had to look it up. The drop was phenomenally fast, too. People froze solid.'

Jack thought. There had to be imagery that would flesh this thing out, prove that it wasn't just a once in a millennium freak.

'Can we get a satellite image of Scotland?' Jack asked. 'Two hours ago?' He asked Rapson, 'How do you know all this, Gerald?'

'Our monitoring stations captured everything. We've got mountains of data, but nowhere near enough computing power to analyse it, and every super-computer in the UK that's not doing something urgent seems to be down.'

'That's gotta be a lot of data,' Jason said.

'Drop it on our FTP site,' Jack told Rapson. Assuming that the internet was still working, that is. Things were getting dicey. All sorts of web-based communications systems were having trouble.

Janet had imagery up of Scotland from the DSRS geosatellite. 'This is what was over Scotland when they experienced that temperature drop,' she said.

'It looks like a hurricane,' Frank said.

Jack stared at the white cloud, giving special attention to the eye, which was not a distinct feature. Still, there was rotation, no doubt of that. He had never seen a mega-cell before. Such thunderstorms only existed in theory.

He stared at it, thinking that this was the most menacing object he'd ever seen, right up there at the top of the list of nature's most dangerous hazards. He wondered, if he could pull together satellite imagery of the whole northern hemisphere, how many other of these demons he would see. 'Not over New York,' he thought, 'please, not over my boy.'

CHAPTER 9

It was still pouring in New York, and Luther was confused. Yes, that was it, he was confused. He and Buddha were dry, though – at least, a little dry. They were under the awning of a very fancy building, and the doorman was not there.

Then he was. 'Hey you, you can't stay here. Get a move on.'

Get a move on. How many times had he and Buddha heard that? Well, they knew from long experience that the guy didn't raise a stink and the dog didn't bark, not if somebody didn't want to get kissed with a billy. And all doormen had them, concealed under those fancy coats of theirs.

They got a move on, back out into the rain, but they took their sweet damn time, until the dago twit slapped his thigh – or rather, the billy that was evidently on his right hip.

Maybe the schlubway. They couldn't stop you from being in there, not as long as you kept moving. The transit cops weren't too bad, most of 'em. They'd give a guy a little break in the rain. Most of 'em.

But when he tried to go down he couldn't, because so many folks were coming up. Now, this was the damnedest thing, here. Who would be *trying* to get out of a place of shelter? It was raining at least an inch an hour, and it was cold and getting colder. In fact, the rain had a kind of a freezy feel to it, and Buddha was starting to shiver.

They were down about ten steps when Luther saw that the damn subway was filling up with water! It wasn't just a little, like, ankle-deep water. This was serious, and it was happening fast. It hit him that people could be dying down there, it was flooding that fast.

Buddha gave Luther a fantastically pitiful look. 'Don't look at me like that,' he said. 'I can't swim, either.'

Buddha was a sinker. He'd jumped into the reservoir in Central Park a couple of times going after ducks, and Luther had needed to go down and get him off the bottom. Damnedest thing. Some dogs were sinkers, though, like some people – weird dogs like Buddha, anyway.

A couple of hundred feet up and in very different circumstances, four brilliant young people, the kinds of kids who filled the human future with promise, watched television. The family room was the size of a small movie theatre, with a huge TV, and on that TV was a reporter who did not look very happy. In fact, he looked scared, his face pale, his eyes flicking back and forth as if he was waiting for all hell to break loose.

'It's a mob scene here at Grand Central,' he shouted above the roar of a very large crowd. 'Over half of the platforms are flooded and service has been suspended . . .'

Sam was just as scared as that reporter. He felt very far from home, and he knew Laura did, too, because her hand was holding his tightly. Brian sat with his arms folded – or rather, clutching his shoulders. J.D. was on the phone. 'Don't worry, Benny, I'll be down there in a few hours. I'll see you soon.'

'My dad's driver is coming to pick me up. Do you guys want a lift to the station?'

'Not anymore,' Brian said.

J.D. watched the TV for a moment. 'I'm going to pick up my little brother. I can give you a ride.'

'Where is he?' Laura asked.

'At boarding school just outside of Philly. I'm sure you guys could get a train or a bus from there.'

'The Dow tumbled a catastrophic sixty-one per cent this morning before trading was halted moments ago . . .'

A mile and a half away, on Wall Street, Gary was feeling as if an angel of mercy had come down and lifted him out of SEC hell. Yesterday, the market had been strong. Top of the world.

Speaking of which, Paul said, 'It's like the end of the world.'

'Billions of dollars gone,' Tony whispered, 'billions . . .'

Gary smiled. He wanted champagne. 'So much for the Voridium merger.'

Paul looked at him like he was insane. 'Voridium. Yeah, that was something that was gonna make this firm a little dough.' He stared at the TV like it was trying to bite him. 'What're we gonna do?'

Gary couldn't stand it. He had to just damn well raise a glass to a life that had been saved. 'I'll tell you what we're gonna do. We're gonna go out and damn well celebrate.'

Up on Park, J.D. was still pretty calm, as far as Sam could tell. Pretty calm, still in control. Sam clung to that. He wanted somebody to be in control. He wanted not to panic and he was about to do just that, no question.

'Victor is stuck in traffic over on Fifth,' J.D. said. 'It'll be easier to head straight out of town if we meet him there.'

Brian's mouth dropped. 'You mean walk? In this?'

'It's only a few blocks.'

Just then the lights flickered. Oh, God, thought Sam, electricity, don't go out, not that, too, because I don't want to cry in front of these guys, and I am about to. Laura seemed to know, or maybe to be falling apart herself. Her hand became like steel. Warm steel, comforting. Sort of.

Morton's Bar was open and jammed, mostly with a double dip of brokers at the bar knocking back shots. Tony wanted to join them, but there was no way he was going to make it far enough forward to get to the oblivion section, which was the front, where every time you dropped a five on the bar, another dram of bourbon or vodka or whatever hit your glass.

Back here, it was a matter of handing money forward, waiting, waiting some more, and hoping that some asshole didn't just down your shot for you. 'I just took out a second mortgage,' Terry said miserably.

Gary felt oddly superior. It wasn't his doing that his ass had been saved. But still, miracles on this scale didn't happen every day, did they, now? So he must have some kind of preferred stock with somebody upstairs. Had to.

'You know what your problem is?' he told Tony.

'Yeah, everything's gone to shit.'

'Your problem is, you worry too much about money.'

Paul actually put a hand on Gary's forehead. 'You feeling all right?'

Gary had bought some Camels on the way in. He unwrapped them, took one out and then rummaged in his pocket for the lighter he'd also bought.

'I thought you quit,' Paul said.

'From here on in, I'm living every day like it was my last, brother. You never know what's in store for you. One

98

minute, you're lookin' at ten million dollars, the next you're lookin' at ten years in prison. Whatever.' He knew he was getting louder. He knew that. He knew, indeed, that he was getting so loud that people were noticing, even over the din of weeping that filled the place. 'I pay five grand a month for an apartment my maid spends more time in than I do. What is that about? I'm telling you, Paulie, it's about time to make some changes. Say goodbye to the old selfish, materialistic, greedy Gary. I am no longer gonna be a slave to the almighty dollar!'

'Maybe you should sit down, Gary.'

'From now on, it's all about the moment. Money means jack-shit to me! From now on!'

'Gary, sit down!'

Gary picked up a bill and rolled it like a coke stick, and lit it with the lighter. 'This,' he said, 'is worthless.'

'Jesus,' Paul said, 'that's a damn C-note, man!'

'It's a piece of paper.'

The lights went out. There was silence. Shock. The darkness was broken by only one small light, the hundred dollar bill burning between Gary's fingers. It went out.

Pandemonium.

J.D. had just hit the button to call the elevator when the power failure hit his building. 'Maybe we should take the stairs,' Sam said.

'We're on the top floor,' J.D. replied.

They waited. This time, the power did not return.

'Guess it's the stairs,' Brian said.

They made their way down the stairwell, which was illuminated by harsh emergency lighting from the battery-powered floods that hung at each landing.

It wasn't a tall building, so being on the top floor

turned out to be not that big a deal. It took only ten minutes to reach the lobby.

Outside the front door, Park Avenue had become a river. Normally, Manhattan was well drained, even superbly drained, but you drop an inch of rain an hour on it, and you keep doing that and doing that for hours and hours, and you are going to get flooding where you have never seen it before or believed it possible.

Laura suggested that they just stay there. Sam thought she was probably right, but he could not quell his urge to return home. This was all very, very wrong. It was worse than the other kids knew. Something was going real wrong, something that his dad would understand and protect the family from. But you had to be together for that to happen, and he secretly thought that, if they did not all get back with their families right now, they might never see them again.

'We need to get home,' he said, striding out into the storm. The water was at hubcap level in the street, deep enough on the sidewalk to get in your shoes if you weren't careful. And the rain, it was a pounding, roaring Niagara of water, coming down so steadily that the idea that it might ever end seemed inconceivable.

Still, though, the city kept on, cars everywhere, traffic jammed tight in all directions. Sam feared that this was because millions of people were trying to cross through two tunnels and one bridge to New Jersey, and it just was not going to happen. Plus, what if the tunnels were flooded? They could be. All of this traffic might be headed in just one direction: the George Washington Bridge.

J.D. tried to lead them. 'This way,' he said, taking Laura's hand. J.D. liked her because she was so damn wonderful, and Sam couldn't blame him for that. He was seeing a different side of the guy now. J.D. was working hard to care for these strangers. Sam had to give him credit. But he did not think that J.D.'s limo was going to get them anywhere any more than the train would, and he was real scared.

Downtown, Gary and Tony and Paul were still not fully aware of the scope of what was unfolding around them. There was a lot of traffic and a lot of confusion, and one hell of a lot of rain, but they still felt basically in control of their lives. If you'd asked them, they would have offered a dozen reasons for the market collapse, none of them correct.

The general public, watching the drama unfold in Europe and now in the US, had not liked what it had seen. Investor after investor had realised that, whatever it was, this disaster was going to cost a hell of a lot. People who had gone through the crash of 2000–2002 had decided to throw in the towel at last. The big boys can rock the market like a mother rocks a baby, but when the little guy speaks with one voice and says 'sell', a broker's hell has no bottom.

Tony was getting soaked as they struggled along the sidewalk trying to hail a cab. 'Look at this, goddamn fifteen-hundred-dollar suit!'

Gary saw a city bus standing at the curb and hurried over to it, his soaked feet splashing in the ice cold puddles. He knocked on the doors.

'Outta service.'

But the guy opened the doors. So what he said and what he meant had to be two different things. Gary stepped into the bus, smiling hard. 'I'll give you a hundred bucks to put it *in* service.'

The driver took the bills, looked at them. He seemed amazed even to see that much money.

'Look, I—'

'Two hundred! Not another word, my friend.'

Tony followed him on to the bus. The driver closed the doors.

Now what?

Every time she noticed a weather report or looked outside, Lucy was more concerned about Sam. Other staff were gathered around a TV at a nurses' station, and she went over.

' . . . severe thunderstorms have caused a major power outage involving all of Manhattan. Efforts to restore power are being hampered by heavy rains and flooding.'

She didn't like that one bit. She wanted her boy back, and she wanted him now. She watched as they went live to a New York street. 'The situation here in Manhattan is very dangerous. There have already been over two hundred reported accidents . . .'

Oh, God, help my Sammy.

This rain was getting to be a serious problem for Buddha, who was soaked and shivering, his tail tucked between his legs. It was colder now than it had been, and it was just totally soaking both of them.

Ahead, Luther could see the big lions of the main branch of the New York Library, and he piloted his shopping cart in that direction. A fair number of people were going up the steps, obviously ducking in to get out of the rain.

He parked his wagon at the base of the steps. There was a lifetime in here, his memories of better days that, when he touched them, brought back his years as a trombone player and a drummer, and even, from long, long ago, the bright days of youth, when he could hit a softball home run right out of a hardball park.

'That dog can't come in here.'

Another security guard. Sometimes he thought they grew them in some cellar somewhere, like mushrooms. Normally, he would have let the harsh words blow him away like the dried up old leaf that he was, but not now, not today, because they were down to the skinny, and the skinny was that Buddha was gonna die out here, and maybe Luther was, too.

'C'mon man, it's pouring and it's getting cold!'

'Read the sign.'

Yeah, there it was, a sign like a wall: No food, no drinks, no pets. So he couldn't bring in his turkey dinner or his pitcher of Cosmopolitans or his damn weasel, either. And if Buddha was going to die, he was just going to damn well do that. 'It's supposed to be a public library,' Luther muttered as he struggled back out into the downpour.

At the Central Park Zoo, there was further evidence of just how wrong things were going. Human beings, long accustomed to living behind walls, to taking shelter from sun and storm alike, have lost the sensitive nerveendings that connect most living things with nature. Animals have not lost them, and for this reason the zoo was a wailing, whooping, flapping, pacing riot of frantic creatures.

But not entirely. One of the keepers, frightened himself and ready to bolt for home, shone a flashlight into the wolf enclosure, which was surprisingly quiet, and discovered that they were not huddled back in the hutches. He'd heard a noise earlier, and he knew what it was now: a tree had come down on this cage and split the back of it.

The wolves were gone, the whole damn pack. If he reported this, there was going to be a huge operation mounted to find them. He would end up stuck on duty for the next two or three days, out there in that mess helping the cops track them.

The hell with that. He cut off his flashlight and hurried back to the office.

J.D. was leading Sam and Laura and Brian through long lines of cars that were submerged up to their headlights. Some engines were running, some were not. J.D. was on his cellphone, which, amazingly, was still working.

'He's stuck a few blocks further up,' he called back to them.

Stuck, indeed, Sam thought. Nobody, but nobody, was going to drive a car out of this mess. In fact, the only way off this island right now was to walk to the shore and take a boat.

Laura said, 'This is ridiculous. We're not going to be able to drive anywhere in this. We should go back to the apartment.'

'I vote for that,' Brian added.

They didn't get it, even yet. Sam doubted that Manhattan was actually sinking, but this water was getting high. They had come all the way down past Forty-Second Street and cut over to Fifth, following J.D.'s quest to reach his driver. Sam very much doubted that they could backtrack. He thought that the lower parts of Forty-Second were probably impassable.

He peered ahead, and saw the library looming ahead like a great island. 'Up there,' he yelled. Now he was in the lead, the other kids behind him.

Laura cried out when her leg hit the submerged fender of a car, but Sam didn't hear it, not in the roar of the rain. He pressed on, passing a Yellow Cab that was going to be completely under water in a few minutes.

But they didn't know that or they would have stopped. Cars don't get submerged in Manhattan. That wasn't the way the world worked – or not like it used to.

Officer Thomas Campbell was not as unconcerned. In fact, he was afraid that the woman and the little girl who were trapped in this taxi were going to drown. The cab was so wedged into the mass of cars just south of Forty-Second that the doors couldn't be opened. The driver was nowhere to be found.

'Calm down, ma'am,' Tom yelled, 'I'll get you out of there.'

But first she had to get the hell away from that window. He needed to break it out, and he couldn't do that if she stayed where she was, pressing her daughter against the glass like that.

'Au secours! Ma fille a peur de l'eau! Sortez-nous!'

Oh, boy, what was that? Some African language? Italian? French? It sounded like French, but that didn't make any difference, did it? 'Ma'am, I can't understand a word you're saying. Get away from the window!' He brandished his nightstick, which made her eyes go wide. She pressed the baby forward even more, as if hoping that the sight of the child would gain her some sympathy. Where she came from, a man with a gun was probably not to be trusted in any way whatsoever.

All of a sudden, a remarkable thing happened. A young

woman, very wet but even so looking like an angel, with her wide blue eyes and sweet lips, came up out of the storm. She yelled into the cab, 'Allez plus loin de la fenêtre!'

Tom was as astonished by her radiant beauty as he was by her perfect French. If there was such a thing as a guardian angel, he was looking at one.

'Le monsieur va vous sortir,' she continued.

Like magic, the woman pulled her daughter away from the window.

'Thanks,' Tom said as he hauled out his nightstick and went to work.

On Liberty Island in New York Harbour, visibility was so low that only the base of the statue could be seen, and then perhaps just the lower twenty feet of it. The harbour itself was completely invisible, except for the small boat bobbing at the Parks Service pier, the boat that carried the staff back and forth each day.

Jimmy Swinton's walkie-talkie crackled. 'What's taking you so long?' his supervisor demanded.

'Just another minute.' He was having trouble with the security system. No matter how hard he slammed the damn door, it wouldn't arm. It had to arm, though. They couldn't leave the island if it wasn't armed. That was procedure.

He heaved again, pushing the old bronze door as hard as he could. And finally, the green light came on and the siren bleated once. The statue was now sealed against all intruders and all the emergency evacuation procedures had been completed.

He turned and began trotting through the park. He was as eager to get to Jersey as any of the others. He wanted coffee, a good meal, and, above all, a nice, dry living room where he could put up his feet, suck a beer, and watch whatever the hell was happening on TV.

As he hurried along, he felt something – or no, heard it. Above the sound of the rain, there was a distinct rumble. It was rising. He stopped. What the hell was that? It got louder still. Christ, look there, a shadow. He saw that it was a ship, black and huge, coming straight at the island.

There was going to be a collision. Except, Jesus, that damn ship was rising, it was bobbing like a cork.

Then he saw. He saw what was under the black shadow of the ship, and was making it bob and turn and rock as it came towards him. The ship was riding on a frothing wall of water.

He turned and ran, thinking only that he needed to get the hell back in the statue and get upstairs, or he was going to be swept right off this island.

The ship veered away but the water came dead on, a forty-foot wall foaming, twisting, raising breakers and dropping them with sounds like many small explosions – boom, boom, boom – as the water came on.

He saw it roil up past the dock, knew that it had swamped the tender, saw fingers of it quest up the island and come racing across the grass and the sidewalks. By then he had his keys out and was getting them into the lock.

The water reached his feet just as he turned the key. Then he felt the cold and found himself looking out into a strange, grey silence, and knew that he'd been overtaken by the wave. He swam, but the surface did not appear. He struggled, kicking wildly now, but it got darker and quieter, and he realised that he was being dragged down, not swimming upward.

His lungs began to hurt, his every instinct demanded more air. He felt his heart becoming a rebel in his chest, then he was seized by a convulsion of air hunger.

He began to take a breath, he could not stop it any more than you can stop a runaway freight train by standing in front of it. Still, he forced himself not to, he even clapped his hands over his mouth and nose.

A flash, another. And then he was breathing, and it was water, and he was coughing but there was nothing but more water. His mother said to him, 'I've ironed those jeans, son.'

It was such a pretty day.

But that was then, this was now: the water sped on, the worst storm surge ever seen on the east coast questing towards the unsuspecting city, dark Manhattan in the rain, laid out before it like a virgin before the ministry of a ravening wolf.

The surge sent long fingers questing against the Battery, that shot straight up in the air like geysers. More and more faces appeared at the windows of downtown skyscrapers as the juggernaut, a black, roiling mass choked with the hulls and superstructures of ships, came rumbling now, blasting up the island.

All along the subway system, a breeze from downtown began to worry the water that stood along abandoned platforms, followed by the booming as if of a rhythm band from hell, as the water exploded down from above into the tunnels.

On the streets above, cars and crowds disappeared, horns honking, sirens screaming, feet sloshing in the little streams and puddles that had been there before the surge arrived.

And then surge covered all, breaking down the

windows of shops and restaurants, blasting into the faces of surprised customers, killing grills in a puff of steam and short-order cooks with hardly even a scream. The water came calling at Trinity Church, speeding up the aisles with a robber's frantic urgency, sweeping across the graveyard and digging up the ancient graves, and now coffins bobbed along the wild way with desk chairs and awnings and jackets and all manner of improbable flotsam. And in the spinning dark below, voices gargled their last and bodies twitched their last, and still the surge raced on.

At the library, all was as it had been before. Or no – unnoticed in the rain, there was a bit of darkness, like some sort of odd blot, appearing twenty or thirty blocks downtown.

Officer Campbell got the little girl through the rear window he had taken out with his club. The angel of mercy helped the mother. They crossed the mostly abandoned cars around them. In one, a massive Expedition, a tiny, infuriated woman honked and honked her horn. Her eyes were like the bulged eyes of a rat, her windshield was spattered with blood from the insane screaming that she could not stop.

And the water came on, slowed for a moment by a building, or the need to go down and fill another tunnel complex, then sped by the long sweep of the avenues.

Laura and Tom and Jama and her daughter, who was named Binata, heard the rumbling now, but they did not heed it. Nothing made sense to them except the rain, endlessly falling, and that one last horn endlessly honking.

'Mon sac! Nos passeports sont là-dedans!'

She'd stopped in her tracks. Tom asked, 'What's the problem?'

Laura said, 'She left her purse in the cab. Their passports are inside.'

'Tell her to forget it.'

Death by water was now less than a mile away.

'I'll go get it,' Laura said. Tom thought she shouldn't, but the cab was just a few feet away, so he didn't stop her. He ushered Jama and the little one up the steps, many and high.

Gary's bus had reached Eighteenth Street, largely because the driver was willing to do just about anything as long as you kept feeding him C-notes. He was actually a pretty good guy, come down to it. There was a time when Gary would have been really, really pissed about all that money, but, truth be told, it was a whole lot easier not to care.

'When was the last time you were on a bus?' Paul asked.

'Dunno. Sixth grade?' Gary remembered that bus, remembered bouncing on the seats. And, say hey, he did it again. He started bouncing. Tony glared at him. Screw Tony. 'This is great, isn't it?' Gary said.

Paul cracked up and started bouncing. Finally, Tony joined in. Here they were, dead broke and without futures, bouncing their way up Sixth Avenue on a bus that, by all rights, was stolen. Only in New York.

They didn't notice how the driver was acting. He was sure as hell not bouncing. In fact, he was noticing that people were starting to run like hell up the sidewalks, jumping out of cars, speeding out of low buildings, running into high ones. His eyes, in his rear-view mirror, were terrible to see, so terrible that they stopped Gary bouncing.

Then the bus stopped, half up on the sidewalk it had been negotiating. There was a rush of air as the doors came open. Then the driver got up and got the hell out of there.

There was a sound coming up from behind. They all heard it. It became rapidly louder. 'From now on,' Gary chuckled, 'I'm always gonna take the bus!'

The roar got even louder. Through the rear window of the bus, had any of them turned around, they would have seen a black wall. Inside it, there were what at first looked like the ghosts of whales. But they were not whales swimming in that water. It was full of buses, cars, trucks, and bodies.

It slammed into Gary's bus so hard that all three passengers were knocked senseless before they even saw the windows implode and the cataract surge in around them and over them.

When Gary found himself on another, very different bus, he hardly missed a beat. He kept bouncing on the bus to hell, bouncing and laughing amid the huddled, despairing shades of the evil dead.

It hadn't taken Sam very long to realise that Laura was gone. In fact, he'd realised it halfway up the steps. But the rain was so dense that he couldn't see. He stopped, turned around, then took the steps two at a time so he could stand in the portico and look for her without water pouring in his eyes.

He was shocked so badly he almost froze. A forty-foot wall of water was coming up Fifth, marching along like a monster truck, and he knew that it was death, and she was in its path. Then he saw her, crouching on the trunk of a cab, rummaging in its broken rear window. She had no idea that only seconds of life were left to her.

Many people, perhaps most people, would have stood rooted to safety, and watched the water take her. In fact, it seemed like there was nothing else you *could* do. The water was coming too fast, surely.

He did not waste a second with ordinary reactions, not even to yell. He took off, leaving Brian behind him calling, 'Where are you going?' He was still oblivious to the danger.

Then J.D. turned, and he saw it, and Brian saw it, and their reactions were the normal human ones: they stood rooted, staring, jaws agape.

Sam passed an old bum who was just scooping up a tatty dog and loping up the stairs. He reached Laura and hauled her out of the cab.

'Run!'

Confusion flickered in her face. Seconds to go. 'What's wrong?'

He grabbed her and hauled her off the cab. 'Go! Go! Go!'

Then she saw it, climbing up Fifth, swooping into Lord and Taylor's, building again, lapping, sweeping ahead. She ran and Sam ran behind her. As they reached the top of the steps, the water did, too, and they pressed their way into the foyer amid a mass of screaming, terrified people.

Outside, a city bus sloshed against the front of the building, followed by a taxi that came crashing through the doors, sliding on its roof in a surge of filthy water and screaming people. The kids scrambled towards the grand staircase across the wide space, the taxi bearing down on them, propelled by a flood of murky death.

CHAPTER 10

Gerald Rapson gazed at the picture; in it the sun shone down on a cottage, beside which a mother, all red and with red eyes, stood beside a father of brown. Their dog, green with green fangs and a curling green tail, sat beside them in the wavy green grass. A little yellow boy stood between his red and brown parents, and Gerald thought he would probably never see the child who had drawn this portrait of himself and his family again. His grandson. His daughter. His son-in-law.

Dennis offered him a cup of tea. 'Is that Neville's work?'

'Neville's far beyond stick figures now. He's six. This masterpiece belongs to my other grandson. David.'

There was a gentleness between the men in this room, almost a reverence. They knew where they were. They knew what was happening. 'Neville's six already?'

Dennis did not have a family. He was not a member of the secret club of people who had loved and been loved by children. He could not know the grace of it, the intensity, the way their innocent delight in you made you feel. 'You wouldn't believe how fast it goes,' he said. When he had been a boy, his father had said to him, 'When you hold your bairns, never forget it.' So true. The way a baby felt in your arms was one of the best things in the world.

Simon's voice called from the communications room. 'Doctor! I've got Jack Hall on the phone!'

Gerald leaped up. His heart began pounding, he couldn't help it. What he wanted to hear was that he'd been dead wrong, that his data were flawed, that the sun was going to come out any time now.

Jack's voice came crackling through on the speaker-phone. 'Did you pull up the file?'

'I've had some problems with the connection, but I'm opening it now.'

Gerald looked at the blue 3D graphic that shimmered on the monitor. 'Were you able to match the thermal cycles?'

At NOAA, Jack heard the question and answered imme-diately. 'Yes. The storm's rotation is drawing super-cooled air all the way down from the mesosphere. That's what's causing those killer cold pockets you're getting.'

Rapson's voice came back. 'Shouldn't the air warm up before it reaches ground level?' He sounded sad, even angry. He was still up there at Hedland. Jack thought that the guy was lucky to be alive.

'It should but it doesn't. It's descending too rapidly.'

'Is this an isolated incident?'

He knew the answer, and Jack knew why he'd asked the question. He wanted another answer. Any other answer. 'I'm afraid not,' Jack said. 'We've located two more of these mega-cells in addition to the one in Scot-land.' Jack pulled up a satellite image that showed three of the nasty circular storms moving south across the Arctic Circle. They looked like tight little hurricanes. At night, a natural light video image would have revealed them to be fantastic engines of lightning. 'One's in north-ern Canada and the other's in Siberia.'

'Do we know their projected paths and evolution?'

Jack did some keyboard work. Normally, thunderstorms are short-lived phenomena, rarely lasting more than twenty-four hours. But these beasts were feeding on a powerful air flow from the south, actually drawing the energy into themselves. 'This is twenty-four hours out,' he said.

According to their model, the storms would have grown by about twenty per cent.

'Forty-eight hours.'

They now covered large regions of Canada and Siberia. Underneath these storms, there would be brutal winds, sleet and hail, with lethal cold pockets forming without warning, freezing everything they touched solid, including living human beings.

'Five to seven days.'

There came a shout over the phone line. Rapson was seeing the same thing that Jack had just modelled. The vortex of the Canadian storm was fifty miles across. It looked like a thunderstorm that had turned into a hurricane.

There was silence on the line. Then, 'My God.'

'It's time for you to get out of there.'

The line crackled again. Jack knew that contact could be lost at any moment. 'I'm afraid that time has come and gone,' he heard Rapson reply. And he also heard the deep sadness in the man's voice.

Static swept the line. 'What can we do, Professor?'

From inside that static, there came back the voice of a ghost: 'Save as many as you can.'

Then there was static. As Jack was hanging up, Jason rushed in. 'What is it?'

'Jack, New York. It's New York!'

A wave of cold, sick fear passed through Dr Jack Hall.

*

The Reading Room of the New York Public Library is one of the great public spaces of the world. In it, thousands of writers have found inspiration and information. On any given day, there are at least three novels being written there, and many more works of non-fiction, articles, papers and essays. Then there are the readers, poring over some of the world's hardest to find books, or just enjoying the latest mystery or the newspaper.

A hundred cold, shivering, wet people huddled there now, in the dark and bellowing of the storm, listening to water surge and lap outside, as hungry waves tested the building that had saved their lives . . . for the while.

J.D. slammed his cellphone closed in rage and frustration. Nobody minded that his filthy face was tear-streaked. They were all crying. Everybody in this room was lost, it was a chamber of the lost.

'I can't reach my brother's school.'

'The circuits are probably overloaded,' Brian said with what Sam thought was amazing confidence. 'Everybody's trying to call at once.'

It was true enough. At least half the people in the room were trying to use cellphones. Sam suspected that the towers were down, that they had no power, that they had been torn from their moorings and swept away by the surge. He didn't say that, though. He wished he could call his folks. He wanted to know that they were alive, and he knew that they would be tormented with worry about him.

It was funny, though, the way you changed. Coming down here, he'd been a frightened kid wanting only to be in the arms of his mom and dad. But now, here, in this situation, he had found a calm place inside, a place to go that could be counted on. He probably wouldn't have put it this way, but the fact was that, under the pounding pressure of this unprecedented situation, a good kid was becoming a good man.

He saw Laura rubbing her shin. 'What's the matter?' he asked, going over to her.

'I cut my leg. It's not that bad.'

He looked at it. At least she was right about the seriousness of the injury. It was cut but not bleeding anymore. Sam guessed that it was going to be okay – unless it got infected, of course.

'Listen,' Laura said, 'I wanted to say thanks for coming back to get me. It was really brave.'

'I didn't really think about it.' They never did, men of action like Jack Hall and his son.

Laura looked down at the sodden purse in her hands. It was made of some sort of cheap wicker material, painted black. It was torn and probably thoroughly soaked inside. 'I'd better give this back.'

Sam watched her go to Jama and present her with the purse that had nearly taken her life. Jama gave her a big smile. Sam could not hear their conversation in French, but he could see the gratitude in the Senegalese woman's eyes. No doubt she was poor. No doubt everything she possessed of importance was in that purse.

J.D. came up to him. 'You should just tell her, Sam.'

Tell her what? Could J.D. mean that he should declare his love? He didn't see J.D. as being that kind of a gentleman. So, maybe he saw him wrong.

Laura was taking a flashlight from Patrolman Campbell, who had known where to go in the building to obtain emergency supplies. 'Conserve the batteries,' Campbell said, as flashlight beams began to dart around the increasing gloom.

Oddly, the librarian, or the one who hadn't abandoned her post long ago, was still at her desk, presiding over an order and a meaning that had slipped, Sam thought maybe forever, into the past. He had an idea that just might work. 'Excuse me,' he said, 'are there any pay-phones on the upper floors?'

The librarian, who had introduced herself as Judith, answered, 'On the mezzanine.'

'Where are you going?' Laura asked him. 'The power's out.'

'Older payphones draw their power directly from the telephone line. Come on, it's worth a try.'

Lucy had made her way across DC from the hospital to Jack's office, and now paced the lobby waiting for him. It used to be that you'd be waved through by the guards. It wasn't that way anymore, and her fear was that Jack would forget all about her the second he put the phone down, but he came hurrying out. She almost hugged him, just by instinct, just because it was so good to see him. But that was all over between them. It was.

'I've been trying to reach Sam.'

'So have I.'

'I tried to call you but I couldn't get through.'

Jack saw that she was trembling, and put an arm around her. She leaned against him. He was warm and strong, Jack was. She just wished to God she could find her boy.

In the murky dark of the mezzanine, Laura's flashlight was essential. 'Are you sure about this?' she asked him.

The water was up to their knees and still rising. It must have taken tremendous energy to push this much water this far inland. Sam could hardly imagine what must be going on out in the Atlantic to cause this. He hoped to God that he was right to come down here. The floor was slick. If the water suddenly started rising fast, they might not get out.

'You have some quarters?'

They pooled their change, and Sam went for the payphone. As he moved along, he realised that the water was now up to his hips. He picked up the receiver.

Jack had taken Lucy to his office. They needed privacy to share the amazing suffering of parents who have lost their child. He brought them coffee. He'd wanted the few moments of being involved with his hands, now he wanted the comfort, and so did she.

'Thanks,' she said. She took the cup. Then she picked up the familiar photo of Sam on the beach, from one of their early trips, taken now, it seemed, back during life in another world. 'I love this picture of Sam.'

'Yeah. I can't remember where it was taken.'

'Florida.'

'I don't remember that trip.'

'Sam and I went with my sister. You were in Alaska doing your doctoral research.'

Jack saw a lot of things, in that moment, an entire lifetime of missed opportunities. Work was important, but now, facing what they were all facing, he saw that there were a lot of other things that mattered, too, and maybe he had made some mistakes.

Lucy gazed at the picture. 'You do remember what he was like at that age?'

'Oh, yeah. He always wanted to hear one more bed-time story.' Jack smiled at the memory, and then his heart filled with pain.

'Jack, how bad is it going to get?'

The pain increased, in fact, the pain seemed to flood out of his heart and into every pore of his body. He laid his hand on hers. He decided that he had no choice here: the truth and nothing but. 'It's going to get worse than you can possibly imagine.'

At that moment the door flew open and Frank burst in. 'Jack! It's Sam! Sam is on the phone!'

The world swayed, came back, and then Jack was running, Lucy behind him. He wheeled into the conference room and grabbed the phone that Sam had come in on.

The water was up to Sam's chest and it was cold and dirty, and he was scared that they might have trouble wading back to the stairs. 'Sam, it's dad,' the voice in the phone said, and Sam's heart almost broke into pieces, and tears stung his eyes. 'Are you all right? Where are you?'

He had to be strong. He could not tell his dad just how terrible his situation was. His dad would do anything to get here if he knew. His dad would die, if necessary, in the effort. 'I'm okay,' Sam said, and Laura's eyes widened. 'We're at the Public Library.'

Jack and Lucy huddled around the speakerphone. 'Your mother is here,' Jack said. He knew well that Sam was very far from okay. He knew that Sam was in mortal danger. But he admired his son's courage, to try to keep his situation from his parents, to prevent from worrying them.

'Thank God you're safe,' Lucy said, and hearing those words Jack had a realisation. Divorce and separation do not end the marriages of people like him and Lucy. Nothing ends them, not really. They were married forever, the two of them, in the blood of their beloved son.

'We're all right, Mom,' Sam said carefully. That's right boy, never lie. Tell what part of the truth you must. 'All right' made his dad's heart thunder with relief. Whatever was really happening to him and around him, Sam did not feel in enormous and immediate danger. 'Can you call Laura and Brian's parents,' he continued, 'and tell them?'

Sam was now up to his armpits. The water was coming up fast, and he knew that he had to put an end to this little miracle, a phone call that had gone through despite impossible odds. 'The water is rising,' he said – and immediately wished he hadn't.

Lucy stifled a scream, and Jack grabbed her hand, held it tight. He had to do his best to instruct his son. Just maybe, the knowledge he was about to impart would save Sam's life. 'Listen carefully, Sam,' he said. 'Forget what I told you about heading south. It's too late now. This storm is going to get worse. It's not like anything anybody's ever seen.' He paused to let that sink in, but only for a second. Given what was happening in New York, Sam probably already knew that, in spades. 'It's going to turn into a massive blizzard with an eye in the centre like a hurricane. Except the air will get so cold, people will be freezing to death in seconds.'

Laura was motioning to Sam. The water was rising too high, they were beginning to need to swim. But Sam had to hear this incredible thing his dad was saying, he had to hear every word. He knew well that their lives depended on it.

'Don't go outside. Burn whatever you can find to stay warm. Wait it out. I'll come for you. I promise. Do you understand?'

Sam did not fear that his dad would risk his life, not

after hearing those calm, authoritative tones. His dad had the measure of this thing. 'Yeah, Dad, I understand.' Laura was treading water. 'I have to go.'

'Wait,' his mom yelled. 'I love you! Oh, Sam, we both do!' His dad added, 'We love you—'

Just as Sam went under, the line went dead. When he emerged, Laura was frantically shining her light around, the beam darting across the mean little waves that filled the hallway. 'I was afraid you'd drowned,' she screamed, her voice producing a dull echo in the confined space.

Sam understood how close she was to panic, to absolute, mind-twisting, insane panic, the kind that led to shock, to helplessness, down the path to death.

He waded to her. 'Come on, Lady,' he said, mustering every scrap of courage he had left and putting it into the calm voice with which he spoke to her. 'We've got to find some dry clothes for you.' And he led her towards the staircase.

Lucy wept, openly and frankly. Jack held her, feeling her slim frame against his body, pressing her head to his shoulder. Secretly, he feared that they had lost Sam, even more that the world itself was lost. He knew that the storm was coming south, and that it could easily get this far. It could be that the Potomac would come striding out of its banks, propelled by billions of gallons of rain, and then would follow a killing freeze unlike any mankind had known, and he thought again of mammoths and daisies, and the last summer day of an apple tree.

He had to release his wife. He did not want to, but his work demanded his involvement. It could not wait, and even though he would have held her forever if he'd been able, he gently pushed her away.

He turned to Frank, who had been waiting – hovering, really – just across the room. 'Where'd you store our Antarctic gear?' he asked.

Frank's face registered confusion, then surprise, then understanding. 'Oh, no,' he said, 'no way. You can't make it to New York.'

'I can try. I've covered as many miles on foot at the poles.' What was it, he wondered? About two hundred miles, and a lot of it was liable to be under water . . . at the moment.

Frank's face had gone the colour of heavy cream – a sick colour in a man who was in robust good health. Jack saw it for what it was: the colour of fear.

'Jack, this isn't any arctic trek you're talking about. Lucy—'

She remained silent. She would not stop him and Frank knew why. If he made it, he would save their son. No mother would have stopped him.

'I have to go,' Jack told her. 'I have to do it.'

She nodded slightly. Jack wiped away her tears, tried to ignore his own. She gave him the steadiest, strongest and bravest look he'd ever seen on her face. It made him proud of her, that look. It washed away years of disappointment and misunderstanding. She smiled a little, and he knew she was proud of him, of his bravery.

He touched her cheek. Her eyes closed. Only another divorcee could understand that gesture. For divorce is as mysterious as marriage, and the real life of couples is known only to couples, a life that is lived through the medium of a secret language of gestures and coded sentences.

He had touched her like that the first time he saw her, and it had made her close her eyes and press her cheek against his fingertips. Again, standing beside their marriage bed, when they were just two trembling kids, he had touched her like that, and in the gesture there had been the shadow and promise of pleasure in the night, the promise that would one day become that precious soul up there in the land of chaos.

This time, when she leaned gently against his fingers, it said, 'I remember all that has come before, and I approve what you're doing now, and if you give up your life for our son, I will love you until my own days are done.'

There could be no more profound moment than this between two people who are snared in the cords of marriage . . . whether they be divorced or not.

In the clammy, dark library, echoing with the rush of swirling water and the strange throbbing of the stricken city, as the occasional cries and sirens that sounded as boats, makeshift and otherwise, plied past outside – in the dark, Laura and Sam explored. The lower reaches of the building were lost to them, of course, but it was a large structure and there was much to be learned and found.

They explored, though, because they were already freezing in their soaked clothes, and his dad had warned Sam that it was about to get very much colder. She was a little drier than he was, and had a coat, so she was not in quite such desperate shape. He was barely able to walk, he was shivering so much, and if he let himself go, it felt like it might turn into a sort of a seizure or something. The word 'hypothermia' came to mind, and he wondered if that was what he was suffering from. If so, shock was on the way, and then the sleep of the very cold, followed by the gradual darkening of dreams that ended in death. Sam had read, in his efforts to understand the perils his dad faced on his polar expeditions, all about what it was like to die of cold. As they died, they dreamed of their lives, just like the drowning do.

And then, in Laura's flashlight beam, there was a door with what could be a very, very useful sign on it: Lost and Found.

It was unlocked, so they opened it and went in. A worn counter, a desk with some papers on it, and boxes and boxes of stuff. Sam gasped at how many. People lost a *lot* of stuff. He doubted that he'd find many pairs of underpants or socks, but he might just get a shirt and over there he could see a whole array of coats, some of them hanging on a rack, more in boxes.

'Come on,' Laura said, 'we need to get your clothes off before you get hypothermia.'

What did she mean? What was he going to have to do, here?

'This is no time to be shy,' she snapped as she started pulling his shirt off. He helped her with the buttons, but she tossed it aside like it was a rag. Then she dropped his pants and ordered him out of them. He complied, and she went down on her knees and helped him out of his socks. Without blinking an eye, she took down his underpants.

It was dark but not that dark. He thought, 'I'm seventeen and this is the dreamiest girl I have ever known, and I am naked.' He was shivering so uncontrollably, however, that nothing happened down below. Then she opened her coat and wrapped him up in her warmth, and that was like being swaddled in an angel's wings. But not a heavenly angel. No, these wings were steeped in girl smell, and this warmth was not heavenly, it was bodily. Very.

'Wha-what are you doing?'

'I'm using my body heat to warm your core slowly. You can't let the cold blood in your extremities rush back to your heart too quickly. It can cause heart failure.'

She knew more about hypothermia than he did. But she did not know about the male body, the way that it cannot conceal its enthusiasms. Or did she? 'Wh-where did you learn all this?'

'Some of us actually paid attention in health and safety class. How are you feeling.'

'M-m-much better.'

Her arms surrounded him and pulled him to her, and he realised that nothing was going to happen that might embarrass the two of them. Because she had been absolutely right. He was seriously cold. He was farther along than he had realised. Just like it said in the books, death by cold had been creeping up on him. His grateful body was interested only in one thing: this delicious, wonderful, life-giving warmth. Later, it might long to be in these arms for other reasons. But right now it was life, and life alone, that it sought.

He thought, 'We're seventeen, we're not about dying, we're about being alive and having fun.' The water echoed, a lapping tinkle. Outside the wind rose, and the old eaves of the building moaned, and its ghosts.

CHAPTER 11

Like all of the great federal buildings in Washington, the Department of Commerce headquarters had been built to last for ever, and packed with more rooms than its planners could conceive that the agency would need in a hundred years. Which was why it was stuffed to the rafters with people and equipment after just a few years, and NOAA was spread out across nooks, crannies, hallways and conference rooms. The headquarters of the National Oceanic and Atmospheric Administration was like Los Angeles: there was no there there.

But Frank knew it as well as a grizzled old cabbie might know LA, and he led Jack straight to the cache of equipment that they'd brought back from the Antarctic. He had stored it with the skill of an old-line civil servant. It would take another old-liner even to understand that the cryptic file notations concealed a treasure trove of superb cold-weather gear. And nobody, but nobody, was going to find this storage space within a storage space without a map, a guide, and more than a little luck.

Jack pulled out a crate of gear, and began sorting through the familiar parkas. They were all fur lined, not out of choice, but because only nature could really handle cold as intense as they had to withstand. But would they still be pliant, and still retain enough warmth to keep a man alive at, say, a hundred and fifty below?

The lowest temperature ever recorded on earth was

127

minus 128.3 at the Russian Vostock II base in Antarctica, back in the winter of 1983. These parkas were rated to minus 130. But below that, who knew what might happen?

At minus 140, exposed skin would freeze hard in about six seconds. At minus 150, a healthy man's blood would freeze in thirty-four seconds, despite the most vigorous activity possible.

He heard somebody behind him. He kept assembling his kit. 'Frank told me about Sam,' Tom Gomez said.

Jack ignored him. Frank had obviously sent him down here, and Jack wished he hadn't.

'I'm not gonna try to talk you out of going. But there's something I need to do, first.' He had a printout of Jack's results, which he held up like a flag – of surrender, Jack thought. 'You need to explain your results to the White House.'

That had been tried and he'd been humiliated by that jackass of a Vice-President, and he wanted no more part of any of it. Let the idiots freeze to death, and the folks who elected them.

No, not them. They'd been lied to, or the administration wouldn't even be in power. But how could he re-explain something to people who'd already dismissed him? How did you do that? 'I've already tried, Tom,' he said.

Gomez shuffled uneasily. His guilty expression revealed that there might have been something between him and Vice-President Becker, something along the lines of Tom assuring the VP that Jack was just a harmless crank . . . in order to preserve his job.

Because Tom had not believed him, either. Tom had dismissed all of this as nonsense, even when the tragedy was well advanced. Now that it was too late – well, here he was. 'This time, it's going to be different,' he said. 'This time, you're going to brief the President.'

So, Tom had bought the model and informed the White House that it was real. You didn't speculate at a Presidential briefing, you informed.

'When?' Jack asked.

'There's a car waiting to take us now.'

At the New York Public Library, Patrolman Campbell was getting things organised. Sam had explained who his father was and the information that he'd offered. Before that, everybody had been waiting for the water to recede. The consensus was that it couldn't be long. People did not understand the behaviour of massive surges like the one that had inundated the east coast. They have an inertia of their own. They do not recede as fast as they rise, not when the scale is as massive as this.

In truth, a terrible race was on, on a scale much too large to be understood by anybody in the library. Probably not even Jack Hall himself was fully aware of it. Or no, he knew, but it would not be in his briefing or in his thoughts, not this secret: that the world was hanging in an extraordinary balance.

If that water did not slide back into the ocean before it froze, and if there was enough snow, then the earth would begin reflecting the sun's heat back out into space. It would be reflected from massive fields of white that would cover a huge circle of land from New York west to Washington State, from Vladivostok to Moscow, and on deep into Europe, to Paris and London and even Marseilles on the Mediterranean coast, to Rome and Athens and Tehran. In the end, almost half the world would be involved.

And if summer didn't heat it enough, then it would not melt, and next winter would add to it and the winter after that, and on and on, until global warming would come to seem like the memory of a lunatic, and another ice age would have begun.

So the world hung in the balance. If the cold now building in the north captured this water and turned it into a sheet of ice, it would be a hundred thousand years before it would melt. If not, then maybe, in the spring, mankind would be given another chance.

It wasn't a new thing. It had happened before. In the past three million years, in fact, it had happened no less than twenty-three times. But the scale of time was so unimaginably large that it was hard for people to understand the truth: the whole of human history, from the cave paintings of Lascaux to the Space Shuttle, had unfolded during one of the brief warm periods that punctuated the earth's normal state, which was to lie sleeping beneath massive sheets of ice.

Couldn't happen again? On the contrary, it happened all the time. But still, in the tremendous history of earth, even three million years was just the flicker of a fly's eye. Indeed, most of the time there was no ice on earth at all. Polar caps were rare on our planet. Mostly, there was a dusting of snow at the south pole, and that was it.

Mostly, but not since Central America had risen out of the sea, cutting off the great trans-equatorial current that had ruled earth's climate for twenty-five million years. That, and a period of instability on the sun, had created this little spat of climatic turbulence that had caused the past three million years to be, well, just a little wilder than normal.

In the library, Sam and Laura and Brian had quickly

assumed roles as authorities and organisers. It had ever been thus: back when the glaciers last ruled and the winters in Provence and what is now South Carolina could see temperatures of fifty below, the smartest had been the leaders. The ones who could trap and sew and measure the seasons in the majesty of the stars – they had kept mankind going.

'Is that the last of it?' Campbell asked as J.D. and Sam and Laura brought in a load of coats.

'Pretty much,' Laura replied. 'We also found this radio, but I don't think it works.'

The silence that followed that remark was pregnant with sorrow. Every soul in that room knew just how valuable a functioning radio might be. Just as, twenty thousand years ago, every soul huddled at the back of some winter-choked cave had known just how valuable a little spark of fire would be.

'Let me see it,' Brian said.

She handed it to him, and he began examining it. The thing had been lost for a long time. It was an ancient transistor radio, something from back in the eighties, before walkmen and microcircuitry.

Then there came a sound so unexpected that a couple of people actually screamed. It was barking – Buddha had started to bark. He and Luther were keeping to themselves at a table across the reading room. Luther was embarrassed because he was so dirty and he smelled, or suspected that he did, or perhaps he was exhibiting the wrinkle of mind that had made him a street person in the first place.

The barking soon subsided to a series of whines. Buddha kept pricking up his ears, too. He was obviously uncomfortable about something, and that was making

131

the whole group uncomfortable, too. The role of the dog had changed. Now, he was an essential part of the community, just as his ancestors had been back when winter howled and fur made him a good friend on a cold night, and his nose told of the silent approach of the sabre-toothed tiger long before human eyes and ears noticed.

Sam's head turned, then Laura's. Then they all heard it – the high-pitched screeching sound that had made Buddha so uncomfortable. He still whined and yowled, but between the whines, the noise got louder and louder.

Sam's first thought was that it was girders straining in the basement. Maybe the building was caving in. But that couldn't be. The water filled the structure all the way down to the bottom, so the water was supporting its own weight. It wouldn't be placing any extra strain on the structure.

Sam, wearing a comfy lined raincoat over the sweats that he'd found still in their bags from Bloomies Sports Store, went out into the long hallway that fronted the reading room.

'What's going on?' Brian said, joining him.

'I have no idea!'

Laura and J.D. came out, followed by the others. They crossed the hall and entered the Salomon Room that overlooked Fifth Avenue. At the moment, the room housed a collection of Native American written objects from deerskin story sheets to Iroquois wampum. Here, the sound was loud, crunching and screeching, loud cracks and long metallic groans.

They went into the small Special Collections office with its tall windows, and looked out over one of the strangest sights that anyone, in all the colourful history of Manhattan Island, had ever seen.

Wreathed in snow, which was already beginning to flurry, was the grey steel side of a huge cargo ship, which had somehow been swept through the streets, by whatever maniac trick of tide and wind, and was now grinding and scraping slowly along, pushed by the slight current that still remained, and the whipping, nervous wind.

There was silence in the crowded little room, as each of them thought the same private thought: this is the very image of chaos itself, a world gone mad, life turned inside out.

Jack was also experiencing one of the strangest things he had ever known. He was giving a briefing to the most powerful people in the United States, and nobody had coughed, snickered, yawned or even so much as glazed over, not for a second.

He had laid the situation out as he saw it: since 1999, there had been a series of events that he had been concerned might be warning signs of a much more dramatic event. After an unseasonably warm autumn in 1999, tremendous storms had swept Europe with winds that were unprecedented in recorded history. In total, something like three hundred million trees, many of them hundreds of years old and as solidly rooted as trees could be, had been uprooted across the continent. Even trees planted by Marie Antoinette at Versailles had been destroyed, making wreckage of its legendary park.

In 2003, a devastating heatwave had caused temperatures as far north as Lapland to rise into the eighties. All through this time, there had been increasing signs of trouble, prompting the British government to deploy the research buoys that Gerald Rapson managed from his station at Hedland. Those buoys had been recording a steady weakening of the North Atlantic Current – data that this President, facing him now, had worked to keep out of the hands of NOAA experts here in the US.

He was not a happy man, was President Blake. He was well aware of the fact that millions of his fellow citizens were going to die on his watch, and that history was going to lay the debacle at his doorstep, and for good reason.

'When will it be over?' he asked in a hoarse voice. It was, Jack reflected, the voice of a man who had been crying.

'The basic rule of storms is that they continue until they're out of energy, which happens when the imbalance that created them is corrected.'

Jack didn't want to look these men in the eye, because he knew how painful that would be for them. But part of him was compelled to, to see the guilt. Between the left, which had always used environmental problems to push for more control of business, and the right, which had rejected environmental reality in order that business as usual could continue, everybody had missed the point.

This happened all the time on Earth, just not frequently enough for it to be part of human experience. There had been no factories spewing pollutants when it happened ten thousand years ago, and a hundred and twenty thousand years ago when it had been so ferocious that it had led to a full-fledged ice age, the automobile had not exactly been invented.

Jack's message had always been the same: paleoclimatology is warning you. No matter what, this thing is coming again, not because of anything you do or don't do, but because it is part of the nature of the earth. As long as there is no way for the oceans to circulate through the tropics and the sun remains a variable star, it is going to keep happening.

Therefore, the smart leader plans for it, gets ready for it as the British had been trying to do, and the Italians with their efforts to protect Venice, and a few others. Human pollution had probably sped it up somewhat, maybe even intensified it. But Jack's message, that these men had scoffed at, was, 'get ready for it because *it happens all the time.*'

Too bad that every hundred thousand years, which was the blink of an eye in Earth time, made almost not one damn bit of sense to anybody except a scientist. 'Yeah, yeah,' they all thought, 'but it ain't gonna be while I'm around.'

He looked from face to face: sad, mad, too dumb, some of them, to understand even yet. Others understood all too well. They were the ones with clenched fists, the ones whose eyes never stopped moving.

'We're talking this time about a global climate realignment,' Jack continued. 'These storms will end after they've covered most of the northern land mass in ice. That could take weeks.'

Jack pulled up a graphic, created for him by Jason in about twenty minutes of the most frenetic keyboard activity that he'd ever witnessed. It showed the ice spreading south. 'The snow and ice will reflect the heat of the Sun, and the Earth's atmosphere will re-stabilise, but with average temperatures closer to those of the last ice age.'

General Arthur Watkins Jones Pierce, Chairman of the Joint Chiefs of Staff, was one of the ones with eyes that never stopped. He was one of the smart ones. 'What can we do about this?'

'Head as far south as possible.'

Becker's face darkened. Like most dumb men in high office, his main activity was ass-covering. Damned if this mistake was going to end up on *his* plate. 'That's not amusing, Doctor Hall.'

'I'm not joking,' Jack snapped, then fought back the anger. He would not shout at this creep. That would only give him the upper hand. 'People have to run while they still can. Those who aren't already trapped.' An image of Sam appeared in his mind's eye, and his heart filled with a number of things. He wished that he was the hell out of this jerk shop and on his way. But if he somehow prevailed among these men, he would be saving millions of Sams and Lauras and Brians, all those precious souls.

Now the Secretary of State, who had been sitting with her arms folded and her chin jutting, looking for some reason to scoff and leave, leaned forward. 'Where do you suggest they go?' She was a lovely woman, was Angela Linn.

And, possibly, given that question, a convert. One, at least. 'The further south they can get, the safer they'll be. Texas, parts of Florida. Mexico would be best.'

'Mexico,' Becker yapped. 'Maybe you should stick to science and leave policy to us.'

Jack had a chance to do something at this moment that he was really going to enjoy. He fixed his eyes on the President and addressed him directly. He knew that Becker had stiffened, then turned red. Men like him were always sensitive to a slight.

'Mr President, if we're going to survive – and I don't mean survive personally, I mean survive as a species – we're going to have to stop thinking nationally and start thinking globally. It's not just America that's in danger.'

Becker scoffed. 'It's our responsibility to protect America first.'

'Then protect the American people – not their national identity. Take a look at this thing from a long term perspective. The prospects for agriculture in North America are slim to none. Now is a good time to start thinking ahead. Make alliances, ask for help. Before long, we may have to beg.'

The silence was deafening. Becker broke it. 'What exactly are you proposing?'

Jack was quietly amazed. That was the kind of question somebody who was buying your story asked. But Becker? Stranger things had happened. Maybe.

Jack walked over to the map wall. He raised the map of south-east Asia that had been used earlier in God knew what capacity, and pulled down the map of North America. He took a black grease pencil from the trough below the maps, and drew a line that roughly paralleled the old Mason–Dixon line.

'Evacuate everybody south of this line.'

Now the President spoke. He raised his eyebrows first, as if asking Jack for the floor. Jack nodded at him. 'What about the people north of the line?' His voice was heavy.

The President knew. The President understood.

In the privacy of his heart, Jack thanked God. This meeting should have been held three days ago, and it should have been a matter of activating a whole elaborate predesigned plan. But at least it was happening now, instead of not at all.

But because this meeting was so late and there had been no pre-planning, Jack had to say one of the hardest things he'd ever said in his life. 'I'm afraid it's too late for many of the people to the north. If they go outside or try to travel, the storm's going to kill them.' And maybe my own boy, maybe my Sam.

Jack could not resist giving Becker a hard look. The man turned away as if Jack's gaze had acid in it.

Jack continued. 'At this point their only chance is to stay inside, try to ride it out, and to pray.'

The President thought for a moment. Jack could see the names going through his mind, Pittsburgh and Cleveland, Gary and Chicago, Minneapolis-St Paul, Omaha, names from the deep song of America. The numbers, too, no doubt. President Blake was famous as a numbers man.

The President stood up, then, and thanked Tom Gomez. This meant that Jack's presentation was finished, and it was time for him to leave. Jack tried to conceal his eagerness. But the fact was, all he could think about now was Sam. He'd done his duty for his country, now it was his right to do the same for his loved ones.

Gomez came out with him. He put a hand on Jack's shoulder. Job well done. Too bad it was such a sad job, in such a tragic situation. 'What will he do?' he asked Gomez. He hoped that he'd been reading the President right.

'I don't know,' Tom answered.

That was honest, anyway. They could still do nothing, of course, still pretend to themselves that their ideology – that man's pollution couldn't affect the environment – meant that nothing they didn't like would ever happen. Too bad nature doesn't have ideology, just numbers. And two and two are always going to equal four, no matter how hard you try to believe the truth away.

As Jack went off towards the security station, the meeting continued behind closed doors.

'We can't evacuate half the country because one scientist *thinks* the climate is shifting,' Vice-President Becker burst out. He'd felt the contempt radiating from Jack Hall, and he hated him now. He wanted him to be wrong, he wanted him the hell out of NOAA and off teaching grade school or something somewhere far, far from Washington DC.

Secretary of State Linn said, with that mildness of manner that had so often deceived her enemies, 'Every minute we delay is costing lives.'

'So what about the other half of the country?' Becker persisted, 'when all these people come down on them, what do they do? Where's the infrastructure to handle that, Angie?'

'If Doctor Hall is right, sending troops north is only going to create more victims. We should save the people we can, right now.'

General Pierce spoke up next. Like the Secretary of State, he was moving towards the edge of shock. 'We, uh, use triage. Same approach a medic takes on the battle-field. Sometimes it's necessary to make hard choices.' He cleared his throat.

'I don't accept that abandoning half the country is nec-essary,' Becker almost shouted. Or rather, screamed.

This gigantic, almost unimaginable, catastrophe had come out of nowhere. Just thinking on the scale that it demanded would not have been easy for a skilled profes-sional planner, let alone a small group of desperate men with no plan at all.

Tom Gomez watched them squirming, as well they should. 'Maybe if you'd listened to Jack Hall sooner, it wouldn't be—'

Now Becker did scream. '*Bullshit*! Hall's a loose cannon. It's easy for him to suggest this so-called plan. He's safely here in Washington.'

Tom looked at Becker. He'd always been told that choosing a weak Vice-President was a sign of a weak President. 'Jack's son is in Manhattan,' he said. His voice was quiet, but they all heard, Becker included.

Becker turned back to him. 'What?'

'Doctor Hall's son – he's in Manhattan. I thought you ought to know that before you start questioning his motives.'

The faces changed, grew more grave as each man realised the significance of what was being said. Jack Hall, in stating that it was too late to evacuate the northern part of the country, was including his own child among those left behind. And they all knew, then, just how completely convinced he was of his data.

The President also realised it, and as he did, he slowly came to his feet. Normally content to watch and listen and allow his aides to come to consensus, he had finally seen that debate was over. It had been over, probably for months, maybe for years, but nobody had been willing to face that.

The President of the United States faced it now. He took a deep breath, sighed a long sigh. And in the crossing of that breath, gave nearly a hundred million of his fellow citizens into the jaws of the storm and the hands of God. 'General,' he said, 'give the order for the National Guard to evacuate the southern states.' Now his eyes rested on his Vice-President, as if daring him to utter one single word of protest. 'We're going to follow Doctor Hall's plan.'

Tom Gomez hurried out, his heart thundering. He had an enormous amount of work to do. NOAA had to be informed, all the field offices prepared, the National Weather Service alerted. Plus, he had to get his headquarters staff to safety with whatever essential equipment could be salvaged. He recognised that his agency's services and skills were going to be essential to the survival of the nation, not only now but in years to come, more essential than ever.

If this thing left a sheet of ice too large to melt over next summer, a new ice age was going to begin. Human life was going to be different, very different. The northern hemisphere, where the strongest countries and the best educated people were concentrated, was going to disappear under the weight of trillions of tons of ice, and stay that way for the next hundred thousand years.

General Pierce picked up a telephone. 'Get Case Unicorn up,' he said quietly.

CHAPTER 12

Case Unicorn was the closest of the Pentagon's thousands of case scenarios to an evacuation of the people of the United States. It would not be perfect, not nearly, but it would be a beginning. He paused. 'Restrict case activation to First Army and Fifth Army.' First Army was commanded out of Georgia, Fifth Army out of Texas. According to the President's order, there was no point in activating the case in the other continental army commands.

Before he had even hung up the phone, the command structure of the Joint Chiefs of Staff was going into operation. The 'case' the General had referred to covered only the evacuation of populations from major cities into surrounding countryside, not a wholesale movement south of millions.

But it didn't take an announcement from the government to get most people moving. They saw the clouds coming, and they saw on Fox News and CNN what the storm was doing farther north. Toronto ceased to report, then Montreal, Bangor and Minneapolis, and the silence from Europe was frightening.

In Houston and Atlanta, Europe-bound flights began to be held at their gates. Farther north than Atlanta, nothing was flying anyway, so the matter was moot. The President had already grounded domestic flights, as if anybody would dare to take a plane aloft as a sheer wall of clouds fifty thousand feet high and five thousand miles long came slipping and sliding across the continent.

It darkened the fields of Minnesota and the ranges of Montana, the rolling lands of Iowa and the sweet Ohio flats that, until just a few weeks ago, had been the bread-basket of the world. Running before it like leaves before an autumn wind, the quick and the smart were getting out. Even some from as far north as Chicago and Gary made it, by jumping in their cars and racing southward the instant that they heard that a strangely powerful blizzard was on the way.

But most people followed their instincts, and our instincts tell us to go to the back of the cave when danger threatens. So storm windows went up and grocery stores were stripped and kids brought home from school. The TV was turned on, and then they waited.

When people in the northern half of the country realised that their more southerly neighbours were being evacuated and they weren't, many more of them hit the roads, and the snow-choked interstates began to fill up with long strings of cars, creeping south with pitiful slowness – pitiful and fatal. Not one human being from one car was destined to survive. In fact, as the snow closed over them, most of them would not be seen again for stretching cycles of years, when the ice would once again fall back, leaving their rusting, twisted remains on a scraped plain that nobody in those days would ever imagine had once been fragrant with cornflowers in the moonlight, in the long ago.

Farther south, there were those who had recourse to their Fourth Amendment rights in order to resist the sol-diers' attempts to force them to leave. Their names and addresses were noted, and they were left behind. They died with their rights intact, at least.

Evacuation was proceeding efficiently at Lucy's hospital, so when Jack's call came in, she took it without delay. He explained more to her about what was happening than they'd so far been told. She thought that the government should have said how incredibly cold it was going to get, but she understood that this would have spread unimaginable terror among those millions already trapped, who did not yet understand that their lives were over.

'It'll be impossible to reach each other,' Jack said. Her heart almost broke to hear that. She had faced the fact, in recent hours, that she'd loved this man too much *not* to divorce him. What she had been unable to bear had been the endless waiting and the struggle of his prophet's life, preaching to the hostile and the indifferent, his unwanted message of doom. He added, 'Leave a message for me at the American Embassy in Mexico City.'

She wondered if she would get that far south in a caravan of ambulances full of sick kids. She said, 'All right.'

The silence that came between them wasn't really silence at all, but rather another part of the mysterious life of couples.

Jack answered it in just the way she'd hoped he would: 'I love you.'

Now it was her turn. 'I love you,' she replied and it felt better, she thought, than anything she had ever said before in her whole life, except for one thing: the moment that they had laid her purple, wrinkled baby boy on her belly, still damp from her own waters, and she had said, 'Hi.' 'Tell Sam that I love him so much. And Jack, God be with you.'

Slowly, blinking away the tears she didn't have time to

cry, she hung up the phone. Out the broad glass front of the building, she could see young patients being loaded into waiting vehicles, attended by hospital personnel and parents.

Dusk came early, and with it worrying flurries of snow. The trees were already bare, and their limbs rattled softly in the uneasy air. Overhead, low, ragged clouds raced south, reflecting the lights of the city in hues of grey and rose. Once, it would have been beautiful, a moment like this, with all the lights along Connecticut Avenue flickering behind the dancing tree limbs, and the snow making a curiously lonely place for itself in the heart. But not now, on this night, when the souls of the dead were already thick in the storm wind.

Jack fought the sled into the back of a white Tahoe with NOAA's blue seal on the doors.

When another pair of hands grasped the other side, he almost jumped out of his skin. 'You're supposed to be on a bus heading south, Frank,' he told his long-time partner.

'I've watched your back for twenty years, Jack. You think I'd let you tackle this alone?'

Jack laughed. 'And all the time I thought I was watching your back.'

And then another surprise, scuffling at the steel door that led to the parking area, and Jason came trundling out, burdened by a case of equipment, which he tossed into the back of the truck as well. He headed around to the cab.

'Where do you think you're going?'

'Neither one of you can navigate your way out of a shower stall. Without me, you'll end up in Cleveland.'

Janet Tokada came hurrying out. Wrapped in her

overcoat, with her dark hair flying in the freshening wind and her cheeks flushed by the cold, Jack thought she was incredibly attractive. And then he wondered, 'Is this battlefield effect?' To men on their way into battle, women were supposed to be overwhelmingly beautiful. 'I'll try to give you updates on the storm as it heads your way,' she said.

Jason, ever the optimist, responded, 'Maybe with a little warning we can get our butts inside before they're frozen off.'

Janet took Jack's hand. 'Good luck, Jack. It's been a privilege working with you.' Translation: since I'm never going to see you alive again, this is goodbye to whatever probably wouldn't have happened between us anyway.

Jack took her hand. 'The privilege was all mine.' He meant it, too. She was one of that rare band of people that Jack Hall truly admired: those who were totally committed to excellence in all they set out to achieve.

By dawn of the next day, it had been snowing for eighteen hours, and it was still getting harder. In front of the library, the cargo ship sat jammed in ice, its superstructure a fairyland of gleaming, icy wires and frost crazed portholes.

Inside, Brian was working on the radio. He had the back open and was tracing the circuitry. He didn't know how well he could repair it, but he thought he could at least get something out of it.

'Maybe you should let somebody help you with that, son.'

Brian raised his eyes, looked at Campbell's broad, red Irish face, his twinkling green eyes. 'I'm in the chess club, the electronics club and the Scholastic Decathlon team. If

146

there's a nerdier nerd here, please point him out. Or her.'

The cop smiled slightly. 'I'll leave you to it, then.'

'Thank you.'

The idea that Buddha might make a mess inside the library was horrifying to Luther. His sense of order would not allow it. So as soon as first light began sifting in from outside, he was headed out with the dog.

It was a strange experience, crossing slippery ice instead of the floor that lay twenty feet below, but they made it out onto the rough white plain that stretched to the fourth-storey windows across the street. It was as cold as a Riverside Drive sidewalk in January, and them was the worst nut freezers in Manhattan, when the north wind came cutting down the Hudson, sweeping them with snow.

'Come on, Buddha,' he said, 'nobody's damn well looking, buddy.'

But that wasn't quite true. Buddha was distracted because he was seeing and smelling people. He let out a bark, a loud, curious *wowf,* but not nearly what he could generate when he got going. A 'protecting our grocery basket' bark this was not.

A crowd went past using a car hood as a freight sled. On it were the contents of an apartment: chairs, a table, an elderly TV. They were working damn hard to save their stuff, for sure. Luther could understand that. His own treasures were under about ten feet of ice, which he suspected was not doing his collection of John Coltrane LPs a whole lot of good. Or was that a collection of Duke Ellington LPs?

But hell, there were a lot of people out here, and the folks inside needed to know this. Risking the worst from Buddha, he headed straight back into the library.

'There are people out there!' he yelled as he slid across the ice and up the six stairs that were all that remained between its surface and the third floor. 'People all over the place!'

Everybody went running to see. The library security guard who had appeared during the night said, 'They're getting out of the city before it's too late.'

Folks started crowding around, trying to get a look. 'All right, everybody,' Patrolman Campbell shouted, 'quiet down!'

He looked over the crowd of about sixty people he had been wondering what the hell to do with. What were they going to eat in here, shoe leather and hair? Books sure as hell wouldn't do it, and the water fountains were history. Even the toilets were dry. Not frozen, damn well dry. But maybe this meant the end of the food and water issues that had been worrying him. 'All right,' he said, 'it seems pretty clear that we can get moving, too. The water's frozen enough that we can walk. So we need to do this before the snow gets too deep.'

'So let's do it,' Jama's cabbie said. He started bustling out.

'Hold it! Slow down. We're gonna help each other, it's the only way. Let's get ready as best we can and make sure nobody gets left behind. So if you need help, sing out!' A few people raised their hands, an older guy with a limp, a young woman who'd sprained her ankle yesterday.

Sam watched this carefully, saying nothing. The cop was a natural leader, but Sam was just going to let this one play out a little longer.

'When's the last time anybody got a signal on their cellphone?' Campbell asked.

'I got through to my cousin in Memphis a few hours

148

ago. They're being evacuated,' a young woman said.

Another, older lady added, 'I talked to somebody about the same time who said the same thing. The whole country's headed south.'

Dad. Doing his work. How many lives had he saved? Twenty million? Fifty? What he was hearing told Sam exactly what he had to do. Also, that his dad was out there somewhere for sure, and he was not heading south.

Sam turned to his friends and said softly, 'We shouldn't go.'

'Everybody else is,' J.D. pointed out.

Sam stopped Laura, who was trying to explain what was happening to Jama in French.

'Hold off,' he said, 'when I talked to my dad, he told me we have to stay inside. This storm is gonna kill anybody who gets caught in it.'

Laura looked around her. People were loading coats from the lost and found on their shoulders, layering as best they could. 'Sam,' she said, 'you have to say something.'

Sam did not relish going up to the huge, authoritative cop and telling him he was totally wrong. But he knew she was right. He had to do it. He went over to where Campbell was helping the girl with the bad ankle improvise a walking splint.

'Uh, sir?'

'Yes, Sam?'

'This is actually, uh, it's a mistake.'

Campbell looked at him, his broad face full of surprise. 'What?'

'We – it's a mistake.'

'Listen, Sam, we're all scared but we've got no choice.'

'No, sir, that's not it.'

'C'mon, son, get ready to go.'

Campbell patted the splint and bustled away. Sam did not like to be cold-shouldered like that. Shades of second grade, when his smarts had intimidated his teacher so much she wouldn't allow him to ask questions. 'If you go outside now,' he blurted, 'you'll freeze to death!'

Speaking of freezing, that froze the entire crowd. Faces turned towards him. He found himself looking into a whole lot of eyes, all of them scared, some of them flashing with anger at his challenge to the accepted wisdom.

'What is this nonsense?' Campbell said.

'It's not nonsense! This storm is going to get even worse. It's going to get too cold to survive.'

One of the crowd, a guy with round glasses and fuzzy hair, gave Sam a long, thoughtful look. 'Where are you getting this information?'

'From my dad. He's a climatologist. He says that this storm is like nothing we've ever seen before.'

He had the attention of a few more of them now. A couple more, anyway. 'What are you suggesting we do?' the guy asked. Jeremy, Sam remembered. He was a computer technician and his name was Jeremy.

'Stay inside,' Sam replied. 'Try to keep warm until the storm passes.'

'Look, the snow's getting deeper by the minute. We'll be trapped in here without food or supplies. If we want water, we're gonna have to eat snow.'

'It's a risk,' Sam admitted.

Campbell shook his head. This kid was an idiot. 'Better to take our chances leaving with the others. And it's time to do that.' He raised an arm. 'Come on, everybody.'

'Don't go out there!' Sam was surprised at his own intensity. But lives were at stake here. 'It's too dangerous.

You gotta believe me!'

But their shuffling exit had begun and it was obvious that they were going to follow the police officer and the word that the rest of the country was evacuating, not listen to some kid who said the opposite.

'Où va tout le monde?'

Sam knew enough French to understand that Jama had innocently asked if everybody was leaving.

Laura replied, explaining that they were going south, but she and her friends were staying here. She said that Sam's father was a scientist, and he'd said that it was dangerous to go out.

Elsa, who'd got through to Memphis on her cellphone, was also hanging back. Sam heard her say to Jeremy, 'I've got a bad feeling about leaving. What are you gonna do?'

'Well, with all due respect for New York's finest, I'm going to put my trust in the climatologist.'

Elsa turned to the librarian, who had reoccupied the space behind her desk as soon as she'd waked up. 'How about you, Judith?'

'I'm not leaving the library.'

Some people are funny about libraries, Sam thought. He hoped that would stay true in the future. The internet was going to be down for a long, long time, but a book was still a book.

Luther's dog was whining nervously. 'Don't worry, Buddha, we ain't goin' back outside.'

Sam and the others followed them, if only to watch them go. When he reached the street, Sam saw that there were literally hundreds of people on their way south. Was the Hudson also frozen? Could be. Probably was. You could probably walk all the way home from here, without ever getting your feet wet.

He thought of their places in Alexandria, of his room with its model of the Constitution left over from childhood, and his various scientific collections, his trilobites and his hundred-and-fifty-million-year-old ferns, all correctly preserved under non-acidic coatings.

They watched a crowd of at least eighty people file past them . . . and past a cab frozen in the ice, with frozen people inside, their blue faces peering out of the windows. Sam thought, 'If it hadn't been for Laura, that Jama and her little girl would be in one of those cabs.'

Death has a surprising tendency to blindside you. Who would ever have thought, the previous morning, that Manhattan Island was going to be a frozen wasteland in twenty-four hours?

After the crowd had gone, there were exactly nine people left – nine people and a dog.

Luther turned to J.D., who still looked kind of resplendent in his fur-lined coat, despite the growth of beard, despite the hairstyle from hell. 'Name's Luther,' he said. 'And this here's Buddha.'

J.D. looked down at the extended hand. Sam thought, 'It has a crust.' J.D. looked sick, but he grasped it firmly and shook it, and Sam was proud of him for doing that.

CHAPTER 13

Interstate 95, which runs between Washington and Boston via New York, can be one of the windiest roads in the United States. More than one eighteen-wheeler has been caught by a gust during a nor'easter and sent hydroplaning to truck heaven, its driver frantically working his air brakes and cursing the air blue.

Gusts of upwards of forty miles an hour blew snow to whiteout and made life hell for the National Guardsmen directing traffic southward on all six lanes. The ribbon of cars stretched from horizon to horizon, and Jack knew that it was unlikely, at the rate they were moving, that a single occupant would be alive by this time tomorrow. And those poor National Guard kids – they were standing in their own graves and they didn't know it.

Inside the Tahoe, the air was warm, and would remain so unless the temperature dropped low enough to freeze the fuel in its gas line. Jack knew that temperature – 150 below. He also knew that, fifty to seventy thousand feet overhead, it was even colder than that . . . and that the air rushing upward, cold as it was, was warm by comparison, and was thus getting sucked into those hostile realms as the storm continued to boil ever upward.

At some point, it would begin snatching at that super-cold air, dragging it from its accustomed place above the stratosphere – whereupon it would communicate its coldness to the denser air below, and the whole mass would plummet downward, smashing into the ground and killing all that it touched.

He knew that, but he kept his show on the road, because Sam was at the end of that road, and he'd promised his boy that dad was on his way.

Jason was consulting a map and his GPS at the same time. The GPS frequently lost itself, because of the thick clouds, but he was managing to get a sufficient number of readings to maintain their course.

With the snow as deep as it was, signs were few and far between, and those that were visible were so ice-choked that they couldn't be read. So Jason had been needed, for sure. A navigator was as essential as he would have been in the Sahara.

Jack inched through a line of cars waiting to get onto the interstate, being led by a snowplough. Then the road was more or less clear. It had been ploughed in the past few hours, too, so it was also passable. 'At least we won't have to deal with traffic going in this direction,' he said.

They had the radio on, but station after station had left the air. Now there was only one still alive, a Spanish language AM station out of DC.

At the International Bridge in Laredo, Texas, there was occurring one of the most bizarre spectacles ever seen there: people were fighting to get *into* Mexico. It was snowing hard as far south as Dallas, just four hundred miles to the north, and from the banks of the Rio Grande the most incredible cloud line ever observed by the eye of man could be seen rolling slowly out of the north, rolling closer and closer.

This far south, it consisted of a fifty-mile-deep band of absolutely fearsome thunderstorms, spawning tornadoes which appeared as long grey worms swinging out in front of it. The lightning and the thunder and the deathly cold wind blowing out of the monster drove people to a frenzy.

Lines and lines of cars were backed up at the bridge. Mexico demands elaborate permits for automobile entry, and the border police were not about to change the regulations just because the *gringos* were being inconvenienced. Mexicans were inconvenienced every day, trying to go the other way.

Car radios were playing, and folks were getting out, standing beside their vehicles, their belongings piled on top and in trunks, their kids jamming the back seats. Many of them had cats and dogs, birds, every kind of pet as well. These were Americans in this evacuation, people with no experience of being refugees. There were cars with things like barstools and remote-controlled model airplanes in them, not to mention televisions, video game consoles, computers and all manner of other things that would be profoundly useless to a refugee. Pound for pound, there was probably as much sports gear as there was food in those cars.

'Half an hour ago,' the radios were saying, 'Mexican officials closed the border in response to the overwhelming number of American refugees heading south.'

Some people shouted and shook their fists, but many more abandoned their cars and took to the walkway, climbing down and attempting to get over the fence that blocked the Rio Grande. The most athletic of them made it, some even with a few possessions, and went swimming out into the flooding, uneasy water, struggling for the far side with their backpacks and suitcases floating around them.

Normally, the Rio Grande was a slow river, often not

even flowing, but today it was steady, and from the darkness that scarred the northern horizon, it looked like it would be in flood soon. Unless, of course, it also froze.

Washington was experiencing a full-scale blizzard. There was nothing abnormal about it yet – it was simply very intense. But the city was still functioning with a skeleton crew of police and National Guard troops out to prevent looting and protect the national monuments.

Six of those men were destined to lose their lives at the top of the Washington Monument when the cold touched it, many others to die in the Capitol, in the various official structures, in the streets.

Alone among all the federal structures, only the White House blazed with light. Inside, it was warm and very quiet, with only the faintest whisper of falling snow, and an occasional wail from the wind as it compressed against the eaves of the private apartments on the upper floor.

Also alone, having even sent his Secret Service personnel south, the President of the United States sat at his executive desk. The building was on its own power and fuel, so he had closed off the largely ceremonial Oval Office.

Vice-President Becker and the Secretary of State burst in. They'd been in the Cabinet Room, which had become a sort of state headquarters.

The President gave them a cold look. He could not help but feel that Becker had betrayed him by scoffing at this man Hall. He should at least have given the President the opportunity to decide for himself.

Like most Presidents, he was most hurt by mistakes made not by him, but on his behalf.

He raised his eyebrows. Becker puffed himself up. It looked like he was about to yell. 'The Mexicans have closed the border!'

Blake had been expecting that. 'Have you spoken to the Mexican Ambassador?'

'He's dead,' the Secretary said. 'A tree fell on his car.'

'Mr President, we can open the border by force if we want to.'

General Pierce appeared as if on command, which was probably exactly what had happened, the President thought.

'What are your contingency plans, General?'

'We already have the Third Corps out of Fort Hood on Threatcon Delta, sir.'

Ready to go.

'Have you lost your minds?' Secretary Linn yelled. 'We're facing the largest ecological disaster in human history and you're talking about going to war?'

'We're talking about survival,' the Vice-President bellowed.

The President thought, 'I must never have another shouter on my ticket. Shouting is always a sign of weakness.'

Becker continued, 'When resources become scarce, nations go to war.'

Yes, the President thought, that had been old Tojo's approach. He'd sent the Imperial Japanese Navy to Pearl Harbor because we'd cut off his oil.

'What about sovereignty?' the Secretary said. 'It's their sovereign right to close their border.'

'America was built on land stolen from the Indians. So was Mexico, for that matter. The only claim nations have on the land they hold is force.'

That was enough. Adolf Hitler, the President thought, had been the last one to buy into *that* argument. 'I will not start a war, Raymond,' he said mildly.

He saw the flicker of surprise in his Vice-President's eyes. He reflected that he'd been passive too long, much too long. How many lives was that going to cost? He dared not think. But he did think this: The Blake Presidency is not going to make any more stupid mistakes.

'Get me the President of Mexico on the phone,' he said to his secretary. 'We're going to ask for help.'

The Trustees Room of the New York Public Library, where people like Brooke Astor and Norman Mailer had held elegant court, was ornate. Were it not for Judith, they might never have found it. And it was important that they had, because it was the only place in this building that they had any chance whatsoever of surviving.

'The fireplace probably hasn't been used in a long time,' Judith said uneasily. She was thinking about things like chimney draw and whether or not the flue could still be opened.

J.D. walked over to it. He sized it up, then bent down and peered inside. He came out, then reached along one wall of the hearth and pulled a black lever. There was a high-pitched crunching sound and a gust of wind came in, scattering ash and snowflakes across the floor.

Sam had worried, also, that the fireplace might be sealed. If it had been, he thought that they might die here. Dad had talked to him many times about what had happened on this planet ten thousand years ago. Temperatures had dropped so fast and so far that huge animals had been frozen solid. There was evidence, also, of massive winds and floods and all manner of mayhem.

Most of the large land animals of North America had gone extinct – the camels, the giant ground sloths, the mammoths and mastodons, and, of course, the sabre-toothed tigers that depended on them for food.

The buffalo had survived because they could run fast and far, and enough of them had done just that to keep the species alive.

As for men, they had been almost stripped off the continent. It was why, when the Europeans arrived thousands of years later, they found a North America that only had about a third of the population that would have been there if the superstorm hadn't taken place.

Of course, most scientists had other theories. Nobody really thought Dad was right – except Dad, of course. Too bad he had only won his battle with his colleagues because all of mankind had lost its war with nature.

'We should start bringing in books from the stacks,' Sam said.

Judith gave him a funny smile, as if to ask 'what are you talking about?'

There was a dictionary on a stand across the room. Sam went over and got it. It was satisfyingly heavy. He threw it into the fireplace.

Judith looked at him like he was insane. 'What are you doing?'

Oh, boy. She'd better face some facts. 'What did you think we were going to burn?'

'We can't burn books!'

Sam felt for her. She was a librarian and she very obviously loved this library. And why shouldn't she? Drowned down below their feet and frozen was one of the world's greatest book collections. But the real question here had nothing to do with whether or not they could be saved.

159

The only real question was whether or not there were enough dry books available on this floor to use as fuel to save their lives.

Judith hung her head. She laughed a little, then she cried. Elsa said, 'I'll go hunting for books.'

Brian and several of the others followed her out.

Sam asked Judith a question that was going to become very, very important soon. 'Is there a lunch room or cafeteria?'

'On this floor, just an employee lounge with a few vending machines.'

Sam followed her along the hall to a small room with a door marked 'Employees Only'. Laura and Jama came with them. In the room there were three vending machines, two for sodas and one that contained some Cheetos, some potato chips, Slim Jims and crackers. No candy, nothing anywhere near substantial enough.

He pulled a fire extinguisher off the wall and smashed it into the machine, which rocked but did not break. Of course not. They were designed to withstand vandalism, weren't they? Well, maybe. He gave it another couple of blows, hoping that the fire extinguisher wouldn't explode before the lock damn well broke.

With a satisfying *clang*, the vending machine popped open.

'We're not gonna last long on Slim Jims and potato chips. There's nothing else?'

'Food and drink aren't allowed in the library,' Judith responded primly.

That explained the bias towards the dry and the non-messy. No gooey candy, nothing that could stain a book . . . or sustain a life.

'How about garbage cans?' Luther asked. 'Always

something to eat in the garbage.'

Man, he was cool in his own weird way, Sam thought. J.D., however, went a really pooky shade of green.

'Gross! I'm not eating out of the garbage.'

Luther bowed his head, ashamed. But Sam also heard him mumble, 'Good, more for us.' Then he left, obviously in search of wherever he might find some bread crusts or, joy of joys, sandwiches or something that the librarians might have confiscated and tossed.

Judith hurried out behind Luther. Sam thought that she probably shared the same hope, which was a good sign. Maybe Luther would save them all.

Back in the Main Reading Room, it was getting really cold. Sam did not want to frighten anybody, but he knew that this cold, when it came, would be very fast. They had to get this fire going, and get plenty of fuel for it, and it had to be done like there was no tomorrow. He organised Elsa and Jeremy to load books onto library carts. She began moving along piling up telephone directories, and he started removing books from the ready-access stacks behind the librarian's desk.

When he started reading one, Elsa did the right thing – she snatched it from him.

'Friedrich Nietzsche? We can't burn that, he's the most important thinker of the twentieth century!'

Elsa tossed it onto the cart. 'Please, Nietzsche was a syphilitic chauvinist who was in love with his own sister.'

'He was not!'

Brian called to them. 'Hey, you guys, come down here. I'm looking at a couple of tons of tax law.'

That stopped them bickering. Sam watched them go back to work, satisfied now that they would be able to get sufficient books to the fireplace. The one thing he had said nothing about was matches. He hadn't seen any of these people smoking, not even Luther, so he needed to worry about it. But surely there were some around here somewhere, Judith would know.

There had better be.

An empty hospital is a strange and desolate place, something that practically nobody ever gets to see . . . or wants to. But this particular empty hospital still had running generators and lights, and machines doing whatever they might do automatically. Far off down a corridor, a bell rang again and again, the sound echoing but calling nobody.

Footsteps joined it as a nurse moved past a television anchored to the ceiling of a small waiting area. 'Traffic into Mexico has been moving smoothly since the President struck a deal to forgive all Mexican debt in exchange for opening the border . . .'

She stopped a moment and watched images of a truly gigantic amount of traffic crossing at Laredo, at Juarez, at Tijuana. All of it was going south into the world that Maria Gomez had left so many years ago. Her education, her prosperity, her pride – all of them were part of her American life and her hard-won citizenship. So she was angry at this storm, to see it ruining the adopted country that had given her so much, had really made her life worth living.

She remembered Chihuahua City all too well, with its dirty cops who would rape you as soon as look at you, and its poverty and disease and its miserable few hospitals where only God knew if the drugs in use were even the real thing.

Shuddering, she walked on. As she approached the

162

Paediatric Ward, she heard Dr Lucy's voice softly reading to the one little patient who had been left behind.

Lucy sat on the edge of Peter's bed reading Bill Peet's *Jennifer and Josephine*, one of the most reliable old favourites in the hospital's library. The story of the little old car and the cat who lived in her, and the salesman who was driving the car to ruin, never failed to get the attention, especially, of little boys.

'Doctor Lucy?'

Nobody called her by her last name. Maria wouldn't have been too surprised if she didn't have one. Lucy kissed Peter's forehead, whispered to him that she'd be right back, and went out.

'Is the transport ambulance here?'

That was the problem. That was the big problem for Dr Lucy. 'They've all gone. In the confusion, I don't know what happened. People started to panic, Doctor Lucy. They are running everywhere, the convoys all leaving.'

Dr Lucy regarded her with steady, clear eyes. She saw no fear. She only saw bravery.

'There's a policeman with a snowplough waiting outside.'

'Peter can't be moved without an ambulance.'

'I know! I left messages at the county ambulance service. But, you know—'

Lucy knew all right. The county ambulance service was on its way south with the rest of the USA. So, now there was a choice to make. Leave Peter or stay with Peter. Take a chance at life, or resign herself to certain death. For her, there was no question. It wasn't even close. 'You go on that plough, Maria. I'll stay and wait.'

Maria's heart became very full. Her eyes did, too. Everybody loved Dr Lucy. She was the best of the best, the kindest, the smartest of all the doctors at Washington Paediatric. 'Lucy—'

'You need to go. He won't wait forever.'

Maria pleaded with her eyes. It was not her place to disagree with one of the doctors, she knew that, but Dr Lucy might die here.

'Go, Maria.'

Why had they ever left little Peter? Just because he was so sick and required so much support? Maybe the administrators had decided to abandon him. Well, they shouldn't have, if they did, because that would be a sin. She blinked away tears. Then she turned. She wanted the best for Dr Lucy, but she also did not want that snowplough to leave.

'Maria!'

She stopped. Maybe Dr Lucy was changing her mind.

'When you get to Mexico, leave word for my ex-husband at the American Embassy.'

'What should I say?'

She hesitated for a moment, then smiled slightly . . . a very sad smile, Maria thought. A very, very sad smile. 'Tell him that I had to finish reading a little boy his bedtime story. He'll understand.'

Maria nodded. She would not forget this. She would do this.

Lucy returned to Peter's room. He had no idea what was happening. She went into the soft light, and sat down once again beside the little cancer patient with his bald head and big smile. He had the book open on his chest. He held it out to her.

She began to read.

CHAPTER 14

From Philadelphia to Bangor, the snow was falling, over the vast, silent cities and the whispering forests, along the highways and their immense, choked lines of cars, in the little towns where the intimate lights of evening were turned out forever, falling like a gentle, deadly spirit from the sky, dropping softly when the wind sighed, flurrying when it roared.

In Manhattan, it was literally pouring out of the sky. And yet, it was so cold that the flakes were each entirely discrete. If you put out a gloved hand, you would see individual snowflakes, each a gossamer universe of crystalline threads, and you would share in the wonder that no two of them were ever quite the same.

But that was where the romance of this terrible snow ended. All the rest was nothing but death, death by cold, death by wind, death by a cruel fall.

Inside, Laura was piling books into J.D.'s arms. Once he was loaded up and carrying them out, she picked up a load herself. She intended to tell nobody, but her leg where she'd hurt it was killing her. It hurt even to touch it. And now, she couldn't even put the weight of a few books on it. She could barely walk.

'What's the matter?' Elsa asked when she noticed her rubbing her shin.

'Oh, I cut my leg getting here.'

'Maybe you shouldn't walk around on it.'

Yeah, and not do her part. No way. She forced herself to pick up a stack of books. She headed for the Trustees Room. 'I'll be all right,' she said, forcing herself to suppress every sign of the agony she actually felt.

As Sam came in with books of his own to add to their stacks, he watched Brian holding the old radio to his ear. Then Brian motioned to him to come closer.

'Did you get a signal?'

He nodded. 'For a second.'

'And?'

Brian's eyes met his. 'The storm is everywhere. It's hit the entire northern hemisphere.'

This was incredible. 'Northern hemisphere' covered the US and Canada, Europe, Siberia, most of China. How were the Chinese coping? The Europeans?

'Europe is buried under fifteen feet of snow and they say it's gonna get just as bad here.'

Fifteen feet. That was a hundred and eighty inches of snow. If it had been snowing there, say, twice as long as here, that meant that they had been getting nearly four inches an hour for forty-eight hours. That was unimaginable. An inch an hour for half that time would be a very, very major snowfall.

Sam looked towards the big windows that overlooked Fifth. You could not see across the street, there was so much snow out there.

Brian reached towards him, briefly touched his hand. The two friends were silent together for a moment. 'I don't think your dad's gonna make it,' Brian said quietly.

That was not true, it could not be true, and Sam felt his face get hot. He didn't want even to hear words like that. His dad could handle the Antarctic winter, thirty below, seventy mile an hour winds. He could not face the idea

166

that his dad might not make it. Because, if his dad didn't make it, his heart would be broken and he could not afford that now, no way. 'He'll make it,' he said, measuring his words.

Brian looked away.

What had he really heard on that radio? Was it even worse than the nightmare he'd described? 'He'll make it!'

Brian just nodded. Sam understood that he was only doing it so his friend wouldn't feel bad. And that went deep. He saw the reality of the situation: out there it was going to go *below* minus one-thirty. It was going to get so cold that nobody could live through it without shelter and heat, no matter how expert they were.

Nobody.

He wanted to burst out crying. Until this second, he had not realised just how focused he really was on his dad getting through to them. *He had to*.

Laura came over, dropped some books, and collapsed into one of the luxurious director's chairs that had once supported the fannies of New York's richest. 'Any news?'

She was limping, Sam could see it. Her face was pale, too. But she didn't appear to be in any pain. Maybe her injury was healing up. Sometimes they hurt the most when they healed.

She looked from Sam to Brian, her eyebrows raised. 'On the radio,' she said.

Sam glanced over at Brian. Better not to let this get out, not even to her. They could not give up, they could not panic, not now. He shook his head. 'No. Nothing.'

The Tahoe is a fine vehicle for a tough situation, but this was beyond tough. No automobile designer alive or dead had ever considered that his car might end up pushing across snowdrifts and dealing with cold that was already down around minus fifty. This was right around the minimum for the antifreeze, and the hoses under the hood were already drum tight and covered with frost. One of them, or a belt, or any number of other parts, was liable to just shatter from the cold at any moment.

Inside the car, though, the heater was still producing enough warmth to make it a livable thirty degrees above zero. But if you touched a window with naked skin, you were going to get frostbitten in a matter of seconds, and you just might stick to a doorpost, should you lean your head against it.

At the wheel, it was all Frank could do to keep the vehicle pointed in the direction Jason said they ought to be travelling. Worse, he was now sometimes losing the satellite for minutes at a time. When that happened, they had only a pocket compass to rely on, that and dead reckoning. But how do you dead reckon in a blinding whiteout?

'Where are we?' Jack asked nervously. He was not convinced by Jason's navigation, not at all. His worst fear was that they would leave the general area of the road and plunge into a drift or down an unseen embankment, or off a bridge. Anything could happen at any second.

Jason stared at the GPS. 'Ah . . . north of Philly,' he said at last.

'How good is that fix?'

'Two satellites.'

That was not good. Jason could be off by a mile or more.

Frank drove on, keeping to a steady fifteen miles an hour. Jack knew that he really needed to put a walker out front, but that would be asking one of them to really take his life in his hands. If he so much as stumbled, the Tahoe was liable to run right over him. Plus, some of that supercold air could come down and freeze the guy solid long before he could return to the relative safety of the vehicle.

'You guys okay?' he asked. From long experience, he knew to ask that question a lot. Cold, especially, ate at people's critical faculties. Without realising it, a person who was cold – truly cold – slowly lost his judgement.

They crashed into something. Jack reached forward, pushed frost off the interior of the windshield. It was a snowdrift.

'Sorry, boss,' Frank said.

Frank tried a little burst of gas, stopped immediately when he got nothing but wheelspin.

They were both professionals, they knew everything there was to know about how to control a vehicle in snow and ice – which was why Jack was thinking that this was the end of the Tahoe. He cracked his door. It was cold, but survivable. He stepped out, and the others followed suit.

The truck was in deep.

'Should I unpack the shovels?' Jason asked.

That wasn't going to work. Even if they got it out of this mess, it was going to get into another one in ten feet. No, the Tahoe had done what it could, and it was time for it to go to sleep. Its ruins probably wouldn't get coughed up by this glacier-in-the-making for another fifty thousand years.

'Unpack the snowshoes. From here, we walk.'

They'd done a hundred miles and more in the Antarctic. They'd crossed plenty of treacherous ground, too, glaciers full of cracks that snow cover made appear as smooth as silk. Step on one, though, and down you went, to die of cold and broken bones at the bottom of an ice shaft. Not a fun death.

*

Judith came into the Trustees Room. She'd been combing for children's books, and had actually found a few, a couple even in French. She had done this largely because of the fear that never, ever left the pretty eyes of Binata, Jama's child. The poor little thing spoke no English, so could understand practically nothing of what was being said around her. She clung to a very loving mother, but a little girl needs more than love, she needs it to be delivered in an atmosphere of stability and security, a warm home, friends, a school to go to.

Binata was thousands of miles from the world that she knew, bereft of all friends, maybe missing her daddy . . . and, well, Judith just thought maybe a librarian had a role to play here.

She went to Binata and showed her the colourful cover of *Le Chat au Chapeau* by Dr Seuss and the child instantly lit up and shouted and slapped her hands to her cheeks. The librarian had won one. This little girl had found an old friend. Obviously, she was a Dr Seuss fan. Smiling happily, thanking Judith in French, Jama began to read to her daughter.

Amid the piles of books, Jeremy was holding something close to his chest. It wasn't huge, but it looked really, really old.

'What are you hanging on to there?' Elsa asked.

'A Gutenberg Bible. From the Rare Books Room.'

Sam was surprised. He hadn't even been aware that they had one.

'You think God's going to save you,' Elsa said, an edge of scorn in her voice, scorn and bitterness. Maybe she had prayed over this situation, Sam thought. If so, God had said no.

'I don't believe in God,' Jeremy replied.

'Then how come you're holding that bible so tight?'

Jeremy glanced at their fire. 'I'm protecting it.' As if to illustrate why that was necessary, J.D. dumped in a pile of books without even glancing at them. 'This bible is the first book ever printed. It represents the dawn of the Age of Reason. The Enlightenment. As far as I'm concerned, the written word is mankind's greatest achievement.' He glanced from face to face, his eyes full of defiance and, Sam thought, rage. Not at them, though, Sam hoped. His rage should be directed towards the storm and the morons who'd let it show up with no proper warning.

'Laugh all you want,' he continued. 'but if Western civilisation is finished, I'm going to save at least one little piece of it.'

Was Elsa going to argue? Was she going to say it wasn't worth saving? Her eyes flickered, her mind seemed to be turning over. Then a smile blossomed in a face that was completely transformed by happiness. An Elsa suddenly full of sunshine said, 'I like your spirit.'

Maybe Jeremy had rejected prayer and Elsa had been disappointed with her results, but Lucy felt something she had sensed many times in her career, which was the awesome presence that seemed to draw close to a dying child. Holding Peter's sweaty little hand, she sat close beside him and she prayed over and over the ancient prayer that asks that the will of God be done.

'Our Father who art in heaven,' she said softly, 'hallowed be thy name . . .'

Then she stopped. Had she heard something? She looked towards the door, suddenly apprehensive. This was probably the only building in Washington showing any lights. Anybody might be out there roaming those halls.

Yes, she heard footsteps. No question, heavy ones. They were coming this way, too, moving fast. She thought to get up, to somehow conceal Peter.

And then a flashlight was burning into her eyes. She raised an arm to protect them, to enable herself to see – and she saw a fireman so covered with snow that he looked like a joke had been played on him.

'We heard somebody was left behind,' he said. 'We got an ambulance.'

She looked at his black face, the kindness in the eyes under that old fashioned fireman's hat. He was a small, stocky man with big fireman's gloves on his hands, gloves better suited to keeping heat out than keeping it in.

She found herself crying. But she couldn't do that, not right now, and she choked back the sobs. 'Thank you,' she said, 'thank you for coming.'

Together, they prepared Peter's IVs, getting him ready to travel. Maybe, somewhere down the road, she'd be able to reconnect him with his parents. She'd received two frantic phone calls. They had not been able to reach the hospital. She'd told them, basically, to save themselves, that she would be responsible for their little boy.

She had thought that she was going to die at his side, and she'd reconciled herself to it. Sam was a strong kid, he'd find his way. And as for Jack – well, maybe they'd meet again in another life, if such things happened. She'd love to make it work with Jack, truth be told.

As they rolled Peter along the hallway towards that ambulance, she remembered what she'd been doing when that fireman had walked in on her. She thought to herself, 'He must be working overtime tonight. He sure delivered fast on that one.'

*

Contrary to Lucy's belief, her hospital was not the only building in Washington that remained lit. There were also lights in the Pentagon, in the offices of the planners and administrators who could not leave, not if everybody else was going to be able to. The Commerce Department was also still functioning, because NOAA had left a skeleton crew of coordinators on staff, men and women who had chosen to take their personal chances here so that they could be certain of providing every bit of information that it was possible to obtain. Likewise, out at Langley, Virginia, CIA headquarters was bustling. The eyes of the country could not be blinded nor its ears deafened, not at this moment of great weakness and great need.

In addition, at communications centres both public and private, and in a surprisingly large number of other locations, such as pipeline pumping stations and nuclear power plants, people had chosen to stay behind and take their chances, so that others could have a better chance to escape.

All across the northeast, in fact, engineers kept every operational nuclear plant running, and went through their long emergency check lists, preparing for the moment when shutdown would have to begin. Not one plant had been abandoned. Not one needed worker had left. Nobody had any intention of adding nuclear waste from a runaway reactor to the miseries of the suffering world.

Courage is one of mankind's most precious possessions. It is easy, perhaps, to think that the other man doesn't have it – that *I* would do my duty when others fled. But, when something truly terrible happens, it turns out that it is an abundant human resource, like love, like intelligence.

They got us through the last ice age, after all.

The President had realised the extraordinary scope of his mistake. He had seen that he had wasted many crucial years debating with the environmentalists about global warming – who was responsible, what needed to be done, who should pay. In truth, he should have been planning for this inevitable situation. Earth is in a period of climatic variability. It was certain to change, sooner or later. No matter who was right about the degree to which human activity was affecting global warming, this was still going to happen.

Even if there had been not one single human being alive on earth, it would have happened anyway.

So, where was the planning? Lost in politics, and he was heartsick about it. He had telephoned his mother. In Florida, she was relatively safe. But, as she'd said to him, 'Baby, at ninety-six, nobody is safe.' He had wanted to hear her voice, though, to take with him wherever he might be going.

General Pierce sat on the edge of a chair, his big hands folded in his lap. He had been asked to leave, of course, but as it had not been stated as an order, he had chosen instead what he regarded as a duty higher than his own life, which was staying close to his President in time of national crisis.

As soon as the President put the phone down, though, he came to his feet. Two Secret Service boys entered the office. 'Mr President,' the General said, 'we can't delay any longer. It's time to go.'

'Who's left?'

'Here in the White House? It's just us, sir. We're the only ones left.'

This was the end, then. If Hall was right, this building

was going to disappear now into memory, then legend, then myth, and finally be gone altogether from the life of man.

He was under no illusions. He knew his history. This little house – and it was astonishingly small, considering all that transpired within its walls – had been the headquarters of the greatest engine of human prosperity and happiness that mankind had ever devised, which was the Presidency of the United States.

From here, Harry Truman had saved the lives of millions by snuffing out the lives of thousands with two nuclear bombs. From here, JFK had claimed the moon for the genius of man. Here, Abraham Lincoln had asked Ulysses S Grant to win a war for him. Here, Franklin Delano Roosevelt had declared that the United States would not become a nation of the starving, but that a compassionate government would reach out and rescue its people from a depression that nobody even understood. And here, Ronald Reagan had made the hard, dangerous and unpopular decisions that had caused the Soviet Union to bankrupt itself in pursuit of an arms race Communism was too inefficient to win.

This was the cradle of human happiness, and the devil take the mistakes that had also been made here.

His mistake, for example. A bad one. Real bad.

He went out into the snow.

Patrolman Campbell knew, now, that he'd made a mistake. Here he was out here in this with all these people trusting him, and he was rapidly reaching his wits' end.

If only there had been some planning, some kind of explanation of what to expect from a storm like this, he might have been able to save lives instead of snuffing them out like this, just because his guess about what to do had been wrong.

It had sure *seemed* right. The radio was saying to move south. Everybody was walking down Fifth towards the tunnels. It was an ordered evacuation, for God's sake, and he'd followed the damn presidential order just like any cop in his place would have done. Who was he supposed to believe, anyway, the President of the United States or some high-school kid? Come on, there was no contest.

Evacuate. So okay, we're doing it, Mr President. So now what?

He and his folks were under an archway of the Brooklyn Bridge, and damn lucky to have that much shelter. The tunnels were way under water and they hadn't dared to cross the Hudson with its wobbling, treacherous ice floes and the killing wind that was like a wall. It was probably frozen solid now, but the snow was so bad you couldn't go ten feet without losing your bearings. Worse, the drifts had big air pockets under them, and you could hear people screaming out there when they fell through. 'The Lord is my shepherd,' he whispered in his mind, 'and though I walk through the valley of the shadow of death, I shall fear no evil . . .'

He watched silently as folks woke up, pulling themselves out from under the snow. Jimmy Preston, the cabbie, said, 'Maybe we should just turn back.'

Where to? How? Ollie Starnes, who had been the library security guard, echoed Tom Campbell's own thoughts. 'What for? Half the city is frozen underwater. There's nothing to go back to.'

'We shoulda stayed in the library,' Jimmy grumbled.

There it was, the ugly, killing truth. Tom had set out in life to bring justice and help people. And here he was, helping them to walk the damn plank.

Well, there was nothing else to do but get up and keep trying, even if it was hopeless. There was always the chance of some kind of damn miracle. Fat chance, but it was there.

'Come on, folks,' he said clapping his glove-muffled hands, 'you need to get up and get moving now.'

Ollie and Jimmy got to their feet. Other shapes began moving. One, though, did not. Tom thought her name was Noel. She'd come over here by herself instead of doing as ordered, and sharing body heat. He reached down and shook her. 'Come on, ma'am, we need to push on.'

She rolled over, so slowly at first that he thought she actually was getting up. Then he saw her face, as slick as glass and ice blue. Like anybody who's seen death, he knew instantly that she was gone. He didn't need to feel for a pulse, but it was his duty so he did it anyway. Nothing. He tried to raise an eyelid, but they were frozen shut. Deader. He pulled out his notebook and noted the date and time, and wrote her name, Noel Parks. Then he added, in his careful, Catholic school penmanship, 10-54, the code for a dead body.

He looked towards the others. Nobody was watching him. He reached down and pulled the coat back over her face, covered it with a little snow. No reason to let the others see. It would only demoralise them further.

He went back to his charges, put on a big smile and led them off he knew not where.

CHAPTER 15

J.D. watched Luther methodically tearing the pages out of a book, page by careful page. He had found himself fascinated by this man who lived at the polar opposite to his own world. Before meeting Luther, he'd never given homeless people a second thought, except maybe to assume that they were probably either lazy or paranoid.

Luther was neither. He had, instead, made a complicated and difficult choice to opt out of the world that, as far as J.D. was concerned, was the only one worth living in. Even if you couldn't have it all, then you could at least want it. Wasn't that how things were supposed to work?

Not for this guy. Luther didn't want anything except food for Buddha and to fulfil his own basic needs. J.D. had talked to him – not getting much out of him, because he was a solitary soul – but he'd discovered, among other things, that he hadn't ridden in a car in twenty years. He thought, but could not be sure, that Luther might once have been a journalist or a lawyer or something to do with the corporate world. The amazing thing was that he had not ended up like this through tragedy. He had chosen this life.

And now he was doing something that was interestingly strange: he was tearing pages out of a book and crushing them into balls, then shoving them into his pants and sleeves. He was beginning to look more than a little like a Michelin Tyre Person or the Sta-Puft Marshmallow Man.

'What are you doing?' J.D. finally asked, after spending some little time trying to figure it out.

'Insulating. Newspaper's best, but this'll do.'

J.D. found it difficult to believe.

'You spend some years on the street, you learn how to keep warm.'

Luther also found this kid interesting. He was so damned innocent, it was kind of wonderful. Luther had been through some very dark years, and suddenly here was this handsome, strong, clean and bright kid who had never had a lick of trouble in his life. And he was a nice boy. Just sort of . . . uninformed.

Luther watched him petting Buddha, and that pleased him. Buddha was about as ugly as they came and a whole lot dirtier than Luther wished he was, and he was – well, they were both on the ripe side, that had to be faced. So most of the folks sort of kept their distance. Sort of? They ran like hell, actually. Luther had ended up staying on the far side of every room because he didn't want folks to feel embarrassed by not being able to handle the odour.

J.D., though, he could handle it. Luther watched the young face as the boy and the dog enjoyed each other. There was a lot of sadness in the boy, though. And why wouldn't there be? He was alone here and his parents were nowhere around.

'You worried about your folks?'

'My brother.'

That was a rough one. Little brother, too, Luther didn't even need to ask. Big brother protects little brother, and when he can't, well, that is hard. 'What's his name?'

'Benjamin . . . but I call him Benny.'

J.D. gave Luther a long, appraising look. What was this old tramp up to, asking him all these personal questions?

179

Luther looked right back, and J.D. saw something in his eyes that he knew about but had not often seen. Call it sympathy, call it compassion, it was the look somebody gives you when they sincerely wish they could help, but they can't. He'd seen it once in the face of Doctor Rettie, when he'd separated his shoulder and was writhing in agony on the rugby field. He had seen it in Benny's face, when Dad had lit into him for no good reason.

He let his guard down a little. 'If I just knew he was okay . . .'

Luther nodded slowly. 'That's the hard part, the not knowing.'

J.D. heard a world of pain in those words. Luther had lost a hell of a lot in this world, that could not have been more plain. J.D. decided that they belonged together, the two of them, because they were both in the same situation: they were grieving for people they had lost. Who Luther had lost, he'd probably never say. But he didn't need to, did he?

Luther tore out a page and rolled it up into a ball. He held it out to J.D., who took it and stuffed it down his pants. 'Thanks,' he said. Luther gave him a smile and rolled him another, and was glad to see him put it to use.

Across Europe, the snow continued to fall. By immense effort and with superb coordination, roads in southern France and the west of England were still relatively passable. Elsewhere, though, the situation was impossible. Whole towns were buried in the snow. Trafalgar Square consisted of a white drift of snow punctuated by Nelson's Column. Only the deep tube was running, and officials were stopping trains before they went above ground and sending them back along their shortened routes. Aside from those few tube trains, London's traffic had stopped. Throughout the city, as across the whole northern hemisphere, there were collapsed roofs and people atop others frantically shovelling to keep them from going, too. In London alone, one person was having a heart attack every fourteen seconds, and the telephone lines were jammed with emergency calls to which there could be no response.

At Hedland, the wind howled with a banshee's supernatural fervour, stripping parts of the facility entirely of snow while burying others under fifty feet of the stuff. Inside, practically everything was shut down to conserve power. The project's purpose had been mooted by events. Obviously, the current it had been set up to monitor had done what it had been feared that it would do. It was gone south, thank you, and all the buoys would be flashing alarms if the monitors had been turned on.

The distant sound of the generator changed, going high, then sputtering. As it sputtered the lights flickered. Also, no doubt, the heat. They had closed off most of the facility, leaving heat registers open only here in the monitoring room. When the generator failed, the boiler's electric pumps would stop, and it would automatically shut down. The outcome would be simple: death.

'We must almost be out of diesel fuel,' Dennis said.

Simon opened a drawer and pulled out a bottle. 'Any chance it'll run on this?' It was a fine single malt.

'Are you mad? That's twelve-year-old Scotch.' He took the bottle from Simon and produced some glasses from another drawer. It wouldn't run the generator, but it had a very definite use, most assuredly. He opened the bottle and poured three drinks, generous ones. Then he poured some more. Why not be very damn generous?

Simon raised his glass. 'To England,' he said.

Privately, Gerald Rapson thought that was a hollow toast. England had ceased to exist, was his thought. He raised his own glass. 'To mankind.' His thinking was that surely there was somebody left somewhere.

Dennis laughed a little. 'To Manchester United!'

They all laughed, then, and drank. At that moment, the generator whined again, sputtered . . . and stopped. The lights flickered out and did not come back on. From the heat register across the room, there came a long, declining sigh, followed by a series of bangs.

It was probably under a hundred below outside, maybe even colder than that. Gerald thought that they would lose consciousness from the cold in about an hour. And how strange that seemed, to be in the last hour of life.

Dennis lit some emergency candles. Gerald looked at his two assistants in their glow. They seemed to him to be two very brave men, sitting about with their glasses of Scotch, in the jaws of death.

'I just wish I could've seen him grow up,' Simon said.

'The important thing is, Simon, he will grow up,' Gerald said. Deep in the secrecy of his own mind, he wondered if it was even true. It might be that nobody in the British Isles was going to survive . . . not one.

'Amen,' Dennis said, and Gerald thought that the word meant more than amen to the idea that Simon's son would grow up. It was a final word, a goodbye to life.

'Goodbye,' he said in his heart, 'goodbye.'

It was a damned nice Scotch, smoky, smooth, just enough bite to remind you that it was not some sort of exotic wine.

Goodbye . . .

*

The Trustees Room of the New York Public Library had been transformed from a large and elegant chamber to something very different. The wooden furnishings that could be broken up had been piled beside the fireplace. There were chair legs and arms, stuffing, cloth upholstery, wooden backs and frames. Drawers from a side table had been made into kindling, as had three display cases that had contained a collection of bookplates, some two hundred years old. The plates themselves had been carefully saved by Judith, stacked in the middle of the huge old conference table along with the Gutenberg Bible and a number of other fine editions that had come in with the more humble books.

Sitting together in the circle that the stacks of books had made around the fireplace, were the members of the group, the ones who had taken a boy's word over a man's and stayed put when escape seemed the only logical alternative.

Sam and Laura were speaking so softly together that it might have been thought that they were praying.

'Best meal ever?' Sam asked.

'First time I had lobster. My uncle stuffed them with shrimp and baked them in butter. Unbelievable.'

She closed her eyes, remembering. He closed his . . . imagining.

She leaned her head against his shoulder. 'Most physical pain you've ever experienced?'

That took him back to the beach, and, oh, it was one beautiful memory now, despite what had happened. 'The time,' he said, his eyes closed, 'that I stepped on a jellyfish.' By the beautiful sea, under the sweet blue sky, with a little yellow plane chugging past trailing a suntan lotion sign. And the smell of suntan lotion, and of the sea, the rich, mysterious, devastating alive tang of the ocean.

'Ouch. How old were you?'

'Eleven.' He remembered the astonishing shock of pain that had raced up his leg, causing him to fall forward screaming. 'It hurt so bad I threw up.' Mom had carried him over to the cabana and a lifeguard had put alcohol on it, which had helped.

'My wisdom teeth,' she said. 'After the drugs wore off.'

He noticed her rub the cut on her leg. It looked kind of swollen and red, not like a normal infection. He thought maybe it wasn't too bad – hoped, rather, that it wasn't.

'I got another one,' she said. 'Favourite vacation?'

'Not counting this?'

She rolled her eyes. God, but she was beautiful. How could somebody rolling their eyes be lovely to see? Everything she did seemed to make her prettier. And when she smiled – that was amazing, that was almost, like, supernatural beauty.

'My best vacation ever,' he said, looking back. And then he knew. Exactly. 'A few years ago my dad took me on one of his research trips to Greenland. The ship broke down and we got stuck. The sun was only out like four hours a day and it rained constantly.'

'Sounds kind of boring.'

'My dad and I hung out together for ten days. Doing nothing.' He remembered back to the endless talks, Dad explaining about the way the Greenland ice sheet worked, and how they could drill down the same way they were doing in Antarctica, and find out what the world temperature was year by year, and even the composition of the air, by reading the ice cores. And there had been more, much more. Dad had even quoted poetry from memory – *The Rime of the Ancient Mariner*. 'Water, water

184

everywhere, nor any drop to drink . . .' 'It was great,' he said fervently.

She stared off into space a moment, then nodded slowly. She had understood how much he missed his dad, how much he wanted to be part of his life.

'My father and I were supposed to go look at colleges next month,' she said. 'He wants me to go to Harvard.' She laughed ruefully. 'I guess I don't have to worry about getting in anymore.'

Very suddenly, her laughter turned to tears. She wept bitterly, and he thought to himself that the magnitude of all this had just smashed into her mind. Her Harvard application didn't matter because there was no Harvard.

What did matter? Well, he knew one thing that did. He put an arm around her shoulders and said, 'Hey, guess what? Everything's gonna be all right.'

She reared back, turned on him. Her eyes were running with tears. 'No,' she said, 'it's not.'

Across the vast American plain, the snow fell. It fell on great cities and small towns, whipped by winds that came straight down from the north, that came even faster because its smooth surface offered no resistance. The highways were studded with necklaces of humps, each one a vehicle that had once been full of life and hope. The snow ran in the streets of the cities, the wind screamed around the eaves of houses and the walls of buildings.

In the fields, cattle stood frozen solid where they had been grazing, most with grass still in their mouths. The snow covered them just as it covered the cars and trucks, the barns and the houses, and the long lines of suburbs that had once defined the American dream.

Some of the largest cities remained defiantly alive,

their lights gleaming in the maelstrom, snowploughs roaring in their streets, people hurrying from place to place on foot. Mostly, though, the snow had enclosed a whole world in a frigid, pitiless cloak of freezing death. It was a world that not three days ago had seemed to its inhabitants to be eternal. From Paris, the City of Light to Chicago, the Windy City, and on across to Novosibirsk and Beijing, death danced on winds gossamer with snow.

In his heart, Jack Hall felt that he and Frank and young Jason were just about done. Devoutly, he wished that the two of them had not insisted on making this journey. They were here, though, and his obligation was to do everything he could to both save their lives and reach his objective.

Up to a point. The father was going to save his son if he could. If he had to die in this freezing hell to do it, that was an acceptable sacrifice. It is deep in the nature of the species, no doubt running in the fragments of DNA remaining from the first living things, that the parent will die for the child.

He pushed forward, Jason beside him. Frank was behind the sled, shoving it and guiding them as best he could. The GPS was only occasionally working now. Jack's hope was that New York was a big place, and if they just kept moving east, they were bound to come across it. So he mainly used his compass, correcting when Jason got a fix.

Ahead, there was nothing but a featureless plain of snow, broken only by whiteouts. Snow was still pouring out of the sky. He knew that they were south of Philly, crossing one of the suburbs. His concern was air pockets that had undoubtedly formed under the covering of snow. From his Antarctic experience, he knew how dangerous it was to try to cross a glacier on fresh snow. Covered fissures were often impossible to detect, no matter how good an eye you had.

He glanced back at Frank. He was hunkered down, pushing hard. Jack did the same. The snow felt fairly stable. So maybe they were crossing a field twenty or so feet down. They were over Chester Heights, he thought, moving towards Chester. He was hoping that they would be able to see well enough to cross the Delaware on a bridge. It was a big river, and would probably still have flow in it, meaning that getting across on the ice would take every ounce of skill that they possessed, seasoned with a large dollop of luck.

Was that a shudder coming up from below? He glanced over at Jason. He didn't appear to have noticed. They went on. Now Jack heard a long sound rising over the howl of the wind, a *cr-a-a-ak*. Again he looked at Jason, then back at Frank. All seemed well. Of course, he knew differently. The sound had come from somewhere.

Long experience told him that they were in trouble, also that the smartest thing to do was to press ahead and try to outrun whatever was giving way beneath them.

Crack!

A huge jerk on the safety line that connected the three of them. Jack turned around. For a moment, he saw only the sled, then made out Frank's dark form behind it. He was in a hole, supporting himself on his outstretched arms, his head and shoulders bent forward to maximise the amount of ice carrying his weight. Even in what had to be a terrifying situation, Frank was the consummate pro.

Cra-a-a-k!

Frank disappeared from view. An instant later, the

safety line went taut, yanking Jason off his feet. Then Jack felt himself sliding towards the hole as well. He put one hand on the safety line breakaway, and tried to stop the slide with his snowshoes. No good. Jason was down and could not get any purchase with his own shoes. With his free hand, Jack drew his ice axe out of its holster. He prayed God the snow was packed hard enough not to crumble away. A mighty swing of the axe took it deep, and Jack felt snow building up against his arm as they were dragged closer and closer to whatever lay below.

Then they stopped.

He'd won – for the moment. Now came the hard part. Leaving the axe embedded, he began working his way back along the line.

And then he saw what had happened, and his stomach almost went out through his feet . . . to the floor of the shopping centre fifty feet below. He could see a Toys 'R' Us and a central island planted with tropical flowers, bougainvillea and what might even have been orchids. A Radio Shack had been looted, and a drugstore, and the debris of the violence that had been done to them – radio boxes, pill bottles, and such – lay scattered eighty feet beneath Frank's dangling boots.

With a sickening tinkle of shattering glass, Frank's precarious hold gave way, and he plunged another twenty feet. Echoing up from below came the fainter sound of glass hitting the floor.

If Frank was injured, it was essential that they know that during the rescue. Jack called down to him. 'Are you all right, Frank?'

'Fine. I just dropped in to do a little shopping.'

Beautiful, beautiful guy. 'Hold on. We'll pull you up. Jason, dig your heels in.'

This was going to be a piece of cake. They'd get Frank back up, then take off towards the edge of the damn mall and get the hell off this damn roof.

There was a sound above the wail of the wind, close to him. He looked over, and saw that Jason was hyperventilating. Not needed, kid, not now. 'Jason!'

Jason clutched the ice beneath him. He was too terrified to respond to commands, Jack could see that. He took a deep breath, fought to communicate as much calm as he could. 'All right, Jason, take it easy. Take a breath and roll over onto your back . . .'

Jason looked at him out of the eyes of a hunted rabbit.

'Okay, easy now.'

Jason rolled.

'Good, that's it. Now plant your feet.'

Jason worked the heels of his snowshoes into the icy snow. Now the shoes would operate as a brake, if Frank's weight began to pull him forward.

'Good work. I'm going to come to you. I'll release the pressure very slowly.' He moved a little, allowing the safety line between the two of them to go slack. Then he drew his ice axe free.

Everything stayed as it was. Jason's heels had effectively replaced the ice axe. Jack crawled methodically closer to the opening. He would try to stand up and overhand Frank back to the surface. It was going to be desperately dangerous, but it had to be done.

As he crawled, the wind seemed to come alive, grasping at his arms, whipping around his body, pushing snow in under the edges of his parka, sending freezing tendrils of water down his neck.

There was a sort of shift, as if the weight distribution was changing. Jack thought, quite calmly, that he and

Jason would go through in a moment and they would all die.

So be it . . .

He looked down into the opening. There was Frank, peering up at him. His expression was calm. A professional did not panic at a moment like this. A professional did the opposite, became calm and deliberate, followed the book.

With a heart-stopping *thwanggg*, the safety line sliced into the glass, dropping Frank another five feet.

'Hang on!'

Now a terrible crackling sound radiated out from Jason, who began making little whimpering sounds. Jack ignored them. Let the man weep, he was probably about to die.

'It won't hold all of us,' Frank yelled up from below.

Jack knew he was right. They had blundered onto a skylight that had never in a million years been designed to hold the weight of three men with two hundred pounds of arctic gear and a heavy sled, not to mention the couple of tons of snow that were already there.

Then he saw something in Frank's hand. God, it was a knife!

'Frank, no!'

Frank looked straight at him. Their eyes met. The knife was poised beside the safety line.

'You'd do the same thing,' he said, and sliced through it with the expert stroke of a man who knew just how to cut one of the tough cords.

Frank's face dropped away, the expression turning to one of horror – glaring eyes, mouth opening to scream.

From below there came a thud. Frank hit amid the blossoms and the toys, and bounced into the landscaping.

The sound swept up and down the mall's interior, a fading echo.

The body did not move. The scream had never come.

Moving slowly, arms and legs spread to distribute his weight, Jack began edging back from the hole.

CHAPTER 16

Patrolman Campbell had gathered his brood of refugees into the third storey of a ruined office building. He'd gone hunting then, not for food, which was unlikely to be found above the ice at this point. All the little cafes and restaurants that packed lower Manhattan were on the ground floors. Up here, if you were lucky, you might find an occasional lunch in a desk drawer, hard frozen.

He returned to the building after dark, guided by the flickering fire within, that they had made from furniture and paper.

'What'd you find out?' the library security guard asked.

He was sallow now, the colour of parchment. His liver was failing, Tom Campbell thought, but he didn't know why. God only knew what sort of diseases might emerge among these exhausted people. Poor nutrition, overexertion and stress played hell with the immune system, allowing all sorts of things that had been dormant to become active.

'I talked to some guys who had a short-wave scanner. They'd heard that rescue crews were still picking people up further south on I-95.'

The cabbie bestirred himself. Most folks were huddled close to the fire, their eyes closed, wrapped in their stinking clothes, showing as little of themselves to the cold as possible. Some of them had even taken Tom's advice and were wrapped up in one another, seeking heat. The cabbie asked, 'How much further south?'

It could have been Atlanta, for all Tom knew. But he didn't say that. 'They weren't sure,' he said, and let it go at that.

The guard – was his name Hidalgo? – said, 'It doesn't matter. We've gotta get to them. It's our only chance.'

Tom wondered if he would ever get these people moving again. If you don't get decent food, you sleep longer and feel like doing less, until finally you die. It's called starvation. 'We need to rest, first,' he said. 'Let's stay here till morning.'

And maybe, he thought in the privacy of his secret despair, morning will become forever.

The snow was beyond belief, certainly beyond the capabilities of the equipment that General Pierce had organised to transport the Presidential party southward. He found himself looking at what almost appeared to be new mountains. They were on I-95 north of Richmond, but the snowdrifts were so huge that it seemed more like they must be out in the Shenandoahs, on their way down 81. They weren't though. The superb navigational equipment on board was not confused by clouds. They had an exact fix, second to second.

Ahead of them, their snowplough spewed white fountains a hundred feet in the air. Beside it, a literal mountain of snow rose, it seemed, all the way to the sky. Behind the snowplough, General Pierce sat in a freezing cold Hummer, in constant radio contact with the motorcade.

From moment to moment, gusts of wind made the snowplough disappear, but then its reassuring ungainly form would show up again and they would make another half mile or so.

The wind howled and the Hummer vibrated, and the whiteout became so intense that the driver called a halt.

Then next thing the general knew, he was no longer looking at the back of a snowplough. Instead, a mountainside rose before him.

They did not move forward. There was no way to do so. The driver sat silently, obviously awaiting orders.

The general knew what had happened: a massive movement of snow – in effect, an avalanche – had just buried the plough.

Without a word, he stepped down into the roadway, such as it was. His boots sank almost to thigh depth in the softly packed new snow. For a moment, the cold stunned him. The Hummer's heater must be running full tilt, taking the interior temperature up to, what, maybe ten above? But out here, now *this* was what could be called cold.

General Pierce knew that the motorcade had come exactly two hundred and two miles since it had left the White House nearly forty hours ago.

He watched the Marines fighting to clear the snow from around the vehicles, saw their sweat turning to ice and falling off them in a fine powder even as they worked.

He also understood that this was not going to work. These vehicles were snowbound. There would be no further progress under present conditions, and present conditions showed no sign of letting up.

Wiping off his winter goggles, the General saw a familiar black vehicle ahead. The flags on its fenders were frozen solid. They looked a hell of a lot like ice-covered barber poles.

He pulled open the door of the modified Hummer, and slid into the blessed warmth within. In his formal suit and red silk tie, the President seemed almost absurd. But it was quiet in here, preserving some of the elegance that was supposed to surround the highest office in the land. Despite everything, the men around the President were still efficiently insulating their charge from the freezing hell that screamed around them.

Well, that was about to change. 'It's no good, sir,' Pierce said as he settled in next to the President. 'An avalanche buried our snowplough. The road's completely blocked. We can't stay here. The vehicles are gonna be buried soon.'

'We'll have to try to make it on foot,' the President said.

He was right about that. There was absolutely no other choice whatsoever. The general experienced a rush of frustration. How could the most important man in the world have ended up in a fix like this? The President of the United States didn't get stuck in a damn blizzard. Nature wasn't powerful enough to stop the President!

He wanted to be sure the President knew the risks. 'It's miles to the nearest shelter, sir.'

The President remained silent for a moment. 'Then we'd better get started,' he said grimly.

As a dark, frigid dawn rose over China, darkness swept westward across America. Europe was locked in the horrific cold of the deep night. Unimaginable temperatures were being reached, of a hundred and twenty and a hundred and thirty below in places like Russia and Sweden, and a hundred below farther south.

In Paris, only Sacré Coeur and the Eiffel Tower jutted

above the snow. The temperature was ninety below, enough to shatter the iron of which the tower was made. The windows of the cathedral were dark, like put-out eyes, the glass made so brittle by the cold that the wind simply shattered it.

Across the Seine, Notre Dame looked like the keel of an overturned ship. Only one tower was visible, the other having already collapsed.

Far to the north of Scotland, three brittle bodies sat motionless in the pitch-dark Hedland facility. No light flickered on the control panel. The tea still in Dennis's cup was harder than granite. Every so often the building emitted a sharp bang, as frozen girders and rivets burst. Soon, the snow that had buried it would also collapse it.

Across the tossing Atlantic waters, the *Queen Mary 2* drifted helplessly, defeated by hydraulic failure. Frozen hydraulic fluid had rendered rudder control impossible. Still, it was ablaze with light . . . the only electric light for thousands of miles in any direction.

For over the western world, a great darkness had fallen. In fact, it had not been this dark since before the native Americans had colonised the continent, and Rome had risen in Italy. Here and there, fires flickered, some of them large enough to be visible for miles, but most pitiful affairs, made from what little fuel could be gathered by people who were fast freezing to death.

The triangle of flickering light that glowed across thirty or so feet of snow was not one of the larger fires. In fact, it was coming from a tent, and not from a fire but from a gasoline lantern. Inside the tent, Jack and Jason huddled close to a camp stove.

Thirty feet below them, in a Lincoln Navigator with a crushed roof, lay the bodies of two adults, two children, a dog, a cat and, in a cracked bowl, two frozen-solid gold-fish. But they knew nothing of this. All they were aware of was the small heat from the camp stove on which they were boiling water, and the fact that they both felt as if temperatures were dropping below the minimum rating of their clothing.

Jason got their mugs from their mess kit, and for a moment both of them stared in silence at Frank's. It had been with him for a lot of years, and had the dents to prove it. Like much of the equipment of old hands, it was a treasured keepsake.

Silently, Jack poured split pea soup for himself and Jason. The kid was a problem for Jack. He could not ask him to continue on, because that was virtually certain death. But he couldn't go back alone, either. That was certain death, too.

Jack knew that he should turn around right now and attempt to save their lives. But then he thought of his last words to Sam, 'I promise.'

Jason had known that the promise had been made, and he'd come anyway. To his death, though? If he'd fully understood the danger, would he be here right now?

Part of Jack's conscience said to him, 'Turn back, save this kid if you can.' The other part said in reply, 'You promised. You promised Sam.'

Jack sipped his soup. Even Jack Hall, with all of his experience of the effects of extreme polar weather, was stunned to discover that the mug was already cold.

Sam alone was awake. He was tired just like the rest of them, but if they were going to live, the fire required constant attendance. He watched Laura. She was sleeping fitfully. Her face seemed sweaty even though it was hardly even livable in here, let alone warm, let alone hot enough to make somebody sweat.

He went to her, started to wake her up, then stopped himself. Even here, with her face all dirty and her make-up not even a memory, she was almost heartbreakingly beautiful. His best guess was that she was real pretty, but not the goddess that he saw. No, he saw his love for her, the passion in his heart.

They were young, true, but he'd decided that they ought to get married. What was happening had changed everything. Last week, marriage among seventeen year olds would have sounded really stupid. Now, what he wanted most in the world was to get south, find some way to feed some mouths, and start a family. He didn't know where this ambition was coming from. He just knew that it was there, and it was powerful.

He went back and tossed some Thorsten Veblen and a couple of pounds of IRS rule books into the fire. Sparks flew up the chimney. Outside, the wind *still* howled. This storm was still going full blast.

He wondered why nobody had listened to his dad. If the President was dead, he'd be just as glad. He knew it was wrong to feel that way, but what about his generation, what about him and Laura and J.D. and Brian and all the kids of the world, what was left for them now?

Thinking back, he could not remember anything from any President or any other world leader about planning for the possibility of sudden climate change. What he remembered was a debate about whether or not global warming was real. Of course it was real. It was part of nature.

Why hadn't they listened to Dad?

He gazed across the room towards the big doors that

led out into the hallway. Would Dad ever come through those doors? He did not want to face the fact that he might not – actually, probably wouldn't – so he imagined him as he might look: tall, wearing a filthy parka with the hood framing his bearded face.

Dad. His deepest heart whispered, 'I belong to you, Dad, I'm your son, remember me?' The fire guttered as a frosty gust came down the chimney and spread out into the room. Dad. 'You belong to me, Dad, I'm your son, you took responsibility for me.'

He thought of Brian and his family, where were they? Brian never said anything about it, but Sam had gone over to him a few hours ago, and he'd been quietly crying. Judith, too, and her tears had continued long after Brian's had changed to the sweet breath of sleep. And Benjy, was he lying beneath a snowdrift somewhere? Would J.D. ever gain closure? Probably not. Probably, he'd live the rest of his life, however long that might be, wondering about his little brother.

Sam had hated J.D. at first. But it was only his male nature that made him want to be with Laura. J.D. was also a loving brother, and in Sam's eyes, that made him a good guy. He deserved all the help and comfort he could get, J.D. did. But not, oh please, the hand of the woman I love.

She sort of sighed, and Sam went over to her again. He laid a hand on her forehead and a thrill of fear raced through him, causing him to draw it back as if her skin had burned him . . . which it almost had. She was hot, and she should not be. She was also awake. He could see an eye looking at him.

'Are you all right?' he whispered. 'You feel like you've got a fever.'

'I'm fine. I just can't sleep. My mind keeps going over all those worthless Decathlon facts.' She snorted out a soft laugh. 'Pretty stupid, I know.'

'It's not stupid. It's just that you need time to adjust. That's all.'

'How am I supposed to adjust, Sam? Everything I've ever worked for – it's all been preparation for some future that doesn't exist.' She sat up and wrapped her hands around her knees, and stared into the fire. 'You always said I took the competition too seriously. You were right.' Again, there came that little laugh, that Sam sensed contained a world of disappointment and hurt, just like he was feeling. 'It was a waste of time.'

If the adults loved us, then why did they do this to us? Laura's dad used to scoff about global warming, Sam had heard him do it. Shouldn't he have at least looked at the facts before condemning his own daughter to this hell?

'It wasn't a waste of time,' Sam said. 'I just said that to avoid admitting the truth.' His mouth went dry, because of what he had suddenly decided to do.

She looked at him. Her face was really sweaty, gleaming in the firelight. 'The truth about what?'

He parted dry lips. 'The truth about why I joined the team.'

She frowned. How totally clueless could a person look? He realised that she had no idea at all. He drew closer to her. The others couldn't hear this. This was private stuff. 'Because you were on the team.'

Her eyes widened. Something came into them – he thought it might be laughter.

'It was an excuse to—' The eyes twinkled. It was laughter. She was going to laugh at him. 'Uh, just forget it . . .'

He turned away, but then he felt a hand on his arm. 'Hey, come here.'

He turned back. She reached up and took his chin, and guided his face towards hers.

A second passed, as he gazed into her big green eyes, the most beautiful eyes on earth. Then her lips brushed his and a shiver went down all the way to the hollow of his gut. He reached up, laid a hand on the back of her head and pressed his lips against hers.

Deep in her throat, she made a little sound and he knew it for what it was: a sound of relief, of joy.

She had been hoping for this, waiting for it.

He moved against her, took her in his arms and opened his mouth to her mouth. He felt himself becoming excited, and he knew that the pressure of it would be against her free arm, and it happened, and she did not move.

They kissed deeper, tasting of each other's body and soul, and where their lips met, the storm and death stopped. The little couple, entwined in each other's arms, were like a blazing comet that would push back the north wind and sweep the snows aside . . . at least, here in this room beside this one flickering fire, for the moment.

CHAPTER 17

Hideki Kawahara gazed down at the Earth's surface. As he watched, the station orbited up from the South Atlantic, angling over America. Westward, he could see South America, the centre of which was relatively untouched. Along the distant line of the eastern horizon, though, over central Africa, the flicker of lightning was continuous. What was happening there was that a storm front had almost reached the equator, penetrating the tropical air mass with temperatures not seen in East Africa in living memory. In Djibouti, it was fifty-seven, farther north and inland it was snowing lightly in Timbuktu.

As the International Space Station moved towards North America, what began to slide past below looked more like the surface of the moon than anything one would associate with Earth. The immense cloud cover stretched from horizon to horizon like a huge white plate. Here and there, the vortexes of mega-cells might have been mistaken for craters. But they were not craters, and he hardly dared think what was happening down at the base of those dark glaring eyes.

'There's no point of reference,' he said as he drifted away to let the others look. 'All I can see is cloud cover.'

NASA Houston was still on line, but they were being evasive about when the shuttle might return. The Baikonur Cosmodrome was not responsive, nor was

JAXA communications. NASA kept promising to send word of families, but that word never came, except for Bob Parker, whose wife was safe in their home in Sarasota, Florida.

Nothing had been said, but the three men all knew that their supplies up here were limited. They knew that the shuttle was on indefinite weather delay, and that there would be no supplies forthcoming from Baikonur. They were already rationing food, which would be their main problem. The station's recycling system would keep them in water for another three months, in oxygen for much longer. No, the issue was going to be food. They had about six weeks of it left. Emergency ration protocols would stretch that to three and a half months, maybe four.

So far, NASA had not actually declared an emergency, but they'd heard radio broadcasts suggesting that there had been sustained hundred and thirty mile-an-hour winds at Cape Kennedy. Could the shuttle hangar survive that much stress? For all they knew, somewhere under that cloud cover was wreckage that would mean their lives.

Yuri Andropov began throwing switches. Bob Parker asked him what he was doing.

'Taking infrared image of thermal layers. We send to Houston, to our weather service.' He nodded towards Hideki. 'To yours.'

'I'll help you,' Bob said.

As the images became more complex, they started to take on the shape of a computer model that Bob had seen once or twice before. In fact, it had been in a magazine called *Weather*, a hobbyist's journal. This was the spitting image of the model storm that Jack Hall had postulated would appear if the North Atlantic Oscillation ever moved south due to excessive warming of the northern North Atlantic.

He looked out the window. Back towards Africa, he could see a very definite line swooping across the mid-Atlantic, perhaps five hundred miles north of the Equator. North of that line, the weather was cloudy, indicating the presence of the same extensive storm activity that was directly below them, covering North America. South of it, there were long necklaces of fair weather cumulus, very typical of the place and time of year.

So that was what had happened: that line must be the new route of the North Atlantic Oscillation. Without the current to warm the northern half of North America and Europe, it was going to get very, very cold up there. Much of it was going to be unlivable.

It was selfish of him, he knew, but he was damn glad that Gerry was in Sarasota. It was cloudy and cold there, but he very much doubted that the weather would become life threatening.

Yuri and Hideki, on the other hand, had probably already lost their loved ones. He wondered when NASA would give them a new resupply timetable, or an exit date. Then he thought, 'Not when. It's if. If we will get a resupply date.' He gazed long out the window. *If.*

In normal times, the Texas–Mexico border, from El Paso–Juarez to Matamoros–Brownsville, has a total population of four million, half of them packed into the slums of Juarez.

Not now. Texas' Rio Grande Valley had tripled its population from one to three million in a matter of days. And the lucky ones – another two million – were across the border in Mexico. In all, the United States now had a population of around a hundred million living souls, five million of whom were even yet in jeopardy. A hundred and fifty million brothers, sisters, mothers and fathers were entombed, not to be seen again for vast cycles of years; indeed, not until the equinox had marched its stately way backward around the pole four more times, taking twenty-two thousand years to make each journey.

Scientists, politicians, the media – they had all scoffed that nature could do something as radical as this. 'Where's the energy for a storm like that?' scientists had sneered when Jack Hall had published his papers.

The energy was there. What was not there was the will to see the truth. And so nature had done her worst. Ironically, proper planning and greenhouse gas management could have staved off the disaster for years, possibly until ways were found to interrupt the ice cycle that had the planet in its grip once and for all. Alone among world leaders, the Canadian Prime Minister had pointed out that simple voluntary measures that could be done in the home at virtually no cost could have so reduced human greenhouse gas emissions that the catastrophe would have been averted.

At no cost. Maybe for years, maybe forever.

Now, instead of these millions of people living out their precious lives, there was vast death across the northern half of the planet, a civilisation thousands of years old had fallen, and along this border, in wretched camps, huddled the pitiful remnant of its greatness.

Still, though, the Americans were organised. Thousands of tents had been found, and stood in long sentinel rows, their flaps shuddering in the blustery north wind, light snow flurries hissing against their peaked roofs.

There were people everywhere, listening to radios, watching what little television they could pick up, but mostly watching the sky. The National Guard distributed food from large centres that would spring up as soon as another truckload of supplies arrived from the north.

The United States was vastly harmed, but it was not killed. The West Coast was functioning as far north as San Francisco – wet and storm battered, but not killed. Much of the Southwest was intact, also, as was southern Texas. San Antonio and Houston were hubs of organisation and the source of food supplies for the millions.

Ominously, though, those supplies were dwindling fast, and neither Fourth Army planners nor local grocery chains were able to obtain anything like what would soon be needed.

In Mexico, the price of *masa*, the tortilla flour essential to life, had risen a thousand per cent overnight. The result was that the poor were gathering along the borders of the American camps, and it would not be long before there was friction.

The world was like a great ocean liner that had taken a torpedo and was filling fast, but there were still people aboard with hopes, with dreams, gazing out across the empty ocean for rescuers who were, themselves, already dead.

The Emergency White House consisted of an elaborate series of tents. Inside, staffers moved about in every direction, as this flimsy, inadequate nerve centre struggled to make some sense out of chaos, to get itself going, to offer meaning and support to the American people.

Secretary of State Linn was pressing through the crowd. 'Where's the Vice-President?'

Then she saw him. Sitting over there in that corner he

looked, well, small. Very small. Shrunken. It was as if the suffering of the nation had literally diminished the man. Well, he needed to find his strength and his courage fast. She went over to him. 'Raymond?'

At first, he didn't react. Then he raised his eyes . . . slowly. 'What?'

'The President's motorcade got caught in the storm.'

His eyebrows raised. She saw fear flicker in the eyes. One of the most ambitious and outspoken Vice-Presidents in American history was obviously terrified at what he thought he was about to hear.

Well, that was his problem. 'They didn't make it,' she said. No point in mincing words. What was, was.

If Becker leaned away from her any farther, he was going to fall out of the tent. 'How . . . how could this happen?'

How, she wondered, could you have been such a dumb jerk for your whole damn worthless life, or how could the President of the United States have got himself frozen to death in a snowbank in *Virginia*, for the love of Mike?

'He wanted to be the last one out the door,' she said. Blake had realised the incredible scope of his mistake, the tremendous, historical immensity of it. No doubt of that, he had known that his name would be cursed for millennia, as the names of the demons were cursed.

He hadn't wanted to live.

She patted the Veep's perfectly manicured hand. If ever a man had a chance to grow into an office, it was this man, and this office. 'Good luck,' she said, 'and God be with you, Mr President.'

It was the beginning of the third day in the Trustees Room, and Jeremy had lost his energy to a rattling cough.

Elsa, as well, huddled close to the fire, coughing and staring at the flickering flames.

There were not nearly as many books in the room as there had been at first. Not nearly as many.

Laura was shivering in Sam's arms. Earlier, she'd been talking, laughing to herself. There were beads of sweat on her forehead, and sweat was running in rivulets down her cheeks. Sam was so scared he could hardly think straight, his mind just kept turning over and over. He was trying to remember what did you do – was it starve a fever, feed a cold? What did you do for somebody who was real sick, and Laura, he knew, was real sick.

'Maybe she has the flu,' Brian said. He and J.D. were sticking close.

'It's not the flu.'

Then Judith came over. She tossed a dictionary into the fire, having made sure it was open so all the pages would burn, and then turned to them. 'Okay, let's go over the symptoms.'

She'd tossed away the dictionary, but she had in her hands a thick blue book called *The Meck Manual*. It was a couple of thousand pages of fine print, all the diagnostic knowledge of mankind, gathered between two covers.

'She's got a fever and her skin is cold and clammy.'

Judith flipped pages. 'Books can be good for some-thing other than burning,' she muttered.

'Some books,' Sam thought, 'now, just *some* books.' He tossed a James Hilton novel on the fire, watched it burn. *Goodbye Mr Chips*.

'How's her pulse?' Judith asked.

He lifted her wrist, looked down at her soft hand, lying limp and hot in his. He closed his eyes, found the pulse. *Wumpwumpwumpwump*. 'Beating really fast.'

Judith turned more pages. 'Does she have any injuries? A cut or something that could've got infected?'

Sam remembered the flood, the car bumper down there under all that dirty water, Laura's blood flowing. 'She scraped her leg in the flood. I noticed she kept rubbing it.'

He pulled up her pant leg, and what he saw caused him to gasp, caused them all to gasp. Angry red lines marched up her leg under the skin, which was so swollen that it looked like it'd pop if you pricked it. The wound itself was an angry, puckered mass of swollen skin and pus.

'That's septicemia,' Judith said, 'blood poisoning. She's at risk of septic shock.'

Sam felt like he was going to throw up. 'What can we do?' he asked, frightened that the book was giving Judith an answer he did not want to hear.

'She needs a massive dose of penicillin or a broad spectrum antibiotic immediately.'

She stopped. Sam saw her jaw working, saw the wet that had appeared at the corners of her eyes.

'Or what?'

There was a silence. She looked at him with hollow eyes. He took the book from her, read it himself. 'In untreated cases, death would follow within hours, or at most days, but modern treatment protocols make this an extremely unlikely outcome.'

Death? But she was just a kid. He threw his arms around her.

The National Oceanic and Atmospheric Administration had assumed an enormously important role in the life of the country and the world, with control over most environmental satellites, the National Weather Service, the National Hurricane Centre, the Severe Storms Laboratory and almost all of the reporting and analysis facilities possessed by the United States.

The problem was, despite the fact that Tom Gomez and his staff had actually moved the headquarters facilities to the government compound on the Mexican border, the vast majority of their data collection facilities were not reporting. The National Weather Service was intact in only the southern tier of states, and it was presumed that the stations not reporting had been destroyed.

Still, the NOAA tent presented an appearance of lots of activity. One of the main tasks at hand was making use of all the personnel who'd found their way here after being displaced from their stations. Many meteorologists had realised early on that something was very wrong, and had moved south with their families in the first wave of migration.

Janet Tokada moved quickly through the milling groups of scientists, some of them standing around jerry-built terminal stations, all, inevitably, trying to make sense of the spotty data they were receiving, and having trouble doing so.

The greatest loss was probably in the satellite department. The storm hadn't reached the satellites, of course, but cloud cover was causing signals acquisition problems, and many ground stations were no longer reporting.

Janet found Tom on the cot he'd had installed in the tiny area behind his desk, which he now called home. He was not about to leave this headquarters, not for any reason, lest he miss a crucial development.

NOAA had been using the National Emergency Alert System to alert travellers of much more than weather conditions. The system was also being used to inform about things like food and gasoline supplies along the highways, traffic problems, the availability of medical support, and anything else that might help refugees.

Janet shook Tom's shoulder. 'Tom, wake up. I just received some images from the International Space Station. You'd better take a look.'

Tom rolled off the cot, rumpled but fully dressed. He followed her to a monitor and there, for the first time, saw the storm whole. He stared down at the pale mass made weirdly beautiful by infrared imaging that saw through the cloud tops into the structure of the storm below. A map was overlaid on the storm, and it could be seen that its northern border was involved with additional heavy weather over Quebec somewhere north of the St Lawrence Seaway, while its more clearly defined southern border reached well into Alabama, Georgia and South Carolina. From there it curved up across the north half of Texas, where it became involved with another system plunging down from the north, that was now blizzarding across the western half of the country, with snow falling at the rate of three inches an hour, and wind gusts on the flat prairies reaching past a hundred miles an hour.

'The vortex is fifty miles in diameter,' Janet said, pointing to a spot approximately over Detroit. 'It's growing. And the cells over Europe and Asia are even bigger.'

'Good God.'

She pointed to a nasty bulge in the overall mass of the storm. 'This mega-cell's going to hit New York inside of an hour.'

Even now, every communications officer in the system was using all means available to try to let the people facing this thing know of their peril. Tom thought, though, that very few of them would be able to save themselves, even if they did know. This was one of those monstrosities whose vertical circulation was going to get so fast and so high that it would bring supercold air down from the upper levels of the atmosphere, air that would, briefly, drop ground temperatures to a hundred and sixty below, cold enough to freeze a human body solid in seconds.

He looked up at Janet, his tired mind focusing on a small detail that suddenly seemed intensely important. 'Does Jack know?'

'We can't reach him.'

Tom thought it ironic that a storm of a type that only Jack Hall had believed was even possible was going to kill him.

Jack had been in willpower mode before, so he knew that it was a matter of making sure that one foot went down ahead of where the other one had gone down. The wind swirled around him and the snow slid downward, but he was aware that it seemed less thick now. Even the worst storms, it seemed, played themselves out. Of course they did, he knew that. He was just beginning to have a hard time believing it.

Suddenly the rope around his waist went taut. He turned, and for a moment didn't see Jason. His heart started hammering: he was full of guilt for what had happened to Frank. Losing Jason was totally unacceptable.

He hauled himself towards the lump that was Jason, being careful not to let the line go slack. When he saw him, he realised that he hadn't dropped into a hole, but had simply collapsed. He bent down. The kid's eyes were closed, he was breathing normally. Jack reached into his parka and felt the pulse in his neck. Normal.

The kid was exhausted, that was all that was wrong

with him. Jack got his arms around his chest and lifted him onto the sled. Then he went behind it and started pushing.

The air was definitely lighter. The snow was less. It had warmed up so much that Jack was actually feeling a little sweat under his arms, deep beneath his six layers of clothing.

Had he been less exhausted himself, he would have recognised these danger signs. Instead, he pressed on, even allowing himself to hope that he'd soon see the sun.

CHAPTER 18

Sam had found some chairs with cane seats. He cut into one now, struggling to turn it into something that would work as a snowshoe. Without snowshoes, you'd sink to your waist out there. Ten feet out, you'd stop, too exhausted to go any farther. Struggling to turn around would take you down to chest level. If you made it back to your starting point, it would be a miracle.

'What are you doing?' Judith asked.

What Sam was doing was either saving Laura's life or giving up his own. He gazed out towards the wrecked cargo ship that was visible through the windows. 'That ship has to have medicine aboard.'

'You said it was too dangerous to go outside.'

His dad had warned him about lethal downbursts, but they'd been here for four days now, and so far there hadn't been a sign of one. They were out there, for sure, but they were apparently more rare than Dad had thought they would be. He continued working on the snowshoes.

'Where'd you find those chairs?' Brian asked. He had been sitting with J.D. The two of them were caring for Laura, making sure she was as warm as possible. When the wind slacked off, you could hear her teeth chattering and the steady murmur of her delirium. 'Where'd you find those chairs?' Brian repeated.

'Why?'

'Because I'm going with you.'

J.D. came over. 'Me, too.'

Sam might have been worried, once, for their safety. He was beyond that now. Just getting up on that ship was going to be a tremendous job, and he had to save Laura. Anybody willing to help was welcome.

They bundled themselves up as best they could, but when they jimmied open one of the ice-encrusted windows, they all knew immediately that it was hardly enough. The cold that hit them was brutal, it shot through them like a jolt of ice lightning. It seemed to attack their skin, then their blood with a billion tormenting pinpricks. J.D. gasped, Brian cursed, and Sam started out into the snow, holding his head down, moving towards the grey hulk that was dimly visible ahead in the roaring blizzard.

He came up on something swinging back and forth, a ghostly, strange presence. At first, he was mystified by what this bizarre object could be, but when he got close he saw, inside its crust of ice, a dimly visible image of a yellow stop light. It was the traffic light at Fifth and Forty-Second. The snow here must be at least thirty feet deep.

Moving slowly, hoping that their jerry-built snow-shoes would hold together, the three of them approached the ship. It wasn't really all that huge, but up close it seemed impossibly massive. Its bulk stretched off into the driving snow, creating the illusion that it must be miles and miles long. Craning his neck, Sam looked up to the Cyrillic lettering on the prow. Between the unfamiliar shapes of the letters and all the ice, he couldn't even begin to read it.

Now came the hard part – how to get into the thing. He thought of Laura in there dying, and he knew he had to hurry. He'd read more about septicemia, and he knew just how unpredictable it could be. At some point, Laura's heart would give out. When depended on a whole host of factors that he had no way of knowing.

She could have died five minutes ago. She might die in ten minutes, in an hour, in three days. All he knew was this: he had to get penicillin in her, or she was lost.

Brian went past him, hurrying ahead. Then Sam saw why. There was a rope ladder there that led to a narrow steel stair that rose up the side of the ship. The port-entry. Sailors could use these steps to get down to a tender when they wanted to go ashore in a port that was too shallow for the ship to enter. Somebody must have used it to get off the ship. What an experience *that* must have been, riding a ship up Fifth Avenue on a storm surge.

They left their snowshoes tied to the bottom rung of the rope ladder, which was frozen iron-hard. It was exhausting, dangerous work, climbing the ladder in the wind, but the stairs were even harder. They offered absolutely no traction. J.D. had found some decent boots that fit him, but shoes were a scarce item in the lost and found, and Sam and Brian had to make do with the sneakers they'd been wearing when this started.

The thing was, Sam's feet were already getting numb, and he knew that Brian's would be, too. How much time did they have before the cold incapacitated them, then killed them? Sam guessed half an hour, maybe a little more, maybe a little less.

The deck was a complicated riot of cables and jumbled equipment, all of it thickly encrusted with ice. The ship's superstructure was at the rear of the vessel. That was the crew's living quarters. Their medical cabinet would be there. He hoped to God that this Russian vessel had been observing international sea law, which required vessels to carry safety equipment that included antibiotics. One hopeful thing was that it had obviously entered New York Harbour, which meant that it had passed a harbour master inspection. They looked at safety equipment. But how closely, and could they be bribed?

They reached a door – a hatch, really – that was frozen closed. At first, getting it open seemed impossible, but then Brian found a piece of metal that was flat enough to force into the small gap between the hatch and the metal wall of the ship.

With a report like a rifle shot, the door came open. Inside, it was dark, but not pitch black. The portholes were covered with snow and ice, but they still let in enough light to see. Thank God for small blessings, Sam thought.

They climbed a stairway, passing through a kitchen area, a dining room, then another stairway. There were beds here, bunks in small cabins. The crew lived simply, but it looked cosy enough.

At the end of the corridor was a door with a small red cross painted on it. 'Over here,' he yelled to the others, who were searching different parts of the deck.

He tried to open the door, but it was locked. He kicked it. His foot bounced off with a clang and a flash of agony. Be careful, if you break anything, that's death. Out here, that's death. Like in the Antarctic, where the simplest problem could so easily escalate into disaster.

They struggled for a time with the door. Their little piece of metal wasn't going to help them. Whoever had run this ship had thought that the medical station was vulnerable to break-in. Probably full of painkillers, drugs that bored sailors on a long voyage might like to take advantage of.

Sam saw a porthole nearby. He remembered something about this part of the ship, that he'd glimpsed from the street far below. A frozen-solid fire extinguisher made an excellent battering ram, and he and the others took turns slamming one into the glass.

Finally, it gave way, shattering along with the ice that covered it. Sam went out on the catwalk – and when he did, noticed something odd. Far below, where they had come in, their own tracks were already covered by the snow. But there were other tracks there, deep, round tracks that looked like they belonged to some sort of animal. What would be out there in this? Dogs, probably, he decided, that had gone feral after being abandoned by their owners. The poor creatures were probably starving. He saw that the footprints went alongside the ship for a distance, then simply stopped. Maybe the dogs had found a way in. Good for them.

It was precarious out here, all slippery ice. His numbed feet were insensitive to slippage, and the wind buffeted him as he struggled along. He could be blown off here in a second.

It got even more dangerous when he started smashing what he hoped was the window to the medical cabinet. Of course, it could be that the room was small, and this would lead into another space behind it.

Smash!

He almost lost the extinguisher, it bounced back so hard. Then he slipped, fell back against the railing, felt it start to give way – and righted himself.

Again he hefted the extinguisher, aiming it at the centre of the craze marks left from his last blow. This time, there was a satisfying crunch, and the extinguisher didn't bounce back. Taking aim at what was now a hole, he slammed the extinguisher against the window with every ounce of strength he possessed – and it crashed through, leaving his hands and landing inside the room with a clang that echoed off into the storm.

He peered through the window and his heart started crashing in his chest so hard he was afraid he'd given himself a coronary at the age of seventeen. It was a beautiful, meticulously kept and well-equipped medical station. He pulled away the shards that remained in the window frame and climbed in.

He opened the door for Brian and J.D. Frantically, they began searching shelves and opening drawers.

'It's all in Russian,' J.D. moaned.

They could have penicillin in their hands and not know it. Sam was about to scream, he just could not believe this. He threw open another drawer – Russian, Russian and more Russian.

He looked along the shelves. There must be fifty different kinds of pills here, plus all manner of other medicine. But they couldn't give her everything in hope that one bottle would be right.

'I think I've got it.'

Sam turned on Brian like a famished wolf going for a fat goat. Brian held up a vial with a hypodermic kit attached by tape.

'But how do you know?'

Brian looked straight at him. 'It's labelled "Penicillin" on the bottom.'

Sam took the six precious vials – then stopped and distributed them, two each. Two doses would probably do it, so even if not all of them made it back, she'd still have a chance.

They took off down the corridor, running as fast as

they dared, each aware that he was racing death for Laura's life.

Then Brian stopped. 'Hold on a minute. I think this is the mess hall. Shouldn't we look for some food while we're here?'

'We don't have time!'

J.D. put a hand on Sam's shoulder. 'None of us are gonna survive much longer,' he said gently, 'unless we get food. Laura included.'

Sam had to admit that it was true. He did not stop to think how he would feel if he got back and she'd just died, because this was a chance to get something they all desperately needed. Like Dad said of his Antarctic expeditions, 'You never put anything off, because now might be your last chance. Things change fast in extreme places.'

'All right,' he said.

They went into the mess hall, with its long tables and tumbled mass of chairs. This was a ship that was getting ready to sink, obviously. Instead, it had ended up here, above water but still dead, and this room looked like that – it looked dead.

They crossed the mess to a door at the far end. No question where it led – the kitchen. Had to. And indeed, as soon as they stepped through it they were rewarded with a magnificent sight: shelves of canned food.

'Jackpot,' J.D. said.

Brian opened a steel cabinet. A large yellow package fell out. A moment later, there came a click, then a loud hissing sound – and a life raft started inflating at his feet, its frozen plastic crackling loudly as it took shape.

'All I did was open the cupboard.'

They were pushing the life raft out of their way, preparing to leave the boat with their wonderful haul of penicillin and all the canned goods they could carry, when something happened.

It happened so fast that at first Sam did not know what had made J.D. go flying off against the wall like that. Then he saw the grey shape standing over him, and J.D. shrieking and trying to fend off its snarling, snapping jaws.

That wasn't any dog, that was a damn wolf! Brian hurled a can at it, but it didn't help. Sam grabbed a chair from the mess, came back into the pantry and hit the wolf with it. The creature let out a yelp and fell aside. Its eyes were open, it was still breathing and half-growling. Stunned.

He went to J.D., but another wolf started through the door. He threw the chair at it, and he and Brian dragged J.D. through into the kitchen proper.

Brian slammed the door shut behind them.

There followed a thud, then another and another as the famished wolves threw themselves against the door.

Sam went down beside J.D. 'Are you all right?'

'I – I think so . . .' He started to his feet, but then winced and fell down. 'No, I'm not. I don't think I can stand.'

Brian found a long-nosed propane lighter, obviously used to light ovens. He clicked it a couple of times and it lit, giving them enough light to see that J.D. had a deep bite on his thigh. Blood was flowing, but not spurting. Sam had been reading every medical text he could find in the library, and he knew that this meant that no vein or artery had been opened. Still, the wound was a bad one.

He looked around, and, sure enough, saw a first-aid kit on the wall. Every school kitchen he'd seen had had one. Restaurants probably did too. Certainly a ship's galley would, given all the rocking and rolling that would be involved in cooking while at sea.

221

Mostly, the kit contained burn stuff, but there were plenty of bandages, and he was able to get a good covering on J.D.'s wound. He would be in for some of that penicillin when they got back. Sam would give Laura two doses and J.D. one, then wait to see what happened.

Over the next few minutes, the sounds at the door increased: growling, frantic digging and whining, horrible barking and howling.

There was a whole damn wolf pack out there. And that appeared to be the only door.

Judith sat with Laura's head in her lap, gazing down at her sweet, sweating face, listening to her rattling breath. She thought this might be the infamous 'death rattle'. She thought this lovely girl was going to die any minute, right here in her arms.

'How's she doin'?' Luther asked.

'Not so good.'

She wiped Laura's brow. Where were those boys? Had they got lost out there, or frozen to death? If they didn't get back here very soon, their effort wouldn't make one bit of difference.

Laura coughed again, the long, rattling sound echoing in the room. Luther threw some more books on the fire. Judith found herself praying. This was a child, a wonderful girl child just starting out in life. She'd seen her kissing that sweet beau of hers, Sam Hall.

She found herself praying very damn hard.

Janet and Tom were watching the monitor as a new set of images appeared, relayed from the orbiting Space Station to NASA's still intact communications centre in Houston. 'It should be over New York by now,' Janet said softly.

They were both thinking of Jack Hall. He'd be right under it, assuming he had reached New York. But also, the city probably had lots of survivors in it, folks clinging to life in whatever shelter they could devise. They'd be out there, under bridges, huddling in buildings around makeshift fires, you name it. People were amazingly resourceful.

But nothing could have prepared them for what was about to strike them now. Tom gazed at the bizarre tower of clouds that swept up out of the broader cloud cover. How could anything be like that? What unknown mechanism of nature was driving that air upward like that? Somewhere, the storm was drawing warm air into its belly from the tropics, carrying it towards its eye until, at some point, it let go of it and the air shot upward at inconceivable speed, driving right through the stratosphere, up past thirty then forty thousand feet, up to fifty thousand feet where it froze and fell, speeding downward like a stone towards the earth.

Temperatures on the surface were going to drop a hundred degrees in a second or two. He watched the killer moving slowly south, imagined the desperate, clinging lives that were being snuffed out beneath its awful mechanism.

Sam listened at the door. Nothing. He motioned to Brian to listen, too.

'Maybe they've left,' Brian said.

Sam went to the door and pounded on it with his closed glove, the thuds echoing back flatly from the pantry beyond.

Snarling and growling erupted, scratching at the door, frustrated whining.

'Where the hell did they come from?' J.D. moaned.

When he looked back at J.D., who was lying against a counter trying to prop himself up, Sam noticed that the room was distinctly lighter. He thought to himself that the lessening of the storm that he noticed earlier was developing nicely. Too bad it was an illusion.

Brian noticed it, too. 'Looks like the blizzard's finally letting up,' Brian said happily. 'That's one bit of good news.'

'No it's not.' Sam knew what this meant. If it had tapered off, the wind dropping, the snow would have stopped falling and the sun would have begun to appear through thinning clouds.

Instead, there was this strange translucence, as if the nature of the clouds themselves had somehow changed. 'We've got to get back right away,' he said.

He took J.D.'s penicillin from him, gave one vial to Brian and took the other one himself. The odds were against J.D. That had to be faced. J.D. did not protest. They all understood that death was just an inch away. In this case, less than an inch. The door into the pantry and the dining room beyond was made of tin, that was all.

Sam went to a window and smashed it open. The air outside was weird, as if the sun was shining through a window covering made of pearl. He'd never seen anything like it. The wind wasn't blowing anymore, either.

That was death out there, he knew it, the very storm that had killed the mammoths and the rhinos across Alaska and down into the Midwest all those thousands of years ago. Science had come up with every kind of nonsense explanation that could be conceived of to explain away what had happened to those animals. They'd dropped through permafrost into subsurface bogs and drowned. They'd got stuck in crevasses and frozen to death.

The *one* thing that must not have happened was the only thing that really could have: they'd been quick frozen by a rare and extremely powerful atmospheric phenomenon.

Sam peered out along the catwalk. 'I'll lure the wolves away from the door. When they leave the mess hall, lock them out.' He started out the window. 'If I'm not back in five minutes, get the penicillin to Laura.'

He moved out along the catwalk. The light was now eerily pale, with an odd yellow tinge. The air had become still, and a profound silence had fallen over everything. To the north, the sky was a clotted black mass. Immediately overhead, clouds bulged down towards the land, so low that they scraped the top of the Empire State Building to the south, and the Chrysler Building immediately to the east.

It was like a sky that belonged to another planet. Sam scuttled along the catwalk, hating the poor damn wolves, his skin clammy with fear.

The air now became filled with electricity, and distant rumbles began echoing off Manhattan's skyscrapers. Sam reached the medical station window and crawled in. As he did, some glass fell to the floor.

He reached the interior of the room and froze. Had the wolves heard? Of course they had. Their hearing was naturally superb. And they'd probably smelled him by now, too. A moment ago, he had been afraid. Now it was worse. A hand that was shaking so badly he almost couldn't control it went to the doorknob. Outside was a terrible death – to be eaten by wild animals. 'A week ago,' he thought, 'if you had asked me how I thought I would die . . .'

What a world. You just never know.

He turned the knob and stepped out into the hall. The wolves were still milling around in the pantry, but they heard him and came yapping their horrible eagerness, their claws scrabbling on the metal deck.

Sam leaped down the stairs into the bowels of the ship. He turned and saw the eyes of the lead wolf, and saw in their grey, glaring fury a truth that mankind had almost forgotten: nature is savage, relentless and far more powerful than we like to believe.

He ran, not knowing where he was going exactly, just hoping, somehow, that his death would not be the agony of being eaten alive by wolves.

On the deck above, Brian opened the door from the galley to the ship's larder. He opened it just a crack.

No wolves. He hurried across the mess hall to latch the swinging doors – and couldn't find any way to latch them.

As he ran, Sam pulled out his knife. The wolves were fast, they moved with the eerie grace of ghosts, their dewlaps flying, their tails circling. They yapped with excitement. And why shouldn't they be excited? Dinner was on the table.

The knife was small and not real sharp. The wolves were on him now, he could feel their muzzles brushing his legs, his thighs, hear the snapping jaws as they strove to grasp an edge of his clothing and bring him down. This was how they did it with moose, he remembered – their method was to grasp the loose skin of the belly between their teeth and disembowel their prey.

Nature is a ruthless mathematician, his dad used to say, and man is always trying to make two and two come out five.

Not today. Desperate now, he came to a long hall. He threw himself down, his knife held in both fists, and slid on his back like a baseball player sliding into base. The lead wolf leaped straight at him—and he turned the tables on it, slicing it from sternum to scrotum. As it howled in agony, its steaming entrails poured out over him.

Then he was on his feet again, racing down the next set of stairs. The wolves had got in on this level. He knew this because the snow was up to the portholes. They could not have come in lower or higher. Somewhere, he was going to find a door.

He ran along another hallway, now smelling the outside clearly, with its strange, hard clarity, the sharp scent of very, very cold air. Behind him, there was a riot among the wolves, as they fought and devoured their own leader.

The door was wide open, light glaring into the dim ship's interior like the glow of neon. He plunged out into the snow, struggling in the depth of it, stepping wide, pressing forward towards the ladder. He reached it, grabbed on. He began heaving himself up.

Brian had secured the galley doors by jamming a broom through their handles. He thought it might last about ten seconds. Then, from behind him, he heard pounding.

'We have to hurry!'

Sam watched Brian's confusion and surprise. Then he blinked, as if he simply didn't want to think about that now. Wise decision. The wolves would not waste any time. They would be back.

They got the inflatable life raft out onto the deck and dropped it down onto the snow. With J.D. between them, they made a precarious journey down to the snow's surface. Finally, they reached the snow, got their snowshoes back on and helped J.D. into the raft with the food.

From high overhead, there was a strange, high-pitched wailing sound. Sam learned what it meant to feel your blood run cold, because he thought it was the wolves. But it was not the wolves, it was something that terrified him even more: wind screaming through the rigging of the ship.

But the air – everything had changed again. Now there loomed up around the city a great, curving wall of cloud. Its calm was on the surface though. Sam thought that they must be in the eye of the mega-cell. Which would mean . . . he started to run, dragging the raft with all his might. The whistling in the rigging wasn't just the wind blowing through it, it was what he was feeling deep down inside, this blisteringly cold down draught.

Even as a patch of blue sky appeared behind the Empire State Building, Sam screamed to Brian, 'We have to get inside! *Now*!'

Brian didn't ask questions, thank God. Instead they pulled with all their might, plunging through the snow on their makeshift snowshoes. If one of the shoes were to fail – well, that would be it. Death was moments away.

There came another strange sound, a tinkling noise, and Sam saw the Empire State Building becoming an odd grey colour, as if it was turning to ash.

He knew what was happening: a supercold down draught was hitting it.

Behind them, a savage face appeared in the doorway

of the ship. Then another. Then more, and the wolf pack emerged out onto the snow.

Sam and Brian reached the library. They climbed up to the window they had come out of – and couldn't get the raft through.

'Take this and go,' Sam said, handing him his share of the penicillin. Brian just stood there. 'Go!'

He dove through the window. At least the penicillin would definitely make it now, no question.

Sam got J.D. out of the raft and, supporting him as best he could, moved towards the window. Across the short distance between the library and the ship, there came a great howling. The wolves were coming and they were coming fast.

J.D. was weak, and getting him into the library was an agonisingly slow process. As he worked, he could hear the wolves panting as they plunged through the snow, panting and yapping, and he could see their breath coming in blue bursts and their flanks smoking as they worked against the deep snow.

Then J.D. was in. Sam tore off his own snowshoes and began half-dragging, half-carrying J.D. down the hall. As he hurried along, he saw frost forming on the interior walls around him. Frost! The supercold down draught was hitting the library now.

Behind him, he heard the wolves scrambling into the library. They were growling, yapping, some of them uttering sharp, eager howls of frustration and excitement. He could hear the fear in those sounds. They were eager to reach their prey, but they also sensed something wrong, some indefinable danger.

Ahead, Brian stood at the door of the Trustees Room. His face urged them on. Behind them, the wolves scrambled quickly closer. Again Sam heard that terrible sound, *pantpant, pantpant*, as the leader drew within striking distance.

He and J.D. went through the door and Brian slammed it shut. From the other side, there came the loudest, most ferocious growling Sam had ever heard, and thudding, and scraping, but the big old door was going to hold, despite the fact that it was hopping on its hinges. The past had built to last.

'What's happening?' Judith asked, her eyes wide.

As the growling outside changed to echoing, woebegone howls, the windows of the room turned abruptly white. Ice crystals began forming on the ceiling, literally growing before their eyes.

Abruptly, the howling stopped.

'More books,' Sam shouted, hurling books into the fireplace. 'Don't let it go out!'

Then a blast of cold air laced with fog came *out of* the fireplace, and the flames burned low, becoming little more than coal glows in the mass of blackened paper that now choked it.

Frantically they stoked the fire, they fed it more books, they assisted it in its struggle to survive. The room became so cold that Judith and Luther almost went into convulsions, and Buddha came back from the door, where he had been standing sentinel against the wolves.

Sam looked at Laura. She was the colour of marble. She did not look alive. He reached out to her, touched her with his fingers . . . and nothing happened.

She was dead! They'd let her die and they didn't even know it, look at them, look at the damn *fools*!

Then something touched him, grasped his hand. He turned back to her, and saw that her hand had come into his. So she *was* alive, she was!

But for how long? Minutes? Seconds?

Patrolman Campbell's group was barely two dozen now. They had left body after body behind them, at first stopping to speak over them and honour them, then silently covering them with snow, then simply leaving them where they dropped, as the group continued its shuffling, hopeless progress south and west along what they thought might be the turnpike.

But then something happened. The snow stopped. Tom raised his eyes, looked up at the sky for the first time in days – and saw blue!

Beautiful, beautiful blue! The storm was ending! Then a long shaft of sunlight came down and they began gathering in little knots, pointing upward and laughing.

Along with the sun and the still air came wonderful new visibility. They could see down a long slope for miles . . . and all along the vastness of it they saw lines of black dots in gradual motion. As they realised that these were other groups of refugees just like them, the cheering slowly died away . . . and then it stopped.

Tom Campbell was surprised to feel that the air was getting colder. Then he hurt all over, his skin pricking angrily. Then his bones began to ache deep within, setting off cutting bursts of pain, as if they were being twisted inside his muscles, as if they were breaking. His next breath seared his lungs, and he thought it was fire, he had breathed in fire.

A fist reached into his throat and closed it. He tried to breathe, could not . . . and ice formed over his eyes, an intricate tracery, frosted lace between the veins. His body did not fall over. None of them did. They remained like that in the searing cold of the burst from above, corpses like statues, that would stand there until the snow covered them, and would remain standing, just as they were, across the vastness of time; to a time so far in the future that it could scarcely even be imagined, when the ice age that was starting in this place, in these days, would finally end.

CHAPTER 19

Objectively, Jack knew that, if he did not find food and water and shelter very damn soon, he was going to die trying to drag Jason to safety. His heart would burst. That was what happened to men who had the capacity to force themselves to keep on even after their bodies had told them to quit. Eventually, the heart simply exploded.

Still, he was adhering to his old method of just making sure that one foot always landed in front of the other. He was navigating only by the compass. He had kept the GPS, of course, but its batteries were too cold now to power it. He had it close to his chest, under his clothing, in hopes of warming it up again. So far, no good.

He stopped. He knew he shouldn't, but he was hearing something. A change in the sound of the storm. What the hell was that? He pulled back his parka and listened.

Whistling . . . in the sky.

Then he knew what it was: some kind of a wind aloft was making the ice crystals that filled the air blow against one another. But the wind was not here at the surface. Here, the air was still.

He looked up, and it was as if he was staring into the face of an angry God. He knew at once what was happening here. The storm of legend, that he had theorised and predicted, was about to break right over his own head.

He had minutes, maybe just seconds. Glancing around, he saw a pair of yellow McDonald's arches jutting up out of the snow. They must be the tombstone of a highway rest stop. If he could dig down, he could maybe find shelter – assuming that it hadn't caved in.

The whistling was becoming a rushing sound. Far overhead, he knew that a supercold mass of air was crashing towards the earth, a descending banshee of instant death.

He was almost to the arches when he felt something hard beneath his right snowshoe. He bent down and began digging, pushing away snow, clawing until he saw a large mushroom-shaped exhaust vent. He threw his arms around it like it was the loveliest woman in the world and, with a growl of rage and urgency, ripped it from its moorings.

An aluminium shaft now lay exposed to the air. He leaped over to the sled, pulled Jason off and pushed him into the shaft.

Now the freezing wind hit. An American flag, which was visible on the top few feet of a pole near the arches, suddenly began to flap its tattered hem – and then froze solid, jutting out as rigidly as if it had turned to steel.

Jack dove into the shaft, reached up, and pulled the sled over the opening. Then he dropped down with Jason, pushing him along as tendrils of what felt like searing heat went up his trouser legs and worried the bottoms of his boots.

They went crashing down through the exhaust vent over the grill, and fell in an ungainly heap on the cold altar of the hamburger. Jack checked himself for broken bones, then Jason. He pulled Jason off the grill and raced around the kitchen looking for – and he found them, matches!

Would the grill light? This far out on the road, the

restaurant would have its own propane tank. But were the lines frozen?

He turned one of the burner switches, struck a match and held it out.

The match went out. Overhead, there was a loud crinkling sound. The surface of the grill suddenly turned frost white. He felt freezing air pouring down around his feet. He struck another match – nothing.

Whoompf!

Fire! It was working. Frantically, he opened up all the burners.

The grill turned black again. Soon, it began to smoke. The temperature began to rise. Jack drew off his boots, looking for frostbite.

His toes were red, and there was some bite, but it was not all that bad.

He lay back on the floor. His body took over, then. Jack's eyes closed. He thought, 'This is like anaesthesia—'

That was all he thought for a long time.

Gradually, the kitchen heated. The grill smoked. Fortunately, there was sufficient heat that the snow above melted and the fumes the grill was making escaped.

Jack woke up as suddenly as he had gone to sleep. One moment, there was the blackness of death itself, the next there was full consciousness.

And hunger, he was full of damn hunger, too. Jack was a big man who had used just about every microgram of nutrition his body possessed, and he found himself so hungry that it was almost fantastic.

He was on the floor of a kitchen, though, with a hot grill ten feet away, and a freezer that might not have power, but certainly wouldn't have spoiled anything. He went in and found neat stacks of various different types of hamburger patty, arranged according to the type of burger they were for. Even the refrigerator was good news: the vegetables were still nice and crisp, not frozen solid as he had feared.

He took ten hamburgers to the grill and laid them out, then found buns – very cold – and put them face down to warm. He'd done plenty of grilling. They had equipment a lot like this on some of the Antarctic stations where he'd worked.

Jason suddenly said, 'How long have I been out of it?'

Jack smiled. He looked at his watch. 'About twelve hours.'

Jason sat up, rubbed his head. 'What happened?'

Jack pointed towards the vent hood. 'We had to get inside in a hurry, so I kind of pushed you in.'

Jason, still rubbing the part of his head that had hit the grill, said, 'I should be used to you pushing me around.'

Jack thrust one hell of a nice looking approximation of a Big Mac into his hand. Slowly, Jason sat down on the floor. He stared at it. Jack began to wonder if he had a concussion. 'You don't like my cooking?'

Jason looked up at him, his face stricken. 'I've been a vegetarian for six years. My old girlfriend convinced me it's better for the environment.'

Jack just stared. This was not a world that was going to be treating vegetarians real kindly. He bit into his own hamburger.

'What the hell,' Jason said at last. He took a bite, chewed, then wolfed it down just as Jack was doing. As he ate, he asked, 'What's going to happen, Jack?'

Jack could have answered the question in a lot of ways, beginning with 'I have no damn idea whatsoever.'

But he tried science instead. 'A mass extinction cycle. Large mammals will go first, probably on the order of the Cretaceous event, maybe eighty-five per cent of species will go down. This ice age might last a hundred years, or a hundred thousand.'

'No, I mean what do you think will happen to us?'

'To me,' he meant – the primary question on the mind of any young person, especially one in trouble, and Jason and Jack were certainly in trouble. Jack's answer might once have been little more than a 'Who the hell knows?' But he owed Jason more than that. The world might have forgotten that the young are owed a debt of responsibility, but Jack had not.

'Human beings are the most amazing and resourceful creatures on earth. We survived the last ice age, and we're certainly capable of surviving this one.' He gestured up-ward, thinking of all the arrogance and mistakes in high places that had led to the catastrophe. 'It all depends on whether or not we can learn from our mistakes.' He thought of Lucy and where she might be, and of Sam, his beloved son. Had Sam known how to shelter from down-bursts? If he'd been in one, had he recognised what was happening in time? He sighed. 'I'd sure as hell like a chance to learn from mine.'

'You did everything you could to warn people.'

'I was thinking about Sam. I never made time for him.'

'C'mon, I'm sure that's not true.'

'The only vacation I ever took him on was a research trip to Greenland . . . which was a fiasco.'

'What happened?'

'The ship got stuck for ten days.'

Jason chewed for a minute. 'Yeah, well, he probably had a good time anyway.'

Jack wished he believed that. He wished to his very marrow that he did not have to look back on this unfinished life he'd had with a son he'd probably never see again, who'd probably died a lonely, cold death among strangers.

'I'm gonna get some sleep,' Jason said. He lay down on his side, and in the manner of the young, was instantly asleep.

Jack followed him, and despite the fact that he usually had a rough time at night, fell just as fast into a deep, deep sleep.

The next thing he knew, he was being tossed on a stormy sea. But if only he just kept calm, everything would be fine, the crew would take care of the ship, he could stay asleep.

'Listen! Jack!'

His eyes shot open and the dream receded. He sat up. 'I don't hear anything.'

'That's what I mean! The storm must be over.'

Jack got to his feet. Best to go up and take a look around. If there was any sign of another downburst, they could duck back *tout suite*. He got up on the still-warm grill and pulled himself into the vent. Actually, the grill was pretty damn hot. If he'd stood on it any longer, he would have got burned – which would have been just about the most ridiculous thing that could happen to somebody, given the circumstances.

He slid up the warm vent and pushed himself up through the crust of ice that covered most of it.

He was so amazed that he cried out, then he bowed his head. They were not where he'd thought, in the middle of New Jersey on the turnpike. Looming overhead, sweeping off across the frozen mouth of New York Harbour stood the grandeur of the Verrazano Narrows Bridge. Long fingers of golden light shone like beams from heaven out across the harbour. Manhattan's towers, frozen and dark, stood gleaming in the purest light that Jack Hall had ever beheld. Overhead, the sky went from deep orange on the eastern horizon to emerald green above the rising sun, to rich, sweet blue, the blue of a child's eye, the blue of dreams.

And he saw stars in the retreating night, many, many stars strewn across the western sky still, and the morning star, Jupiter this time of year, hanging low in the rising sunlight, a jewel held in the hand of God.

'Can you give me a hand?'

He pulled Jason up out of the flue.

Then Jason stood, also, before the wonder of the day.

Without a word to one another, they began to walk across the harbour. There was no safety issue. Jack's practised eye told him he was looking at ice as solid as concrete. They made their way past the Statue of Liberty, which had two ships pressed up against it. Jack thought that this place must have endured one hell of a storm surge.

That could happen with a nor'easter, and this had been the mother, father and grandfather of all nor'easters. No doubt Long Island had been devastated as well, cut in two by the surge as easily as a hurricane's surge might split a Carolina barrier island.

Another nail in Sam's coffin. Would he have anticipated the storm surge? And even if he had, would he have been able to get to high ground in time?

They plodded along with the efficiency of practised polar hands, and soon were heading up the desolate canyons of lower Manhattan. The only sound was the whistling of a small wind in the snowy streets. Lip compression made it whip around corners, stinging their red, rutted faces with mean little needles of snow.

Passing an apartment building at about the third-floor level, Jack saw a bizarre sight. Sitting behind a frost-hazed window was what appeared to be a woman in a chair, just as calm and collected as you please.

He went over and pressed his hand against the window. It was ice cold. He broke it with his ice axe. When the glass and frost had fallen away, he found himself face to face with a lady, quite old, but beautifully made up and wearing a green cocktail dress right out of nineteen fifty-eight. On her lap was a cat, its eyes still bright, as dead as the old woman. Her eyes were closed, and on her lips was the smile of fond memory.

He turned and went on, Jason behind him. When he saw the Empire State Building, he quickened his pace. But where was the library? It was a large building. They should see it now but – where were they, in a park? 'How much farther is it to the library?'

Jason pulled out the GPS. They'd got it working again back at the McDonald's. It was an excellent piece of equipment, and had recovered nicely after being frozen below its minimums. 'It should be—' He stopped, looked around. 'Right here.'

Jack saw that he was right. Ahead were the buildings of Forty-Second Street. Over there – what was that? Damn, it was the rigging of a ship. But that was surely impossible. No storm surge could have got this far up Manhattan.

Or no, yes it could. It had come right up the East River and the Hudson, inundating the island from the sides, and bringing with it what looked like a very considerable vessel.

My dear God, New York had been turned into hell, hell on earth. Poor Sam! He felt a hand on his shoulder.

Jason was looking at him sympathetically. 'I'm sorry,' he said.

Jack trudged on, crossing where the library must have stood before the snow had collapsed it or the storm surge drowned it. 'Here is my son's grave,' he thought, 'here in this place.' If he dug down, he knew that he would find Sam somewhere in there, frozen in youthful perfection.

He wanted his son. He did not want to see the suffering that would be on his face.

Then he felt something beneath one of his feet – a beam. He bent down, began to push snow away. The building was far from collapsed. He began to work harder.

In the Trustees Room, all was quiet and dark. The snow had got so deep that it had eventually caved in the windows, forcing the tiny band of survivors to cling together around their dying fire. Now they lay close to one another, Buddha among them, sleeping and resting. The food from the ship was long gone, and their bodies were demanding that they not move any more than they absolutely had to.

They had reached the point that most everybody reaches, when they are dying in the cold. They were dreaming, drifting softly into the golden halls of death, unaware that the cold was drawing them away from life forever.

In the corridor outside, Jack and Jason found the frozen solid carcass of a wolf. Jack bent down, examined it. How in the world had this animal got here? Zoo animal. Had to be. Unless some nut had been keeping wolves in his apartment. Could've happened, this being New York.

241

He noticed that the door the animal was lying beside had no frost on it. He pulled off a glove and felt it. Warm. Definitely.

Jack had to take a deep breath, steady himself. Because he was going to open that door, and if he did not find Sam in there, or he found him dead, it would be the greatest agony he had ever known, soul agony, the howling misery of a dad left behind by his child.

Jack drew the door open and stepped into the room.

It was dim and it stank of smoke and human sweat. It was a grand room, though, all mahogany and a high-beamed ceiling. Two people sat on the floor in front of an enormous fireplace. On the hearth, a fire guttered low. One of the people tossed a book into the flames.

Sam saw Buddha lift his ears, look sharply towards the door.

The wolves!

He turned, went to his feet. Two men were standing there. They were in arctic parkas. Sam knew professional equipment when he saw it. Sam opened his mouth, closed it. The taller of the two men pulled his hood back, revealing a bearded, snow-burned face that – was that—

'Who's there?' Laura asked. She came to her feet beside Sam.

Sam felt his mouth open. He heard the words – the unbelievable words – that came out. 'My father.' Just a whisper.

Then Jack Hall was crossing the room, he was walking towards the filthy kid with the ridiculous excuse for a beard on his face, and Sam was walking towards him, and then their arms came around one another, and the blood of the Halls sang joy to the world, and maybe even the good God above smiled that this love of father for son

242

had defied the worst storm in ten thousand years to declare: I am a love beyond death, and I am stronger than death, and when we part, it will be in *my* time, when I say the day is come for the old man to step into memory, and the young one to lift up his own son.

There was crying, then, before the fire, in the devastated city, beneath the hard blue sky of a new day.

Tom Gomez rode bouncing along in his jeep. They had been going, it seemed for miles, beside the Fence of Hope. This chain-link fence had been hung with tens of thousands of letters, of pictures, of prayers from refugees trying to locate friends and loved ones. 'Sally, me and the kids are in Chihuahua City, Highway 45 Camp Nebraska.' 'George Louis Carver please call Louise my cell is *working*!' 'The children of Mary and William Winston may be reached through any Red Cross Station.' And the pictures, the ribbons, the flowers of hope and memory, on and on and on.

He listened to the jeep's horn as the driver struggled along, being careful to avoid the milling crowd. Finally they turned onto the Paseo De La Reforma and left the Fence of Hope behind them. Here, the Marine Guards in their formal perfection stood before an imposing gate.

They drove through into another world, shaded and quiet, unchanged from before the storm, which had exhausted itself hundreds of miles north of Mexico City.

Tom entered the cool, beautifully elegant building, and was ushered across the broad foyer to a suite of offices. On the imposing door was a neatly lettered sign, brand new: Offices of the President of the United States.

Okay, here was his first real face to face with the despicable Becker. A good man had died to put this creep in office. He did not relish the meeting, the probable cold-hearted turndown.

He found the President standing at his window, staring through half-closed blinds at the Fence of Hope. 'Mr President?'

Becker seemed to freeze. Then, very abruptly, he turned around.

Tom was shocked to his core by what he saw. The arrogant Washington insider had disappeared. In his place was a man with a face etched by deep lines of compassion and regret. Tom thought he had never seen such a sad man. Never. Or so much strength. There was strength in that face.

He was humbled. Before the President even opened his mouth, Tom Gomez knew something about him: God had touched this man. God had given him the grace and strength he was going to need.

'Mr President, I've just received a short-wave radio transmission from Jack Hall. He made it to New York.'

The President's eyes flickered with surprise. Something like a smile played in his face.

'He says there are survivors.'

For a long moment, the President stood with eyes closed. It was as if he was communicating with somebody somewhere very far away . . . and yet very close to his heart. 'Thank you, Tom,' he finally replied. 'That's good news.'

What happened over the next hours Tom Gomez would remember for the rest of his life, but more than just remember: these days would be as if they were still happening, as if they were always happening and would continue unfolding again and again forever, days that had entered eternity.

He had seen an amazing thing: a devastated nation in a hopeless situation deciding to fight back anyway, a greedy man who had found what was sacred within himself organising a gigantic rescue operation that would sweep across America's frozen cities, seeking those who remained, to bring them out to safety, to bring them to a thousand times a thousand meetings beside the Fence of Hope and wherever Americans were lost and needed to be found.

A fleet of helicopters was taking off, and Tom hopped aboard one of them. They would go north, joining a larger force in Houston, then fly across the frozen wasteland where the Air Force was already arranging fuel and supply dumps, to the great cities of the north, Boston and Washington, Chicago and New York.

New York. There they would begin, with the largest city, the most needful city.

As they ascended, President Becker's voice, strong and resolute, the voice of your firm but kind grandfather, came over the radio. 'These past few weeks have left us all with a profound sense of humility in the face of nature's destructive power . . .'

In a rambling medical tent, in an area marked off by ropes on which had been taped handmade paper signs, 'Paediatric Division,' Lucy sat beside a small boy, Peter Upshaw, whose own message she had personally put on the Fence of Hope, 'Peter Upshaw is at the National Emergency Hospital in Matamoros, Mexico. Paediatric Ward. He is getting better every day.'

President Becker's face looked out of a television. You could never tell that he was speaking from an embassy far from home. It looked exactly – heartbreakingly – like the

White House backdrop so familiar to Americans. 'They have also forced us to re-evaluate our priorities. Yesterday we operated under the belief that we could continue consuming our planet's natural resources without consequence . . .'

In the dusty streets of refugee camps, along the Fence of Hope, in the Red Cross villages that had sprung up in the Mexican desert, across the Rio Grande valley of Texas and in still-functioning cities like Miami and Houston, people stopped what they were doing and watched and listened.

'We were wrong. I was wrong.' The President looked straight into the camera. He did not flinch at saying those words of courage. 'Today many of us are guests in the nations we once called the Third World.'

In the International Space Station, the astronauts were watching the broadcast also. Below them, they knew that the shuttle was being prepared to rescue them.

'In our time of need, they have taken us in and sheltered us and I am deeply grateful for their hospitality.'

As the helicopters swept north, the President continued. 'Their generosity has made me realise the folly of yesterday's arrogance and the need for cooperation in the future.'

Tom Gomez listen to the speech, and knew that they were more than hollow words. They were the first utterance of a new man in a new situation, in a very new world.

Resting on the shoulders of those who had paid the ultimate price for it, humanity was gaining a new wisdom.

*

Brian's radio, which was now alive with messages, had told them that help was coming. They had left the Trustees Room and the library behind and marched off towards the open ice that Jack knew lay near the Statue of Liberty. Here, they would be seen, out here on the flat, windblown harbour.

Tom Gomez had insisted on going with the contingent that was bound for New York, and after a day of travelling, stopping to refuel outside of Atlanta and again outside of Washington, they were now flying through the sky of morning, towards the glittering towers of Manhattan.

As they circled the island, Tom saw no sign of life. He listened to the President in the background, who was giving another of what were becoming daily addresses to the nation. 'Working together, we can move past the mistakes of yesterday and look forward to a better tomorrow.'

Still no life. This was not looking good.

'Only hours ago, I received word that a small group of people survived in New York City—'

Tom hoped. Surely they had not ended up losing even this small symbol of human hope, not right at the end.

'—against all odds and in the face of tremendous adversity.'

Tom could not let the President down – not his President, their President. He was going to find Jack and his crew.

'As I speak, a search and rescue mission is under way in New York. Plans are being made to send similar missions to all the cities of the north, all around the world.'

Then Tom saw something – down there, near the Statue of Liberty, just this side of two ruined ships, moving dots. They were barely visible in the grey light of predawn.

The pilot saw them, too, and swung the chopper around.

'The fact that people have survived this storm,' Becker was saying, 'should not be treated as a miracle, but rather as proof that the human spirit is indomitable.'

They touched down on the ice, and as they landed Tom saw that the survivors, instead of running towards the chopper, had turned and were pointing at the city.

And he saw, in windows up and down the island, tiny lights appearing.

Candles. People were announcing their presence to the rescuers. There wasn't just a small group still alive here. Thousands, maybe hundreds of thousands, maybe even millions, had lived and were alive, and were declaring themselves now in a sea of flickering lights in the brutally cold predawn: 'we are here.'

Tom and Jack came together. A young man with badly cracked glasses stood nearby, his breath blasting, a small-ish black book clutched to his chest. Tom recognised it immediately as something very old. 'It's a Gutenberg Bible,' the young man said, stamping from foot to foot.

Jack and Tom locked arms. Sam knew that they would not celebrate wildly, although they wanted to. There was a lot of hope here, but also a lot of destruction and death, and the dead were to be respected.

Then the sun rose. Light poured across the city, strong and warm, and Sam heard something he had not heard in days, had never expected to hear again. It was dripping, loud dripping, lots of dripping.

There was an enormous icicle hanging from the torch of the Statue of Liberty, and dropping from it were mil-lions of particles of fire – water droplets forming as the ice melted.

He laid his arm around Laura's shoulder and drew her close. J.D. stood on her other side – no doubt still hoping against hope. Sam kissed her and she kissed him, and for just that tiny, private moment between two young people standing side by side at the gates of the future, all was well.

The astronauts were gazing down at the Earth. They, also, had changed profoundly, drawing together as human beings in the face of what might have been a lingering death, trapped and starving in the glory of the heavens.

Yuri said, 'Look at that.'

Parker didn't fully understand. 'What?'

'Have you ever seen the air so clear?'

He was right. The air of Earth was absolutely clear. It was like looking through some kind of perfect crystal.

Earth lay like a jewel in the great sky, not only bruised by the storm but also purified, hanging there in space as black as the darkest memory, amid stars as bright as the brightest hope.